THE WIDOW

AND THE

Will

J. THOMAS-LIKE

Dedication

To Ethan,

As always, you were the backbone of our little family
when I was too consumed with my fictional one.
I love you and thank you from the bottom of my heart.

To Molly,

I was afraid that "one" would have to be enough.
But your encouragement, support and *belief* in me was all the
confidence I needed to go for it again.

Acknowledgments

A heartfelt thanks to the following:

As always, my mom, sister and brother. You guys helped out in so many little ways that might have gone unnoticed by you, but were immeasurable to me.

Write Club, as *usual*, was the fuel to my fire throughout the entire process. Powerhouse: you're about the most inspirational, encouraging peeps I could have ever hoped to find. What would I do without you?

Jason Dandy, thank you for answering all the lawyer questions and pointing out when the questions asked were *not* lawyerly (and answering them anyway). You're hired!

Ret. Detective Howard "Butch" Isham and Detective Kevin Kimm of the St. Clair Shores Police Department, your advice and information were invaluable to the accuracy of this story. Also, Officer Jeremy Scicluna answered S.W.A.T. questions I would not have thought to ask and I am grateful for his knowledge and expertise.

Gale Deloney, RN, you were instrumental with all your research and advice. Thanks for helping me to get things right.

Special gold stars on the forehead to Bailey K. Perkins and Natalie Rhymer for their stellar proofreading and editing. You guys were the extra brains behind the scenes. Thank you for being the ones to know and care where the commas go (and oh, so much more), so that I didn't have to think about it.

Chapter 1

The wedding march boomed from the organ and the doors at the back of the church swung open as if pushed by the explosion of air from the pipes.

Jack Kingston's breath caught in his throat as his beautiful bride slowly floated toward him. He'd never imagined Tess could be so stunning. Her bright blue eyes stood out against the white of her veil. Her usually flowing and wavy honey blonde hair was tamed into a high bun surrounded by glittering crystals. Maybe it was the whole bride phenomenon, but Jack didn't care. He would treasure the image for the rest of his life. *That's my girl.*

Prior to Tess's epic entrance, Jack had been nervously chatting with his best man and brother, David. He'd waved to people as they entered and took their seats in the hard-backed pews of the Congregational church. He'd asked David a dozen times if he had the ring. But Jack had mostly been drawn back, over and over, to his mother's stricken and pale face. She looked ill, instead of happy, and he hadn't been able to understand it.

"What's with Mom?" he whispered to David.

David turned and looked at the first row on their left, squinting to see what his younger brother was referring to. "Dunno. Don't sweat it. You're her baby, she's just bummed to be losing you."

As Tess's father lifted her veil and kissed her cheek, Jack forgot all about his mother and every other thing in the world. His nervousness disappeared with one look into Tess's eyes. Taking her hand and turning to the minister, Jack was filled with a calming sense of peace, knowing he was marrying his best friend and the person he trusted most in the world.

* * * * *

"Jack, Tess, by virtue of your pledges to each other of fidelity and trust, you may now call yourselves by these two old and respected names, husband and wife." The minister threw out her arms in triumph.

Tess leaned into Jack's arms, splaying her hands across his back as his lips met hers for their very first "married" kiss. It was gentle and brief, just enough to satisfy those watching, but still sent chills down her spine, causing the hair on her arms to lift. The crowd of family and friends behind them clapped and cheered and Tess felt a satisfaction she hadn't expected. For days, she'd had cold feet about going through with the wedding. But now, she thought she might squeal like a kid at Christmas. Maybe it had been pre-wedding jitters. She sure hoped so.

Pulling away from Jack and staring into his eyes, Tess grinned like a fool. He chuckled at her and pressed his forehead to hers.

"Hello, Mrs. Kingston."

"Hello, Mr. Kingston."

Taking Tess's hand firmly in his, Jack turned them toward the congregation. The shouts and applause were steady and strong, then rose to a gentle roar as he raised their clasped hands in the air. They shared another quick peck of a kiss and then the happy couple scampered down the aisle. When they reached the vestibule of the church, they hugged again, their happiness at its zenith. Then they each reached for a door to close, leaving them secluded.

"It's done and no one objected," Jack teased, swinging Tess around in his arms, lifting her feet in the air.

"Nope. Who would? It's not like we had any exes that would show up." Tess giggled and kissed him a little more passionately in their moment of privacy.

Jack and Tess had given express instructions to their families to let them have a couple of minutes alone after the ceremony. There would be hours and hours for partying, pictures, handshakes and hugs. They wanted to enjoy the first moments of married life by themselves to let it soak in. They even incorporated the signing of their marriage license into the ceremony so they could have this time alone.

Jack danced her around to a tune only he could hear. His warm, chocolate eyes reflected all the love they both felt in the moment. Tess could hardly believe how handsome he looked in his tuxedo. It was a far cry from the usual jeans and t-shirts she knew he preferred. She glanced down at his feet and smiled at the bright red Converse Chuck Taylors. He'd gotten no argument from her when he insisted that he and the groomsmen wear comfortable shoes.

"Oh!" Tess gasped, momentarily interrupting their waltz. "I forgot to show you!" She stepped backward and lifted the hem of her wedding dress. As a surprise, she'd worn her own pair of Converse in her favorite style. They were customized, of course, white with black polka dots and red laces to coordinate with Jack.

Jack's familiar barrel laugh filled the small area and he put out his fist for a bump. "Awesome, babe!"

As she extended her own fist toward his, Jack abruptly stopped laughing. The puzzled look that crossed his face made Tess freeze. "Honey? What's wrong?" She reached for him, her small hand grasping for his arm while she watched the color drain from his face.

"Uh." Jack's eyes scrunched shut and he swallowed hard. When his eyes reopened, they were glazed over. He pitched forward, landing flat on the floor.

All Tess could do was scream.

* * * * *

Tender fingers helped Tess out of her wedding gown. Those same kindly hands of her mother and sister had been by her side all day long. Muffled words from someone made their way to her ears and then a nightgown went over her head. She felt the sides being smoothed down across her body. Tess knew that physically she was in her childhood bedroom at her parents' home, but her brain was still at the church, enjoying a soft kiss. Her mind was still waltzing in the vestibule. Her head echoed with the sounds of her own screams.

"Tess."

That was her mother's voice. Tess swung her head in the direction of the sound and blinked several times, trying to focus.

"Honey, take this."

Ruth Langford stood with a glass of water in one hand and a small pink and white capsule in the palm of the other.

Tess stared at her dumbly for another few seconds before reaching for the proffered items. Reluctance filled her, but then Jack's voice popped into her mind. *It's okay this time, T. You can take it.*

"Go on, honey," Ruth urged. "You need to sleep."

Years of parental obedience overruled Tess's hesitation and she placed the pill on her tongue. Sipping a bit of water, she jerked her chin back, making the medication slip down her throat. Ruth took the glass from her and set it on the milk crate nightstand beside the bed.

Tess didn't move. She continued to sit on the edge, staring at her hands. Her diamond engagement ring twinkled from her right hand and the diamond baguette band sparkled from her left. Tears began to blur her vision, causing the twinkles and sparkles to create a prism surrounding the gems. *I forgot to move the engagement ring to my other hand.*

Ruth waited a minute or so before finally grasping Tess by the shoulders and pushing her gently back onto the bed. Tess pulled her own legs up off the floor and curled into the fetal position. Her mother covered her with a familiar quilt and then softly crept from the room.

"A heart attack," Tess whispered to the emptiness around her. *A fucking heart attack.*

Tess tried to close her eyes, but they were sore from the crying and burning from having rubbed them raw. Drugs or not, the grisly images seared into her brain following Jack's collapse would never have allowed her to sleep. The rush of people who poured into the vestibule when they heard her screaming. Being torn away from Jack's body as someone tried doing CPR. The multitude of phone calls made to 911 for an ambulance and then the endless wait for paramedics to arrive. The nasty things she had said to someone when they tried to stop her from climbing into the ambulance to be with Jack. The guilt she carried because only hours before she had wanted to postpone the wedding.

Sitting in the waiting room at the hospital for news, any news, that would change the course of events and then not getting that reprieve. Many people had surrounded her, as she wept piteously, unable to believe such a tragedy could happen today of all days. Tess remembered her mother and father, her sister, and her newly minted in-laws.

Tess tried to cry quietly but gave it up when the tears came faster and her breathing grew heavier, turning into moans and then outright wails. She pressed her face against her pillow to muffle the sound. Somewhere in her heart she knew she was frightening her parents, but couldn't bring herself to stop the hideous sounds. Exhaustion finally overcame her and she circled downward, drowning in a pool of nightmares.

Chapter 2

It took more than a year to plan the wedding and less than a week to bury Jack.

Chapter 3

A little over six months after burying her husband, Tess stood in the tiny dining room of their two-bedroom apartment, surveying the mountain of prettily wrapped wedding presents in the early morning sunshine. A thin layer of dust covered them, along with cat hair shed from the two resident felines. Tess's stomach clenched, knowing she should have sent them all back before now. No matter how many times her mom and Lilly assured her that she could take all the time she needed, Tess couldn't help the guilt she felt. What if people thought she kept the gifts and spent the money? Yet that fear hadn't motivated her to deal with the job, either. Timothy the tabby appeared beside her, winding his way around her legs.

"Meow."

Looking down, Tess sighed. "I know. I have to deal with all this."

"Meow!"

"If you had thumbs, I'd make you do it," she muttered, lifting a foot to rub his side. With a heavy heart, she turned away, trying to focus on something that wouldn't remind her of the horror of those months. She shuffled to the couch in the living room and slumped down into the soft cushions.

The truth was, everything reminded her. Jack's absence was the biggest one of all. He was a freelance graphic designer and she was a medical transcriptionist, both working from home. From the day they declared their love for one another at the age of sixteen, they had not spent more than a few hours apart. Theirs was the hokiest of romances, meeting when they were eight years old, and it was love at first sight for Tess. He was the prince from all the storybooks her mother read to her, and she knew she would marry him some day. Jack wasn't as convinced. It took him about five years before he noticed Tess as a girl instead of one of his buddies. Oh, but when he did notice her for the first time, she was infused with a confidence and power she'd been waiting for since Mrs. Grabowski's third grade class.

At sixteen, Jack gave Tess a promise ring and she gladly accepted it. Stereotypical high school sweethearts, they attended every dance and function as a couple. After graduation, they went to the same college and graduated together four years later. When they got back home to St. Clair Shores, they moved in together immediately. They settled down with jobs and the joy of living life, getting engaged when they were twenty-three. They wanted to be married by the time they were twenty-five. They planned on starting a family at thirty.

All gone. Every bit of it. All from a freak heart attack because Jack couldn't give up the energy drinks. A faulty heart tore him away from Tess, leaving her with a broken one.

Tess's mind wandered back to the days before the funeral, but they were all a blur. The only thing that had gotten her through them was denial. Cloaking, heavy, thick, non-acceptance. It wasn't until she was confronted with the open casket containing Jack's body that her veneer cracked wide open. The memory of that moment still made Tess's stomach ache and her head pound. Even now, waves of nausea washed over her like the ocean at high tide.

Without her mother and Lilly, she might have had a total nervous breakdown. They had held her hands and whispered in her ear that everything would be okay. Over and over, they repeated their platitudes until Tess was able to keep herself from screaming and bolting from the church. The same church where the same minister conducting the funeral had married them not six days before.

Weeks of tears, not eating, not sleeping followed. Then the tables turned and Tess began sleeping all the time and eating everything she could get her hands on. Only the crying remained constant. Her family let her be for the first couple of months, hoping she would bounce back on her own, but when it didn't happen, Lilly was the one to step in. Big sister took control and forced Tess to get out of bed, shower, leave her apartment, go back to work. Slowly, things improved until Tess was finally able to put her happy mask back on. She faked feeling better until she did. She pretended that she didn't feel lonely until she didn't. She acted like her life was back on track until it was.

Still and all, the only thing she couldn't seem to conquer was the guilt. That was what was really killing Tess. For several weeks before the wedding, she had been filled with self-doubt and fear, wondering if she was making a mistake. Even though she knew she loved him, Tess couldn't help feeling they were getting married only because it was the next logical step. It was something they'd dreamed about for so long that marriage was a foregone conclusion instead of the culmination. More than once, Tess had considered postponing the wedding. As the date got closer, the embarrassment over canceling outweighed her fear of going through with it, but even as she sat in the hairdresser's chair, Tess considered not showing up at all.

It had nothing to do with wanting to see other people. She wasn't filled with doubt because she thought she might be missing something better. Tess knew Jack was about as special and wonderful as she could hope for. No matter how hard she tried, she couldn't pinpoint why she felt so unsure of the future.

But who could she share all these feelings with? No one. Not even her sister. Lilly had always taken every opportunity she could to remind Tess of how lucky she was. How grateful she should be to have found her prince charming. Tess took Lilly's words to heart because her sister was about the unluckiest woman in the world when it came to love. Lilly's track record contained a divorce from one husband, then emotional and mental abuse from her next boyfriend. For every perfect moment she had, Lilly's experience was the polar opposite.

Tess carried the guilt and shame around in her heart like a shackle around her neck. Everyone thought she was mourning and grieving for a dead husband, and she was. Even more so, she lamented the fact that she hadn't changed courses. If she had canceled the wedding, would Jack still be alive? Had the stress of a big fancy affair caused the heart attack that killed him?

Questions that would never be answered, even though she asked them constantly from the night she left the hospital. When would she be able to stop asking them? When would she finally feel normal again? Tess felt sick and tired of taking one day at a time. She wanted to imagine a future for herself again. She loved and missed Jack, but she wanted to feel happy again, hopeful again. Anything *but* sad and grief stricken.

It was the noisy meow of an ignored and hungry cat that brought Tess back to the present, as Spencer called to her from the doorway into the kitchen. His bright yellow eyes stood out against his black fur, imploring her to pay attention. She glanced over and could see the food dish was nearly empty. She wearily hauled herself up to go put more food into their bowl. Timothy appeared from out of nowhere to add his voice to Spencer's chorus of displeasure. "Yeah, yeah, I'm gettin' there." Howling as though they hadn't been fed in days, Tess scooped the pebbles of kitty chow into the dish until it was almost overflowing. They attacked it, heads side by side as she stepped backward. After a couple of bites, they both turned and looked at her as if to say, *Thanks, Mom.*

"You're welcome, boys," she whispered as she watched them crunch and munch their way through the top layer of cat chow.

Tess took a deep breath and let it out slowly. She was so very tired, literally exhausted from going over the scenes and scenarios in her head, asking the same questions every minute of every hour of every day. She wanted to tell herself to stop. Just be done with it, but she didn't know how. As she continued to stare at Timothy and Spencer as they ate, she noticed how Spencer took a piece of food into his mouth, sat up and then spit it out. He stood up and walked away from the bowl to sit in a patch of sunshine where he began to lick his paws. Within a moment or two, Timothy did the same thing: took a bite, spit it out and then left the food behind to begin his own bath.

As she considered what she saw, Tess smiled a little bit. The cats were full and decided they would stop eating. It didn't seem like they thought about it all that much, they just did it, following their instincts.

Closing her eyes, Tess conjured a picture of Jack. His tousled brown hair, laughing eyes and handsome smile. The twinge she felt in her heart wasn't the same stabbing sensation she was used to whenever she pictured him in her mind. It was more of a dull ache. *Just do it. Just let it all go*, she thought. *Just decide once and for all.*

Opening her eyes, Tess blinked at the bright sunlight pouring in from the outside, making the silver and gold bows on the piled-up gifts shimmer and shine. It was time. Grabbing her cell phone from the kitchen counter, she shot off a quick text to Lilly to head over if she could. It was time to face this one final task. Tess decided that by dealing with the wedding presents, she would finally close the chapter on her marriage and widowhood.

Chapter 4

Hudson Marks arrived at his office promptly at seven a.m., as was his usual habit. Dressed neatly in a fresh pair of tan khakis and a red polo shirt, he had no need to wear a suit to the office that day even though he was a lawyer. He had no court appearances and expected no client meetings. Hudson liked the laid back kind of day he thought he would have.

As he unlocked the door and stepped inside the small two-room-and-a-bathroom suite, if you could call it that, he reached to flip on the overhead lights. The sound of snoring came to him immediately and he looked to the right at the couch against the wall. His brother, Ford, was sprawled on it, passed out and reeking of alcohol and cigarettes. *Dammit.*

Sighing, Hudson dropped his briefcase so that it whacked against the side of the couch. It had no effect on the sleeping man. "Hey!" he shouted. That produced the desired results. Ford snorted and sat up, startled. He snapped his eyes back shut from the bright lights and then placed both of his hands on his head, moaning the whole time. Hudson grinned devilishly. *That's the price you pay, big brother,* he thought, but didn't say out loud. He didn't have to be that much of an ass.

"Shit, man, what did you have to do that for?" Ford whispered.

Hudson shook his head and rolled his eyes. "Because you aren't supposed to be passed out in the office. Where's your bike?"

Ford rubbed his face and head. "I don't remember."

"For Christ's sakes, Ford." Hudson's voice rose, causing Ford to cringe.

"Gimme a second, would ya?" Ford stood up slowly and listed to the right, then steadied himself. "I didn't ride last night. Joe picked me up. He must have dropped me off here instead of at home."

"Ya think?" Hudson muttered as he pulled his truck keys from his pocket. "Are you still drunk?"

Ford opened one eye and squinted. "Yeah, a little, I guess."

"Shit." Hudson shoved the keys back down into the folds of his pants. "I'd tell you to take my truck and go home, but I don't want you for a client. Go back to sleep, it's early."

Ford ignored him and shuffled toward the bathroom. Hudson sighed again and grabbed his briefcase. He crossed the room, which was really a kind of waiting area with the couch, a secretary's desk, and small cabinet housing the coffeemaker, to open the door to his private office in the back. He tossed the bag on the single client chair in front of his desk and then went back out to the main area. While he waited for Ford to relinquish the bathroom, Hudson prepared to make a pot of coffee. Yeah, he was irritated to find his older sibling sleeping off a drunk in the office, but it had become so commonplace he couldn't really get that angry. In spite of his penchant for drink, Ford was responsible enough not to get on his motorcycle in a compromised position. Hudson would rather find him on the couch, safe and sound, than dead in the morgue or sitting in jail. He filled the coffee pot from the water cooler and poured it in. Jamming his thumb on the brew button, he slid the pot in place to collect the elixir of life that would soon come pouring forth.

Ten minutes went by without a sound from the bathroom. No running water, no flushing. Just as Hudson went to knock on the door to make sure Ford hadn't passed out again, his brother emerged looking pale and sweaty.

"You didn't barf in there did you?"

Ford glowered at him. "Yes, I did. Sorry. I cleaned it up."

Hudson growled. "You better have." He looked his brother up and down and shook his head. "You're a mess. I'll call you a cab and you can go home."

"I'll be fine. Let me have a cup of coffee and then I'll borrow your truck."

"Highly unlikely."

The brothers stood silently at opposite ends of the room while the smell of fresh coffee filled the air, disguising any odor of disinfectant that had leaked out of the bathroom. When they both had cups, Hudson went into his office and Ford sat back down on the couch.

Hudson glanced around his tiny inner sanctum and smiled. The space was only about twelve foot square, barely fitting his large oak desk, a filing cabinet and another brown, microfiber couch. It wasn't the poshest of spaces, but it was comfortable and inviting. For as many times as Hudson found his brother passed out in the main area, he'd taken a nap or two himself behind the closed door.

It wasn't often a new attorney, only three years out of law school, could open his own place and keep it afloat. Most of his pals had taken 80-hour-a-week jobs with silk stocking firms just to pay off their school loans and to gain as much experience as possible before thinking about opening their own practice. But Hudson hadn't wanted that kind of a life. He liked to work, and work hard, and the proof was in the fact that he had very little college debt to pay off. Between scholarships and working multiple jobs, he'd managed to get through college and law school without as much debt hanging over his head that plagued so many others. He knew just how lucky he was. Granted, it had taken him a few extra years to do it, but he had. He felt pretty accomplished for 31 years old.

Hudson had taken one of those grueling positions with Hacket & Hacket in downtown Detroit for one year right after graduating law school, and in that time, lived in a studio apartment, scrimping and saving every cent he could. After twelve months, he gladly gave his notice and opened his own firm right in St. Clair Shores where he'd been born and raised.

Hudson found the space on the end of a building right on Harper Avenue, negotiated a rent he could afford, had a sign made and was off and running. For the last three years, he'd managed to stay in business by handling any legal matter that walked through his door.

Of course, it hadn't hurt to have Ford working with him, even if he was the resident fuckup. He'd disappeared while Hudson was in law school, reappearing just in time for graduation and it had taken him a long time to forgive his big brother for not being there. Once Hudson realized that Ford had lots of interesting contacts that provided an endless supply of petty drug offenses, traffic tickets, and other misdemeanors to defend in court, Hudson took him on as an investigator and partner. Ford wasn't interested in college or any other sort of mainstream career, and it helped the firm stay afloat.

Hudson knew he could probably have taken on a couple of other partners, moved to a larger office, and made more money. But that kind of life didn't interest him. He liked being able to take the kinds of cases he wanted and still have some hours in the day to live however he chose.

"Okay, let's get to work," he said to himself, pulling out of the reverie. He sifted through mail from the last few days and found most of it to be junk. Tossing it into the trash can under his desk, he turned to his computer and booted up to check emails. "Crap." There were a half a dozen from his most recent DUI client who was more insecure than a teenage girl in the first flushes of puppy love. He would need some serious hand holding. Then he skimmed past a couple from opposing counsel in a contested guardianship case. And last, his least favorite, was from a judge's clerk informing him that he had been appointed to act as guardian ad litem for a minor in a probate estate. "Great. When it rains, it pours." He pulled up his calendar and checked to see what hearings were soonest and what preparations needed to come first.

As he sorted through his client files and made notes about things he needed to do or be prepared for, he heard the front door to the office open. Knowing Ford was there, he didn't think much about it until the FedEx guy appeared in his doorway. Hudson glanced at his watch to see that it was already 8:10 a.m.

"Sorry," the delivery man said as he stretched his arm out with a regular flat letter envelope in his hand. "The guy out there is asleep."

Chuckling, Hudson took the envelope as he stood up. Dropping it on his desk, he reached to sign for it. "No worries. Thanks." Hudson followed the man out, only to observe Ford still sitting on the couch, his head tilted all the way back and mouth hanging open. His coffee cup was dangerously close to keeling over. Hudson plucked it from his fingers and set it on the end table. Pushing his brother on the shoulder, Ford slowly rolled onto his side. Hudson picked up his legs and put them on the couch so he could stretch out. "Nighty night, brother."

Walking back to his office, the unexpected delivery piqued his interest. The return address listed EJR Insurance, Inc. and he hoped it wasn't bad news. He tore open the envelope and pulled out a letter. As he read it, Hudson felt his stomach begin to twist. It was bad news. One of his clients was dead.

Chapter 5

Ford Marks lit a cigarette and ignored the nasty look from his brother. He put the window of the truck all the way down so he could hang his arm outside. That damn Joe hadn't taken him home the night before. Instead, he'd dropped him off at the office so Hudson could find him in the morning. *When I see him again, I'm gonna kick his ass.* His head was still pounding, but at least his stomach had settled. The couple of hours of sleep he managed on the couch had helped with that. In spite of that, he felt fine to drive, but Hudson had insisted on taking him home.

As Hudson pulled his Chevy Silverado into the driveway of the little house where Ford rented a flat above the garage, Ford flicked his cigarette away.

"I hate when you do that," Hudson muttered.

"Sorry." He wished he could mean it, but in the moment he didn't. His head hurt too much.

As the truck stopped, Ford unclipped his seatbelt. "Thanks for the ride."

"Yeah, call me when you get yourself together. I'm going to need you later."

"Okay."

"Get something to eat. A shower."

Ford rolled his eyes mentally. *Who's the older brother here?* "I'll text you in a couple of hours."

Hudson gave him a two-fingered salute and then backed out to leave.

Ford trudged up the stairs to the studio flat and pulled his keys out of his pocket to unlock the door, hoping his head would stop pounding with some more coffee in his system. That and a handful of Tylenol. Once inside, he sighed and bent over with a groan to pick up the pile of mail on the floor. Sorting through it, he separated a green index-card-sized notice. He had a certified letter waiting for him at the post office to be picked up. *Great, another bill I bet.* He tossed it on the bed, then shuffled past it and toward the kitchenette to toss the rest of the mail into the trash can next to the two burner stove. He squatted down in front of the small refrigerator and opened it to see if there was anything to eat. A six pack of beer, an old package of salami and packets of hot sauce from Taco Bell. He grabbed the lunchmeat and was assailed by the smell of rot when he peeled back the cover.

"Shit."

He tossed it into the garbage on top of the junk mail and then listened to the popping sound coming from his knees as he stood up. Ford looked around, suddenly wondering where his cell phone was. There, on the counter, charging, where he'd left it when Joe arrived the night before. Flicking the screen to life, he saw eight missed calls, five voicemails, and a dozen texts. Some from various women he had sort of dated, a couple from Hudson and, most disturbingly, from his parole officer.

"Great," he muttered.

He deleted the voicemails and skimmed the texts. Luckily, he hadn't missed his scheduled appointment with his PO. The woman was only calling to remind him about the upcoming meeting. Glancing at the clock on the wall, he still had two hours to make it. He damned well better, seeing as it was the last one he'd ever have. How he'd managed to keep his felony conviction and prison time a secret from Hudson, Ford would never know. He didn't plan on fucking that up now. He'd make his appointment and hopefully finish putting the past behind him.

Ford leaned against the only countertop space and rubbed his face with his hands. Just another hangover in a long string of overindulgent nights. He knew his lifestyle was hazardous and would eventually come back to bite him in the ass, but he didn't have the willpower to stop all his bad habits. Not then, anyway.

It if weren't for Hudson, he probably would have been dead by now. When they were kids, his little brother was his focus and what kept him out of trouble. But he didn't need looking after anymore and now the roles seemed to be reversing themselves. The more debauchery Ford committed, the more scrapes Hudson pulled him out of. Deep inside he was guilty and ashamed for not having done something more with his life, but on the surface Ford just couldn't bring himself to care. It would probably be better if he died. Then Hudson wouldn't have to watch him toss his life into the toilet.

Shaking his head, Ford decided a shower was more important than coffee. The tiny bathroom was kitty corner from the kitchenette and he crossed the room to it in only a half a dozen steps. He turned on the hot water full blast and stripped naked, tossing his filthy clothes into a pile near the doorway.

As he let the scalding water ease his aching muscles, Ford tried to remember what he had done the night before. His buddy Joe had picked him up around eight or so, but almost everything after that was a blur. Many shots and many beers had followed. They might have played some pool. They might have even bar hopped a little. "I'm still going to kick your ass for dumping me at the office." His lone voice echoed off the walls of the tiny shower stall. Joe had probably done it on purpose, thinking it would be funny. *If I wasn't such a fuckup, I might have thought it was funny too.* Unfortunately, all humor had dissolved from his life where Hudson was concerned.

Having no clean towels, Ford climbed out of the shower and let himself air dry as he searched through the piles of clothes throughout the flat. Some piles were dirty, but there was one last heap that had some clean underwear, t-shirts and a single pair of jeans. He pulled on the clothes, then gathered up the rest and stuffed them into a green duffel bag. Grabbing a black leather vest from a hook next to the door, he made sure he had his smokes, phone, and the green card for the post office. He slung the duffel over his shoulder and headed down to his bike. Fastening it tightly on the back of the seat, like a little green passenger, he then climbed on in front of it.

Turning the key in the ignition, his old, beat-up Harley Davidson Heritage roared to life. Coffee, food, post office, parole officer and laundry, in that order, was what he had on his mind as Ford Marks rode away.

Chapter 6

"That's the last of them."

Lilly handed over a stack of Priority Mail boxes and envelopes. Tess put them in the trunk of her car along with the twenty others already stacked there. Lilly had been there within the hour to help and together the sisters had opened all the gifts and then repackaged them to go back. She also wrote out the notes of regret and for that Tess would never be able to repay her big sister. She had cried over some of the lovely items, a crystal picture frame, a place setting of china. Things she would never get to use. But there had been plenty of laughter through the tears over silly gifts like a '70s style lamp from one of her fourth cousins and the matching sugar bowl and creamer shaped like elephants. The time had passed quickly enough and Tess had felt closer to normal again. Almost enough to confide in Lilly all of the swirling emotions inside of her heart and brain. Almost, but not quite.

"Thanks, L. Did you lock the door?"

"Yep. Want me to go with you to the post office too?" Lilly stuffed her hands into the front pockets of her jean shorts.

Tess squinted up in the bright June sun and shook her head.

"No, it's okay. I got it."

"Sure?" Lilly raised her eyebrows.

"I'm sure. You've done way more than enough." Tess stepped toward her and opened her arms for a hug. "Thanks for taking the day off work to help."

"Pffft," Lilly rolled her eyes. "I'll take any excuse not to go into that crazy farm."

Tess chuckled. Lilly managed one of the busiest restaurants in town and hated the job, but it paid the bills. "I'll call you later, okay?"

"Okay. I'll be home."

Lilly gave her a pitiful smile and then turned to walk away to her vehicle. Tess watched and waved as her big sister climbed in and drove away. Sighing, Tess turned back to her car and resumed securing boxes in the trunk and back seat. When everything was stowed, she slammed the trunk shut. Pulling the keys out of her pocket, she stepped toward the side of the car to get in. Looking down, she was mesmerized by the flashing diamonds of her wedding rings.

Taking a deep breath, Tess leaned against the door and exhaled. She turned her hand this way and that, watching the flashing jewels on her finger. Picking out the rings with Jack had been one of the happiest days of her life. He'd done a swell job of choosing the engagement ring, splurging on a full carat emerald cut stone set into a white gold band with tiny baguettes encircling it. The wedding band was exactly the same, without the center stone.

Tess had immediately protested. It was too much money. But Jack had shushed her with kisses.

"I think that's when it started," Tess whispered to no one. Until the day Jack slipped the engagement ring on her finger, she'd had no doubts at all about getting married and spending the rest of her life with him. But as the heavy circle settled on her hand, Tess's breath had caught in her throat. She'd taken it for pleasure and excitement at the time, but looking back she knew it was the first moment she wondered whether or not they were doing the right thing.

Gazing down at the thousands of dollars resting between her knuckles, Tess wondered how long she would wear it. Would it still be there a year from now? Two? Five? Shaking her head, she didn't know. She couldn't even hazard a guess. She might be trying to make the decision to move forward with her life, but it would take small steps. Baby steps. Jack's wedding ring was tucked safely into her jewelry box in her bedroom until she could decide what to do with it. Lilly had suggested wearing it on a necklace, but Tess wasn't sure she wanted what felt like such an obvious marker announcing to the world that she was a widow. Someday she would figure it out. Maybe. Who'd have thought his wouldn't stay on his finger?

Tess climbed into her little Scion XB and headed toward the post office. When she got there, she wished she had asked Lilly to come with her. It took her four arduous trips, carrying all of the carefully packaged boxes. On the last one, the man going in right in front of her let the door close before she could wedge her toe in to stop it. *Thanks, jerk*, she thought nastily. But just as fast as her anger swelled, a feeling of relief and gratitude washed over her as another man coming out of the door stepped aside and held it open.

Tess stopped abruptly. She couldn't help but stare at him. He was dressed in dusty jeans, a black t-shirt and a black leather vest. His brown hair had the faintest streaks of gray at the temples and his face was covered with a sexy coat of stubble. His eyes were hidden behind dark Ray Ban sunglasses, but she could feel them on her just the same. There was an air of danger and sensuality about him which Tess was immediately ashamed for recognizing. *Shit, I'm supposed to be in mourning.*

"Would you like some help?" he asked, the corner of his mouth rising in a half smile. His voice was low and gravelly and Tess was doubly embarrassed that it sent a little thrill through her stomach.

"Uh, no." She recovered and cleared her throat. "This is my last trip. Thanks for the door, though."

"No problem." He waited for her to step inside.

Tess shook her head, feeling chagrinned. *Sorry, Jack.*

Thirty minutes later, every gift had been mailed and Tess felt somewhat better. As heartbreaking as the situation was, she knew she'd done the right thing and was glad it was finished. As she pushed her way through the exit, she fished in her purse for her sunglasses. Popping them on the bridge of her nose, she hurried back to the car and drove home. She had more than twenty hours of transcription waiting for her and she felt awful about it. Her boss, Dr. Guildford, had been extremely patient when he'd learned of Jack's death, telling Tess she could have all the time off she needed. The only other transcriptionist in the office had done as best she could to pick up the slack, but Tess had gone back to work a month after the funeral. She had thought it would help to distract her from the grief.

It hadn't. Instead, she found her production slowing to a snail's pace and her error ratio climbing skyward. Having to go back and revise almost everything every time she submitted records was what really spurred her to get her "work" shit together. Jack's voice in her head telling her she was being a slacker hadn't worked. Only the pitiful looks from Dr. Guildford cut through the haze of depression and grief, when he would return printouts to her with enough red pen revisions to make it look like a D-minus term paper. Over time, her content had improved but her speed was still way below what it once was. She was always behind and ashamed at the reminder texts and voicemails that rolled in from the office manager. Tess was pretty sure it was only pity that kept her employed.

As she came through the door of the apartment, the landline phone was bleating its annoying robotic ring. Sighing, Tess dropped her keys and purse to the floor. She was in no hurry to answer it; the relic of an answering machine she used would take a message. She really didn't have any reason to keep the landline. Anyone Tess ever wanted to speak with called her on her cell. But Jack's voice was still on the machine. She stood next to the little black box and its phone in the cradle, waiting for the caller to reveal themselves.

"Hi! You've reached Jack and Tess. We can't take your call so leave us a message and we'll get back to you later."

Since his death, Jack's voice always had a way of bringing tears to her eyes, but this time it didn't. Cocking her head to the side, she smiled a little. *Maybe I am getting better.*

"Good afternoon, this is Melissa from EJR Insurance calling for Tess Kingston. If you could please give us a call back at—"

Tess lunged for the receiver and snatched it up.

"Hello?" she asked, her tone cautious.

"Hi! May I please speak with Tess Kingston?"

"Uh," Tess stuttered, "what is this regarding?"

"It's a personal matter, ma'am. Is Mrs. Kingston available?"

Tess held the phone away for a second and frowned at it. "Well, I am Mrs. Kingston."

"Mrs. Kingston, my name is Melissa and I'm calling from EJR Insurance. It has come to our attention that Jack Kingston passed away this past December. On behalf of the entire company, we'd like to express our deepest sympathies to you."

Pinching the bridge of her nose, Tess forced herself to be polite. "Thank you."

She heard Melissa take a deep breath. "I'm very glad to have reached you, Mrs. Kingston. Every year, we do a periodic check of the death records for any of our client's names and Jack Kingston appeared. You are the named beneficiary on a life insurance policy he purchased in November of this past year."

"What do you mean?" Tess sat down heavily on the couch. "Jack didn't buy any life insurance."

"Yes, ma'am, he did. It's our policy at EJR to confirm the identity of beneficiaries before we disburse any payouts. If you provide me with an email address, I can send you a letter with a confirmation number and security code. When you receive it, call us back and you can speak to one of our benefits agents."

"Okay. When should I expect it?"

"I'll process the letter today and it should arrive within the next twelve to twenty-four hours. What's your email address?"

"It's Tess Langford twelve at my mail dot com."

Melissa repeated it back and spelled it as well. "Do you have any other questions for me?"

Tess snorted. "Well, yeah, about a million, but I'm guessing you can't really answer any of them. I guess I'll just wait for the letter."

"That's probably best, Mrs. Kingston," Melissa agreed. "From all of us at EJR, please let me extend to you our deepest sympathies once again. We are so very sorry for your loss."

Tess rolled her eyes, despising the phrase but knowing it was what people said. "Thank you."

"You're welcome. Goodbye."

"Bye."

Tess put the phone back into the charging cradle, staring at it with confusion. So Jack had taken out an insurance policy and not told her. It was weird, but not completely surprising. Jack had always been a spontaneous and impulsive guy. Someone had probably said something to him about how they would need to get life insurance now that he and Tess were getting married. Still, she thought, why wouldn't he have said something to her?

Should she wait until she got the email? Or should she get up and start rifling through his office for paperwork? Tess didn't know what to do. The spare bedroom had been Jack's space since the day they moved into the apartment. She hardly ever went in there when he was alive, much less since he died. She probably wouldn't have gone into the room for another year, if she could have avoided it. Now, she couldn't. She was going to need information, whether she waited for the letter or not.

Tess rose from the couch slowly and took grudging steps across the room to the hallway. A door on either side represented the bedrooms. One was the master with the door wide open, the other closed off to Jack's domain. She turned to the right to face the closed door. She reached out to lay a flat palm against the cool surface of the door. Her heart was still racing from the phone call, but now it sped up even more, thumping against her chest like a ricocheting tennis ball.

Timothy meowed from behind her, then pounced toward the door. He stood on his hind legs and scratched against it, showing the first bit of interest in the room since Jack's death.

"Okay, Timmy. Let's do this."

Tess took a deep breath, grabbed the knob and twisted, pushing the door to peek in. The room looked exactly like Jack was still alive and would be returning to it any moment. The laptop was open on the desk. There were empty cans of various energy drinks, Coke, and Pepsi piled up in the makeshift recycle bin he'd made out of a copy paper box. The room even smelled like him. She caught the scent of his aftershave and the winter-green mints he liked to chew on while he worked. Her face scrunched up in pain, tears springing to her eyes. *So much for getting better.*

"I don't know if I can," she whispered. From out of nowhere, Spencer scampered into the room and began meowing furiously, as if he was looking for Jack. She looked at him through her wet eyes and swore he was saying, "Where is he? Is this where you've been hiding him?"

"I know, buddy," she said, as she walked over and picked him up.

Tess sunk to the futon against the wall and continued to cuddle with the cat, even though it was obvious from his writhing and twitching that he wanted to get down and explore the room. Finally, she released him and he nosed through the clothes and under the desk. He even went to the closet and pawed at the door. In spite of her sadness, Tess smiled at that. "No, goofus, he's not in the closet."

Spencer hopped onto the desk and sat right on the keyboard of the laptop. The screen jumped to life, much to Tess's surprise. She squinted from across the room, but recognized Microsoft Word immediately. She walked over to get a closer look. Wiping away the water in her eyes, she stared down at the screen.

"Oh shit."

Tess picked it up and carried it into the living room. She plopped on the couch and began to read.

Dear Tess,   *December 12*

I love you with all of my heart. I can't believe I am married and get to spend the rest of my life with you. I feel so lucky. This honeymoon is going to be the best vacation we've ever had. I just know it.

I wanted to tell you all this in person, but I was kind of racked up about a lot of stuff that happened in the last month. I was afraid it would ruin our day and be a big distraction. I figured if I took care of it before hand, without telling you, then it would feel like we won the lottery instead.

I don't really know how to tell you, so I'll just do it like my dad did. Six weeks before the wedding, he told me I was adopted.

Tess stopped reading, glancing at the top of the letter. It was dated the day after their wedding and Jack had obviously planned on giving it to her on their honeymoon, she guess.

He told me the weekend he and I went camping. My birth father was a football star and left me a shit ton of money, which my dad's been managing for me since it happened. He says he never told me because they wanted to wait until I was "of age", but I'm not sure I buy it. We got into a big argument and came back early. Then I had a huge fight with David about all of it. I'm not really sure how I feel about being adopted and a millionaire all at the same time. And then Dad and David started acting real douchey. It was a lot to handle. Yes, I know, I should have come to you, but

"Yes, you should have, you asshole!" Tess yelled, sniffing back the tears filling her eyes.

I didn't want it to get in the way of the wedding. You seemed so happy and consumed with all the details. I didn't want to burden you. I hope you can forgive me for not telling you sooner.

Tess couldn't decide if that statement helped or hurt. It proved Jack hadn't had any idea how conflicted she was before the wedding and for that she was glad. Once again, though, she was overwhelmed with guilt about her ungratefulness for having probably the best guy in the world as her fiancé. Trying to push those feelings aside, she forced herself to focus and keep reading.

Bottom line is this: you and I are set for life. We won't have to work another day if we don't want to. We can travel and start a family and do all those things we said we wanted to do. I went ahead and saw a lawyer to get everything transferred into my name and then I did a will for you. That way if anything ever happens to me, you'll be protected. I was so upset that my parents hid all this from me for so many years that I didn't want to wait until we got back. I wanted it all taken care of as soon as possible. Even now, I'm still really angry. I would have liked to know my birth father.

So right now, you're in the living room talking on the phone with your mom figuring out some last wedding detail and I don't think you've ever sounded happier. I need your help to figure out what to do with my family. Adopted or not, they raised me. They must have had a good reason for not telling me the truth. I want your advice so we can make sure the future

The letter ended there.

Tess stared at the screen, frozen. The words were trying to register in her brain. Adopted? Inheritance? None of it made any sense. She forced herself to read the entire letter again until the meaning of Jack's words began to really sink in. He'd known about it all for weeks before the wedding and said nothing. *Nothing!*

"Why?" she yelled, snapping the lid closed. "Why didn't you come to me?"

How could Jack have kept such huge revelations from her? Tess couldn't figure out how to feel. Anger was the predominant emotion as all of the new information roiled around in her brain. Betrayal was running a close second, making her stomach burn with rage.

Tess shoved the computer off her lap and it skittered across her legs and the top of the coffee table to land with a crack on the floor. Growling, she got up to retrieve it and ended up stubbing her toe on the leg of the table. The pain that exploded in her foot caused her to shriek. Hopping up and down on her right foot, she held the toe of her left in her hands.

Raunchy expletives spewed forth as she lost her balance and fell backwards onto her butt.

"Uh, what the hell is going on?"

Tess's head flew up when she spotted Lilly standing in the doorway, a twelve pack of Labatt Blue in one hand and her purse in the other.

"What are you doing here?" Tess snapped. "I'm having a breakdown. Can't you see that?" Her cheeks flamed with embarrassment. She tore her eyes away and examined her wounded toe.

"Yeah, I kind of got that impression from all the swearing I could hear from the parking lot." Lilly came all the way inside and closed the door behind her. She moved to set the beer on the coffee table, but stopped short before stepping on the laptop. Gingerly, she tiptoed around it to deposit the twelve pack on the floor. Flinging her purse onto the couch, she went to her sister and squatted down in front of her.

"I didn't think you should be alone after what we did today, so I came back. Tell me what's going on, Tess."

Tess's bottom lip quivered and she tried not to revert to her new habit of falling into a blubbery mess, but shouldn't have even bothered. She started to cry and let her sister pull her into an embrace.

"It's okay, little sis. I'm here now."

Chapter 7

"I just don't get it," Tess said softly as she sat in her parents' kitchen sipping coffee with them. As promised, EJR Insurance had emailed a letter but by the time it arrived, it was too late to call the company. The wait for nine a.m. so she could, was agonizing. After finally connecting with the benefits department and confirming her identity, she had been told that Jack had taken out a life insurance policy in the amount of $1,000,000 on December 2, a little over three weeks before their wedding. She would be receiving a lump sum payment within the next seven to ten days, which she could have hand delivered or pick up herself. When Tess had asked why it had taken so long for them to contact her, she was told that it was EJR's policy to research the cause of death and determine that it was not a suicide before contacting the named beneficiary. When the check was ready, she would receive another call. Part of her figured when that call came, the other shoe would drop. The faceless name at the other end of the line would ask her to wire a couple of thousand dollars to Nigeria so that she could get the full million dollars, or some such other nonsensical scam.

A larger part of her felt there had to be more going on than she was aware. After reading the letter she found on Jack's computer, Tess had way more questions than answers. Jack had alluded to an inheritance. A "shit-ton" of money, were his words. So where was it all? Had his family kept it from her? She was going to have to get in touch with the Kingstons and that did not thrill her. Since the funeral, there had been only limited, awkward contact. Even though she had spent as much time at their house as her own growing up, it was as if she had died too. Tess didn't feel like they wanted anything to do with her anymore. Both sides had pulled away, probably because neither one knew what to say to the other. She didn't blame them, but it would have been nice to have support from both sides while she grieved.

Ruth Langford grasped her daughter's hands in her own. "Jack obviously never thought he would die, but he did something to take care of you." The fifty-five year old woman didn't look a day over forty. She shared the same honey blonde hair and blue eyes as Tess, though her frame was plumper after two children. Tess wasn't thin, but neither was she flirting with too much weight. She obviously took after her mom.

"I'm grateful for that, Mom. But why wouldn't he have told me about this?" Tess squeezed her mom's hands back. "What if it's all some weird scam or something?"

"I don't think it's a scam, Padunkin." Harry Langford sat across the dining room table from his youngest girl. "It sounds just like what happened when your Uncle Pat died a couple of years ago and they contacted me as the beneficiary. Jack probably didn't want to worry you. I don't tell your mother about half the financial things I do because I don't want her freaking out and overthinking things."

Ruth pursed her lips and gave her husband a haughty look of derision. "Ha!"

Her parents' congenial bickering made Tess smile. It also made her sad. She and Jack had been the same way, but now she no longer had someone to spar with. She stared into the coffee cup in front of her, feeling more confused and bereft than ever. *Just when I thought I was finally getting my bearings.*

"This is awesome, Tess!" Lilly said, manufacturing a delighted look. "You won't have to worry about anything now!" Tess had called her big sister to come over so she could have all her family available to help hash through what was turning out to be a complete mindfuck. Lilly was sworn to secrecy about her breakdown and Tess had no worries that Lilly would break the confidence.

"Have you looked through Jack's things to see if he left any paperwork?" Harry asked the question no one else was willing to ask.

"Not yet," Tess admitted. "My first look into his office was nothing but chaos. I guess I'm scared to go back in."

Ruth leaned forward and hugged her baby girl. "That's okay, sweetheart. If you want, we could come over and do it for you."

Tess gave her a wan smile. "I guess. I probably need to call Jack's parents, too. If they knew about all this, then why didn't they tell me?"

"They might not know about the life insurance part," Lilly offered. She sat perched on the kitchen counter, next to the sink. She pushed her dark brown hair behind her ears and shrugged. "But they still should have told you about the rest of it." While Tess looked like a carbon copy of their mother, Lilly was Harry's twin, with dark hair and green eyes. Tall and lithe, she had an athlete's physique.

"I don't know what to do first," Tess said, her voice low with sadness.

"Why don't we take a ride over to your place and see what we can find. Then, you can call Emily and Roger." As the matriarch of the Langford clan, Ruth usually made the decisions and plowed the way.

"Sounds like a plan," Lilly agreed.

"Tess?" Harry cocked his head to the side to get her attention. "Are you okay with this?"

"Yeah." She stood up and smoothed her jeans over her legs and yanked on the edge of her plain white t-shirt. "Let's do it."

* * * * *

Lilly sifted through the files in the desk drawer while Ruth poked around the closet in Jack's office. Harry and Tess stayed in the living room, talking quietly. Lilly hoped she would find something, anything, that would give her little sister some answers. It broke her heart to see Tess go through the last six months. Her sister had always been the perky upbeat one, while Lilly was more cynical and pragmatic. Tess's natural effervescence had all but disappeared, leaving her morose and melancholy. Lilly was the strong one, able to survive tragic circumstances and move on. All she wanted to do was protect Tess and fix everything for her.

"There isn't anything in here but clothing. I don't see any papers or anything like that," Ruth said, closing the closet door.

"Come on over and take the other drawer." Lilly was only half way through hers. When she did get through the rest of the files, Lilly sighed. "Nothing on this side. It's all utility bills and stuff like that." Glancing around, she tried to think of where to look next. She spied a black shoulder bag propped up against the side of the futon and crawled across the room to grab it.

"What's that?"

"Looks like Jack's laptop case."

Lilly flipped open the flap and dumped the contents on the floor. It was mostly trash; gum and mint wrappers, crumpled receipts from fast food purchases, a few pens, and the usual dirty grit that collected in the bottom of any bag. Just as she was about to abandon it, a business card fluttered out and landed on the floor. Lilly plucked it up and read it.

"I've got something."

Ruth looked away from her project. "What is it?"

"Hudson Marks, Attorney at Law."

Lilly and her mother went out to the living room and took seats on either side of Tess. "We found this."

She took the card and read it. "Oh boy."

"Call him," Lilly prompted. "Call him right now."

"Okay!"

Tess pulled her cell phone from her pocket and dialed the number on the card. After four rings, a professional, throaty voicemail message came on. When it ended and she heard the telltale beep, Tess hesitated before speaking. "Uh, hi. My name is Tess Lang, er, Tess Kingston. My husband was Jack Kingston. I'd like to speak with Hudson Marks. Please give me a call at your earliest convenience." She recited her number and then added a hasty "thank you."

She tapped the end button to disconnect the call and promptly burst into tears.

* * * * *

Tess looked in the mirror and checked her makeup. In spite of all the foundation she so carefully applied, her eyes were still puffy from crying and she looked too pale. It couldn't be helped, though. She wasn't willing to pile on any more cosmetics. She already thought she might be bordering on clownish.

Tess smoothed her jeans and adjusted the black-and-white striped tunic she had chosen. Going to see her mother-in-law was making her feel queasy and she wanted to do her best to look presentable. Emily Kingston was a proper lady, someone who would have been amongst socialites and high society had she been born to a higher station or married better. She would notice any deficiencies in Tess's appearance, even if she had the good graces not to mention them outright.

Before leaving the house, she grabbed the phone and dialed her in-laws' number from memory. After four rings, the voicemail picked up and she almost hung up. After a few seconds, she blurted out a message.

"Hi, it's Tess. I, uh, need to come over and see you, uh, guys. I'm going to run by and see if you're home. You can call me on my cell if you want."

Tess ended the call and let out a shaky breath. Things had been understandably awkward between all of them with Jack dying only minutes after the ceremony. It didn't feel like a real marriage in a lot of ways, and Tess was loath to admit that. But she'd known Jack for most of her life and she didn't think her association with his family would abruptly end just because he died. If anything, Tess figured their bond would grow stronger, once the initial shock wore off. But as the days after the funeral wore on, there had been no contact with her in-laws to speak of.

Tess left the apartment with a "be good" to the cats, and then drove through the light traffic of St. Clair Shores to Jack's childhood home on Revere Street. The sound of an old fashioned phone was barely audible above the low playing radio and sound of traffic on the street. Keeping one hand on the wheel, she used the other to rifle through her purse for her cell, but by the time she found it, the call had gone to voicemail. *Oh well.*

The closer she got to her in-laws', the more nervous Tess became. She tried to shake it off, wiggling her shoulders and taking deep breaths as she pulled onto their street. "You have nothing to worry about," she said out loud, trying to convince herself that more trouble was not looming ahead.

As if all the crazy shit that day wasn't enough, when Tess got closer to their driveway, she could see their other son's car already parked there. This did nothing to calm her already frayed nerves. She should have been relieved to see that David was there so she could consult all of them at the same time, him being a lawyer and all. Instead, it left her feeling nauseated and more agitated. She and David hadn't always gotten along that well. He thought like a lawyer first, in all instances of his life, and to him, Tess was just another character cast in his courtroom drama.

As Tess parked on the street across from the house, she could see Emily on her knees working in her flowerbeds. Her two little Yorkies snuffled around her and began yapping up a storm when they caught sight of Tess. Emily immediately stopped digging and looked up to see what the ruckus was all about.

"Well, hello," she said as Tess approached the yard. Emily got up and brushed her hands off on her gardening apron, then yanked her gloves off and stuffed them into the pocket.

"Hi-i." Tess's voice cracked with nerves. Emily's eyes looked tired and the corners of her mouth were drawn down. *She looks pretty bad*, Tess thought, but not unkindly. She felt bad for her mother-in-law.

Emily reached to give a half-hearted hug and then stepped back as if to put some space between them. Tess frowned a little, but turned to look at the dogs in order to hide it. She noticed them digging into the bright yellow flowers at the corner of the porch and side yard. Emily saw them too and jumped toward them, waving her hands.

"Renaldo! Francesco! Get out of there!" She raced over and shooed them away from the almost neon blooms. "Those will hurt you!"

Tess stayed where she was, feeling vulnerable and uncomfortable, shifting from one foot to the other as Emily smothered her little dogs with kisses and admonishments.

"Those flowers could take you all the way up to Heaven, you sillies," she murmured to them and Tess felt as though she might gag, mentally rolling her eyes. Jack's mother had always treated the dogs in the family like they were her children.

"I see David's here, too," she said, trying to get Emily's attention.

"Yes, he is. What are you doing here?"

Tess raised her eyebrows in surprise. "I called, but no one answered."

"Oh, of course," Emily shook her head, "David and Roger just got back and I was out here. I must not have heard the phone. But of course you're welcome any time, dear. Is there something wrong?"

I'll say. "Well, kind of. Could I come and talk to you guys about something?"

Emily set the dogs down and reached to link her arm with Tess's. "Yes, come in. How rude of me."

They walked arm in arm up the porch steps of the two-story bungalow. Tess had always loved the modest coziness of the Kingston home, even if the rest of Jack's family acted as if they lived in a mansion along Lake St. Clair.

"Tess!" David looked shocked as she entered the kitchen. "What are you doing here?"

"David!" Emily admonished. "You sound as if Tess isn't entitled to come over any time she likes. She's your sister-in-law."

The hollowness of that statement hung in the air like a vile odor. Roger Kingston squirmed in his chair, refusing to meet Tess's eyes, fiddling with a beer can sitting in front of him. David didn't have the decency to look embarrassed, but he spit out a grudging apology anyway. Emily pulled a chair out for Tess, then one for herself and sat, cradling the canine called Francesco as if it were an infant, shushing and cooing at it.

Tess exhaled a deep breath she didn't realize she was holding. Before sitting, she reached into her purse, pulling out the letter from the insurance company. "I'm glad you're here, David. I got this today and it's a little confusing." She handed it to him and he began to read. Tess watched, surprised to see irritation spreading across his face.

"I hope you don't expect to get anything else from Jack's estate."

"What?" Roger spluttered, nearly dropping his drink making foam erupt out of the can like a volcano.

Tess frowned and took a small step backward. "What is that supposed to mean? I didn't even know Jack had an estate!" Tess hadn't meant to shout, but her voice boiled out of her mouth before she could help herself. Emily flinched and Roger clamped a hand over his face and rubbed it down to his chin, as if he could erase his distress.

"Tess, dear," Emily began, reaching to take one of her hands. Tess pulled back as though it was a snake about to strike. "We thought Jack would tell you."

"Tell me what?" Tess lowered her voice, but she knew the mixture of hurt, anger, confusion, and anxiety were far from disguised. She looked from one person to the other, willing someone to speak. A million years later, or so it felt, Roger did.

"Jack wasn't our real son. He was adopted."

Chapter 8

"I already know that."

All three of the Kingston mouths dropped open at once, but no one said anything to her. Tess wanted to say "ha ha ha" just to be a snot, but thought better of it. Things were already taking a wild turn for the worse and she didn't want to antagonize her in-laws any further. Finally, she lowered herself into the hardback, wooden chair at the oak dining table.

"So Jack did tell you," Roger accused, leaning forward.

Tess was about to answer when the old fashioned phone ringtone blared once again from inside her purse. She scrambled to grab it and silence the noise. Inhaling slowly and deeply, she closed and opened her eyes. "Actually, Jack never said anything. Yesterday I got a phone call from an insurance agency wanting to speak to me. They told me I was the beneficiary of a policy Jack purchased. Then they sent me that and I called to get confirmation." She pointed to the letter still clutched in David's hands. He shoved it at his father as if suddenly the paper was burning his fingers. "I went through Jack's things and found a letter on his computer that he wrote to me."

"Oh!" Emily cried. "Can I see it?"

Tess shook her head. "No, I'm sorry. I'm not comfortable sharing it."

Emily's face crumpled with disappointment but she didn't argue. "Can you tell us what he said?"

"There weren't a lot of details," Tess admitted. "It just said that he was adopted and didn't know until the weekend you went hunting." She looked at Roger then, who was still staring off into space. "He said his birth father played football and left everything to Jack when he died."

"Let me guess." David sneered. "You're here to try and get your hands on the rest of his money."

Tess glared at him. "No. I'm here for answers."

"Good because Jack died without a will. You won't see a penny of his inheritance. You weren't even married five minutes." David smirked at her in a haughty way. A statement like that should have made Tess cry. Instead, she was filled with rage, wanting to bash his face with the peppermill sitting in the middle of the table. Clenching her fists in her lap, she felt her fingernails dig into her palms and the burning sensation kept her from spewing hateful words back at her brother-in-law.

"David!" Emily gasped and held Francesco closer to her chest. She was stroking the dog's fur and whispering nonsense words into its ear. Roger said nothing, but glared at his older son.

"It's the truth, Mother!" David snatched the insurance letter from his father and flipped it in Tess's direction. She had to slap it on the table to keep it from floating to the floor. "Your marriage could be annulled in a heartbeat."

"That's enough," Roger finally said. When David opened his mouth to continue, his father cut him off. "Shut up, David."

David crossed his arms over his chest in a huff but said nothing more.

"What do you want to know, Tess?"

"Everything. Start from the beginning."

Roger sighed, breath whooshing from his mouth like a small explosion.

"After David was born," he began, "Emily and I knew we wanted more children. We tried for years and were unsuccessful. When it finally became clear we weren't going to have any more of our own, we adopted Jack. He was the product of two foolhardy teenagers who didn't use protection. The girl was only sixteen and the boy was seventeen. They were convinced to give the baby up for adoption and we were lucky enough to get Jack. But it turns out that the father went on to make something of himself. He was a talented athlete and got a full scholarship to college where he played football. Then he got drafted into the NFL. You ever heard of Benjamin Thatcher?"

Tess shook her head, too riveted by the story to care about the minor details.

"Anyway," Roger paused to sip some beer, "he had a short but pretty successful career. He took the pile of money he made and invested very wisely in real estate, which earned him an even bigger pile of cash. When he first contacted us, he was at the tail end of playing and wanted to know if we would allow him to see Jack. Long story short, we decided that we didn't want them to meet until Jack was eighteen and then we'd let our son make the decision. We hadn't told Jack yet that he was adopted."

Tess's mouth hung open. "Why didn't you tell him when he turned eighteen?"

"We got word through the birth father's attorney that he'd died in a plane crash and he left his entire estate to Jack, listing me as the primary trustee until Jack's twenty-first birthday. Instead of telling him, we got our own lawyer and invested everything on Jack's behalf. He was only sixteen at the time and we had every right." Roger's tone became defensive.

Tess didn't think the hinge on her jaw was going to hold when her chin nearly hit her chest. "But—"

"Let me finish," Roger insisted, holding up his hands to protect himself, like he thought Tess would climb across the table and attack him. She couldn't help admitting to herself that she kind of wanted to. "I did tell Jack everything that weekend. He was pretty angry with me for not saying something sooner."

"Ya think?" Could there have been a more obvious statement to an equally obvious reaction to finding out you're adopted? Tess wanted to say all the snarky things wandering through her brain, but good sense and Ruth's manners kept her silent.

"Once he calmed down, though, Jack was fine with it." Emily smiled placidly, while staring off into space. By the wistful nature of her voice and the look in her eye, Tess imagined she was thinking of Jack. She couldn't blame her, because she thought of Jack almost all the time, too.

"We told him all about his father's background, the investments."

"He was more pissed off that you made him pay for his own college, when you knew he had all that dough," David muttered. His green eyes were clouded over, too, and his earlier anger and distaste seemed to have disappeared.

As she leaned back in her chair, staring at all of them in shock and awe, she could see it then. Jack didn't look like any of them. The only physical characteristic he shared was his mother's lack of height. Emily was only about five-four and Jack had been about five-eight. Both Roger and David were well over six feet. The Kingstons all had green eyes and blond hair. Jack's had been a chocolate brown. When learning about ancestry and DNA and the like in school, they'd figured it was due to recessive genes. Tess didn't believe Jack ever suspected he wasn't from this family. He'd always taken on enough of their personality traits to make up for the lack of physical resemblance. Still... how could she not have noticed?

Roger looked ashen and twenty years older than the last time Tess had seen him. Emily's usually flawless makeup was applied thicker and more haphazardly. David wasn't as clean shaven and unrumpled as Tess was used to. She wanted to stay angry with them. Furious that they'd kept such a huge secret from Jack, and then her. But in that moment, their suffering was palpable. They'd lost their child and brother. They were hurting as much as she was, if not more.

Desperate to keep calm, Tess let the silence engulf the room for several minutes before she relaxed her shoulders and spoke again.

"When were you going to tell me about all of this?" she asked quietly, leaning forward and lacing her hands together on top of the table. "It's been more than six months since the funeral."

She waited for an answer, but Emily continued to pet her dog. Roger found a piece of lint to pick off his pants. David concentrated on a spot in the middle of the table.

"Were you ever going to tell me?"

"I don't know." Roger made this admission softly, his glance in her direction darting and nervous. "Probably. I think I always knew it wouldn't stay a secret forever. I didn't know Jack had taken out the insurance policy."

"It seems like we're all a bit in the dark then." Tess tried to soften her expression and exude some sympathy toward her second family, in spite of their obvious discomfort with her presence and questions. "What do we do now?"

"There's nothing to do," David said, leaning back in his chair and folding his arms across his chest. "I've already opened a probate estate for Jack and we, as his family, are named as the sole beneficiaries. Since the life insurance policy isn't an asset in probate, then you can keep that."

"What kind of investments did Jack have?" Tess asked, before she could stop and think about the inflammatory nature of the question. She didn't have to wait long for David's explosion.

"That's none of your business!" he shouted, standing up and shoving his chair backward. "If you try and make one move to get your hands on anything, I will destroy you in court!" He took a menacing step in her direction. Tess tried to scoot back so she could stand as well, but her chair bumped into a dog, and it yelped. A similar sound escaped Tess's lips.

"Renaldo!" Emily cried. She fumbled to move one dog into one arm while reaching for the other, upending her chair. Emily cuddled the squirming, yapping dogs against her chest, looking from their faces to the chair and back again. Roger hoisted himself up and went to the toppled piece of furniture, righting it so his wife could sit down.

Suddenly Tess was the accused. Jack had kept vital information from her, even though she was pretty sure he had a good reason. He'd never hidden anything from her before. Dead or not, Tess wasn't ready to stop trusting him. Yet, his family was treating her like she was the one to be suspicious of. "I'm not after anything!"

"David," Emily mumbled. "Tess is Jack's wife. Don't you think–"

"No! I don't think anything. You and Dad took care of Jack all his life. Tess was married to him for all of five minutes! She doesn't deserve anything."

"I think you should leave."

This was from Roger. His eyes pleaded with her to get out of the situation.

"I'm not going anywhere until you answer some more of my questions." Tess's hands found their way to her hips in that indignant way Jack always said she had. Her brain was saying run, but her heart couldn't let go of her confusion and hurt.

"Roger's right." Emily's voice was soft but firm. She looked at her then, with obvious effort to drag her gaze away from her furry children. There was no longer any affection in them for Tess, only sadness and... something else. Fear? Tess couldn't tell.

Who are these people? Tess had just been feeling sorry for them in their grief. She'd known them all her life and they had accepted her like the daughter they'd never had. And now she was being asked to leave because she'd become privy to some deep, dark secret. Something she would have known about anyway. Jack would have told her eventually. *Right?*

Tess reached for the insurance letter on the table. David flinched, looking furious, as though she had done something aggressive. His body was rigid and her gut said he was the one on the edge of snapping. And doing what, she didn't have a clue.

Squashing the page in her left hand, she dug her keys out of her jeans pocket with her right as she hurried to the door. Glancing back, no one in the kitchen had moved and Tess was struck with a profound sadness. She had spent nearly half her life in this house and she knew without a doubt she'd never be back.

Chapter 9

Tears ran down her cheeks, splashing onto her chest as Tess squealed the tires to get away from Jack's family. She tried blinking fast so she could see to drive, but after a block or two she knew she was a hazard on the road.

Pulling over to the curb, Tess rested her head on the steering wheel and sobbed. As bad as it was to lose Jack on their wedding day, as horrible as it was to suffer through the funeral and sending back the wedding presents, even suffering with all the guilt she carried, Tess had thought she was finally finding her footing again. She was back at her own place. She was getting out of bed every day, showering, eating, working. Doing all the things she knew she was supposed to be doing.

Now, not just the rug had been ripped out from beneath her, but the whole house with it. Everything her life had been built on was not what she thought. She needed time to process and she wasn't being given that opportunity. New information kept piling on top of her like a garbage truck dumping its load at the landfill.

Tess's chest was heavy and tight; she couldn't breathe, she couldn't think. She couldn't focus on any one aspect of the circumstances long enough to accept or deal with it. Afraid she would do something stupid, she put the car back in gear and drove to her parents' house.

As she pulled in to their circular driveway from Jefferson Avenue, she could see a strange truck parked in front of the double garage and her heart plummeted into her shoes. *Please God, not something else. Please. Not now. I cannot take one more thing.* Tess climbed out of her car, straightened herself and hurried up the steps toward the front door of her parents' vintage colonial home. She burst through the door into the foyer, spooking the two house cats, Abercrombie and McTavish, who fled to parts unknown.

"Mom?" Tess called out.

"Tess!" Ruth came up the long hallway from the back of the house into the foyer. "Did you get my message?"

Tess didn't answer her, barely hearing her words. She threw herself into her mother's arms and began crying on her shoulder. Ruth rubbed the back of her daughter's head and made shushing sounds as they rocked back and forth. Harry Langford appeared and joined them, hugging both wife and daughter to his chest. Tess wasn't sure how long they had stood there, but it didn't really matter. She felt bad about losing it, but that had always been her way. When some tragedy or misfortune took over her life and she needed her parents, Tess could never keep control before relating the facts. Once she exhausted herself of tears, she could hash things out in a rational manner.

When Tess was finally able to gather herself together, Ruth handed her a tissue from the ever-present stash in her pocket. "Thanks," Tess sniffled, wiping her face and nose. "Sorry."

"Don't be sorry," Ruth scoffed. "You got my message."

Tess's bottom lip wiggled with anxiety and the threat of fresh tears. "No, I didn't. If it's more bad news, don't tell me. I can't handle one more thing."

Harry glanced at Ruth and frowned. She grimaced back.

"Whose truck is that?" Tess pointed back over her shoulder.

"Come on into the kitchen, Padunkin." Harry reached for her hand. He hardly ever used her childhood nickname anymore and Tess groaned.

"Daddy?"

"It's okay, kiddo. Come with me."

Harry led her down the hallway toward the kitchen. When she stepped in the doorway, she couldn't have been more shocked than the day Jack died, and the sound of air sucking into her lungs proved it. The sexy guy from the post office earlier that day was sitting at the table, sipping coffee from one of her mom's familiar mugs. *He held the door for me.* Beside him sat a younger man in a suit and tie, which had been slightly loosened. She stopped short, causing Ruth to run right into the back of her.

"Hello again." Sexy Man said, raising his cup to her in a gentle salute. His voice was as rough and scratchy as she remembered. And still just as sexy.

"Uh, hello?" Tess prayed she wasn't blushing. *Stop that!*

The younger man stood up and extended a hand in her direction. "I'm Hudson Marks, the lawyer who drew up Jack's will."

Tess was having trouble remembering to pay attention to anyone but the leather clad man sitting in what was normally her father's chair. Blinking herself back to reality, she tried to focus. "Will? Jack has a will?" She shook his hand and then sat down heavily in one of the other chairs.

"Yes, he does, and I have a copy of everything for you." He indicated a large yellow envelope sitting on the table. "I'm sorry to meet you under these circumstances and for your loss." Hudson dipped his chin in what Tess figured was a show of sympathy and it made her mentally flinch. *When am I ever going to get used to that?*

"Thank you." Tess lowered her head, grateful for the opportunity to avoid looking at the other man, or feeling his gaze on her.

"Mrs. Langford, could I please get a refill?" Sexy Guy held his mug up in the air.

"Of course!" Ruth rushed to get more coffee while Harry took a seat beside Tess.

"What are you doing here?" Tess asked. "How did you know I'd be here? How did you know where my parents lived?" Her world felt as if it were spinning out of control. Sweat gathered beneath her arms and her fingers began to tremble the same way they did when she hadn't eaten all day. Twisting them together, she shoved her hands between her knees. The words like "will" and "lawyer" were suddenly thudding into her brain like spikes.

"Jack left specific instructions for the delivery of his will. He gave me a list of all your relatives' phone numbers and addresses. I tried returning your call a couple of times earlier, but you didn't answer. When I didn't reach you, I tried calling your parents. They invited me over to wait for you. Ruth thought you might show up here."

Tess's knees began to bounce up and down as she remembered the ringing of her phone from before. "How come you didn't call me right after Jack died? It's been over six months."

Hudson's face filled with sorrow and pity, making Tess want to smack him.

"I did not know that Jack had passed."

Tess snorted. "My husband didn't pass. He wasn't taking a test. You can say it, he died." Immediately, she regretted her words. Every face in the room went stiff with shock and embarrassment from her attack. "I'm sorry," she whispered. "Really, I'm sorry. I just hate that expression." Tess closed her eyes and took a deep breath, conjuring Jack's voice in her head. *Keep it together, T. He's here to help you. No need to shoot the messenger.*

Harry reached for his daughter and rubbed her shoulder. Ruth reappeared with fresh coffee in the carafe and set it in front of Sexy

Man, who busied himself by pouring. Ruth leaned in to kiss the top of Tess's head.

"Please, don't be sorry," Hudson said, his tone kind and warm. "It's totally okay. I received this letter today notifying me that Jack died." He pulled a sheet of paper out of his briefcase and handed it to her. It was from EJR Insurance saying that they would be making a payout to Tess Langford Kingston on the insurance policy.

Tess nodded. "They called me yesterday."

"Well, that makes sense then why I would get a notification too." Hudson jotted some notes on the pad of paper in front of him. "I take it, then, that you don't know anything about Jack's estate planning?"

She shook her head no, but continued to stare at her lap. "I didn't. It's been a pretty hard time, Mr. Marks."

"Please, call me Hudson." He turned to the table to look at the file open there, flipping through pages before looking at her again. "I can't begin to imagine how all this has been for you. I wish I had found out sooner. The last thing I want to do is add more to your plate. Jack was worried about all of the assets he came into very suddenly. He wanted things taken care of as soon as possible." Hudson sighed and ran a hand through his thick, wavy hair. "I would never have believed you'd need the documents so soon."

"Ya think?" Tess muttered, wringing her hands in her lap. She stared at her fingers, lacing and unlacing them together. She had almost successfully forgotten about Sexy Dude. Almost. "When did he do all this?"

"Jack contacted me in November to schedule a meeting." Hudson shuffled through some of his paperwork again. "November twenty-fifth to be exact. We met the next day to go through all of the paperwork and begin drafting the documents. Everything was finalized and signed a few days before your wedding. Usually I don't work that quickly on an estate plan as large as Jack presented, but he seemed worried. Jack wasn't sick, was he?"

Tess scratched her head. "Not at all. What was he worried about?" Dredging up the play-by-play of the last two weeks before the wedding, Jack had seemed happy and excited. He was focused on making sure all his work was finished and clients covered so they could go on their honeymoon without any distractions. He was attentive and patient with her through all the pre-wedding jitters and last minute chaos to make sure everything was perfect for their big day.

Guilt thudded in her stomach, yet again, as she admitted to herself that it was she who had been completely self-absorbed with doubts and fears in those two weeks. She was the one who hadn't thought of anyone but herself and taking care of all the loose ends for the ceremony and reception. Jack could have trotted around the house in drag and she probably would have told him he looked nice.

Clearing his throat, Hudson paused. "How did Jack die?"

Tess felt her bottom lip quiver, but she bit down on it hard to keep herself from crying. "He had a heart attack. It happened in the vestibule of the church right after the ceremony."

Hudson let out a breath and shook his head, dropping his pen on the table in shock. "Oh Jesus," he whispered. "I mean, geeze, I'm so sorry."

Tess waved a hand, struggling to fill her lungs with air. She could never talk about it without seeing it in her mind.

"Are you all right, kiddo?" Ruth had been hovering just behind her, waiting to see if she and Harry should stay or go.

"I feel like throwing up." She could feel her hands trembling and the fuzzy feeling she got when she thought she might pass out.

Ruth was beside her in one sliding motion. "Do you want some water?"

"Yes, please."

Harry jumped up and vanished to fill a glass and bring it to his daughter. He handed it to Tess, while placing a comforting hand on her back. "Maybe we should do this later, Mr. Marks."

Swallowing the water, Tess shook her head. "No. I'll be okay. Let's get this over with. You and Mom should sit down, Dad. I want you here for this too."

"Are you sure?" Ruth didn't move.

"Yes."

Tess watched her parents take seats on either side of her with reluctance. The water sloshed in her stomach but the wave of nausea passed. "Go on, Hudson."

Turning toward her, ever so slightly, Hudson flipped to a blank page on his legal pad and grabbed his pen. "Was there an autopsy performed? What was the cause of death listed?"

"Yes. They said the heart attack was from all the energy drinks Jack drank. Energy Life, Health Boost, you name it. Jack couldn't get enough of them."

Hudson frowned and wrote. "What about a toxicology report?"

"We haven't gotten one yet."

"Not surprising." He glanced over at Sexy Guy and Sexy Guy's face had a matching blasé expression. Tess looked from one handsome face to the other, a thought tickling the back of her mind, but she couldn't put a finger on it.

"They said it would take a few months. I guess we should be getting it any time." Tess's head ached with the stress of the moment and she was filled with worry by the men's reactions. "Is that bad?"

"Nope," Hudson hurried to reassure her. "I don't have a lot of experience with that kind of thing, but I'd take it as no news is good news. May I ask a few more questions?"

"Sure, go ahead."

"Are you aware that Jack was adopted?"

Harry and Ruth gasped and their eyes grew wide as they looked from Tess to Hudson and Tess cringed.

"Y-yes. I found a letter that Jack wrote to me," she whispered. "And I also heard it from his parents. I'm coming from there, actually."

"Is that why you're so upset?" Ruth demanded. "What happened? Jack was adopted?"

"You've just been with them?" Hudson scribbled furiously on the pad but then his green eyes met hers. They were piercing and forced her to pay attention. There was something oddly familiar about them, but she couldn't place it.

"Yeah. After I got the letter from the insurance company, and I didn't reach you right away, I went to them first. I figured they would know something about it." Tess looked at Hudson and then at Sexy Guy, watching for more reactions. That was when it hit her. She pointed to him and then looked back at Hudson.

"Are you two related?" Tess asked, immediately snapping her lips shut as she realized how rude that must have sounded.

Hudson chuckled. "Yeah. Ford is my brother. He's my private investigator and partner."

"Our parents loved cars, if you couldn't tell," Ford said quietly, raising an eyebrow at her, winking.

Tess smiled at them both and Ford nodded. Now that she'd put two and two together, the resemblance was remarkable. Even though Hudson's face was clean shaven, she could see the same shape in their eyes and nose. She had no doubt that Ford had the same strong chin beneath his facial hair and that one day Hudson would have the beginning streaks of gray at his temples and through his brown hair too. *Snap out of it, you twit!* She needed to be concentrating on what the lawyer was telling her, not comparing their cuteness.

Hudson rifled through some pages on his legal pad. "From this point forward, Mrs. Kingston–"

"Tess, just call me Tess."

Looking directly at her, Hudson spoke in a deliberate tone. "Alright, Tess. From this point forward, I wouldn't suggest any further contact with Jack's family. He left everything to you and that will not make them happy, to say the least."

Tess frowned, because she already knew she didn't want to be around the Kingstons after her unceremonious eviction. It hurt hearing it spoken out loud by a stranger. "I sort of figured that out already. They weren't too pleased with my visit. David said he already opened a probate estate."

"David Kingston?" Hudson's eyes never left her.

"Yeah, that's Jack's brother."

"Tell me what else he said."

Tess recounted everything from the time she arrived at the Kingston home until the moment she left. "I'm pretty confused right now. I know they lost their son and they're grieving, but why would they accuse me of anything? They all looked like I'd done something wrong." Tess could feel her heart aching with grief and regret, feeling the loss of not only her husband and best friend, but an extension of her own family. Her second family.

"You did. You threatened their ability to keep Jack's inheritance for themselves."

"But that's not my fault!" Tess shouted. Ruth grimaced and Tess apologized. "I didn't know anything about any of this. I can't help it if Jack gave it all to me. If that's what this is about, then they can keep it."

"Oh no they can't!" It was Harry's turn to get loud. "Something stinks here. Until it's all figured out—"

"You're right, Mr. Langford," Hudson interrupted, holding his hand up. Turning back to Tess, he lowered his voice. "Jack must have had a good reason to do what he did. I can't lie; I'm quite suspicious of it all. But he didn't confide in me his reasons, only his instructions."

Tess bit her bottom lip and crossed her arms in front of her, wishing for the bazillionth time she could turn back the clock. "Jack never said a word to me about being adopted or the money. I know he found out a few weeks before the wedding, but I swear I didn't see any signs." The stone of guilt got heavier. "I was, uh, too busy with the wedding."

Taking a deep breath, Tess reached for her mother's hand. After a good firm squeeze, Tess nodded and was able to let go. Part of her still wanted to bolt from the room, the house, the whole world.

"Everything will be all right," Ruth said, breaking the silence that filled the room like a noxious gas.

Hudson chewed on the end of his pen for a few moments before writing more notes. Ford drank his coffee and kept his eyes focused on the diminishing liquid in the cup. Tess fidgeted and cracked her knuckles, waiting for whatever would happen next.

She wished she could just give the money to Jack's family; let them have it all. She knew she couldn't travel back in time to change anything, but going forward, she wanted nothing more than to just be left alone. Judging by the look on Hudson's face as he pondered the situation, Tess didn't think that was going to happen. Not at all.

* * * * *

Hudson flipped through some pages of notes in the file folder containing an original of Jack Kingston's will. He hadn't liked taking on the estate planning job on such a hurried basis, but Jack had been a kind of a friend in college. They'd had a few undergrad classes together and when he'd called Hudson up out of the blue, Hudson couldn't say no.

Only now he wished he had. Then he wouldn't have to be sitting in this kitchen with Jack's beautiful widow, trying to hash out what was becoming a mystery. Tess Langford Kingston was a woman with dark honey hair and bright blue eyes. She reminded him of Emma Stone as a blond. He had no other recollection of her from college because his own focus had been getting to class and then getting to whatever part-time job he had to pay for school. The sadness locked on her face made Hudson feel a sense of responsibility to make sure things turned out right for her.

Hudson watched as the soft waves of Tess's hair framed her face. Clearing his throat, he looked back to his pen. "I'm sorry to hammer you, Tess. But I need as much information as possible in order to get a handle on all this."

"I know, but if I don't understand it, how will you?"

Hudson was instantly awash in sympathy for her. "Well, I'm a lawyer. It's what I do. You give me the puzzle pieces and I put them together. You said David has already opened a probate estate for Jack?"

"Yes."

Hudson looked at Ford then down at his legal pad. "We need to get those documents."

"On it," Ford replied.

"We also need to make sure we have a copy of the autopsy report and the toxicology report."

Ford only nodded, and Hudson trusted that his brother was committing everything to memory.

"Were you able to sign the Certificate of Marriage before Jack died?" He hated asking questions that brought up such difficult memories, but if he was going to figure out what he was in for, Hudson had to gut it out and ask them.

"Yeah." Tess was smiling wistfully and it gave her an ethereal look. "We did it right in the ceremony. I stole the idea from my friend Natalie. I swear, I think I heard her laugh when we did it."

Hudson smiled as he wrote, glad that he didn't have to look at Tess while she spoke. A twenty-five year old woman had no business being this sad or embroiled in such a mess. Fate had not dealt her a good set of cards. "That's good, then. I'll submit a petition in the case David filed as soon as possible. The Court will know that Jack created an estate plan and that the Court should close the case without making any kind of award to anyone. The whole point was to avoid probate altogether."

"Oh, that's not going to go well," Ruth muttered. "I can just hear Roger Kingston now."

"Hell," Tess snorted, "wait till David finds out. We'll feel the earth shaking from the tantrum he'll throw." Her words were filled with fear and anxiety, not the satisfaction at thwarting David that Hudson thought she might feel.

"You do know you're entitled to Jack's estate, right?" he asked, ducking his head to put himself into her field of vision.

"David said—"

"I don't care what David said." Hudson stared at her hard to make her understand. "You and Jack were legally married. He drew up documents naming you as his sole beneficiary. You have every legal right to every cent that was his."

"Okay."

"You are not doing anything wrong."

Hudson followed his gut and reached out to pat her on the arm hoping it lent more credence to his statement.

"What if…" Tess hesitated.

"What?"

"What if I didn't want to contest it though?"

Harry and Ruth opened their mouths to protest, but Tess held up her hand.

"What if I just wanted to keep the insurance payout and let them keep the rest? Could I do that?"

Hudson shrugged. "Yes, I suppose you could. We would have to draw up a detailed settlement agreement and meet with the Kingstons to hash everything out, but in theory you can do anything you want with the estate. It's legally yours."

"I need to think about it then."

Out of the corner of his eye, Hudson could see her parents struggling to contain themselves. They wanted to argue with their daughter, but kept a hold of their tongues. He found that very encouraging and felt better. Tess obviously had a good support system around her.

"Have you spoken with the insurance company yet?"

Tess pulled EJR's letter from her purse and gave it to Hudson. "I talked to them this morning. They're going to call me when a check is ready."

Hudson read the letter and all the notes Tess had written on the back. He appreciated her neat and tidy handwriting, wishing his own chicken scratch was as legible. He took a moment to look at Tess, trying to determine how much more she could take in the way of questioning and decided it was time to call it quits. She looked pained and exhausted. There were dark shadows marring the fair skin below her eyes. The corners of her mouth were turned down, as if pulled by the weight of all the news she'd gotten. It wouldn't do any good to push her too far, especially when he had a shitload of investigating to do before he could begin to even assimilate all the information.

"I think we should leave this for the time being."

"I think that's a good idea," Ruth said softly, catching Hudson's eye.

"But I'll need to meet with you again very soon."

"Okay." Tess's lower lip quivered as she spoke, but her voice was stronger than he expected.

"Ford and I will get as much together on our own before we set up another meeting. I'll be in touch in the next day or two, if that's all right."

Tess nibbled on her thumbnail and closed her eyes. "Sure."

Hudson gave her a smile he hoped was reassuring and kind. He pulled a business card from the inside of his suit coat and placed it on the table. He jotted another couple of numbers on the back. "Here's another card with my cell number and Ford's. If anything comes up in the meantime, or you need to reach us, don't hesitate to call or text."

"Yeah, okay." She tried to return his smile and let out a shuddery breath as she did.

Hudson nodded his head and turned back to the table. As he gathered his paperwork and stuffed it into the briefcase, he nodded to both Harry and Ruth, hoping they felt some modicum of peace.

After shaking hands with all three Langfords, Harry led Hudson and Ford out of the house. Feeling their eyes on him, Hudson gave them one final wave where the little family stood on the front porch watching their departure. When the doors were closed and they were alone, Hudson snorted. "This is a load of shit, brother."

"I would agree," Ford replied.

"Harry Langford got it right when he said something smelled foul." Hudson started the engine and put the truck in gear. As they drove through the circular driveway, he pounded the steering wheel with his fist. "The problem is, do we dig deeper or just coast and let trouble find us?"

"Couldn't say." Ford was a man of few words. Hudson knew he was only waiting until his opinion was truly required and not just subject to rhetorical questions.

"It remains to be seen."

* * * * *

Ford stared out the window of the truck and smoked, still a little stunned about meeting Tess Kingston. He was pretty thankful for his poker face when she walked into the dining room of her parents' house, recognizing her instantly as the pretty girl from the post office earlier. No one in that room could have ever known how truly shocked he was to see her again.

It had been a long time since Ford thought about a woman as anything other than a bedroom partner. It wasn't that he didn't have any respect for women. Quite the opposite, actually. He had little respect for himself. He was a felon and an ex-con with the beginnings of a fairly serious drinking problem. He had no business thinking about having a girlfriend or, God forbid, a family. The fact that Tess had given him such pause was tickling his brain in a way he didn't particularly care for.

Hudson was prattling on about things to be done for her case, and Ford tried to pay attention so he could get the pretty widow out of his mind.

"Are you listening to me?" Hudson asked as he flicked his cigarette out the window.

"Yep. All ears."

Hudson frowned and looked back to the road. "Doesn't seem like it."

"Sorry, I wandered for a minute. Don't worry."

"Well, I do. I need you to have your shit together, brother. This is going to be a pretty convoluted case with a lot of balls in the air. I can't afford to drop any of them."

Ford smiled and nodded. "No worries. I've got your back."

Hudson dipped his chin and gave him another sideways glance. "Where were you when I called?"

Ford kept his face bland with a great deal of effort. "Doing laundry."

"For four hours?"

"Yep. I had a lot."

Ford hated lying to his brother, but it was a necessary evil. Hudson had no idea Ford had been in jail and he intended to keep it that way. The summer after his graduation from high school, Hudson had been obsessed with worry over how he would pay for college. He'd had no idea his big brother was working on that by running drugs and guns for a couple of local gangs. Ford was able to get away with it long enough to present his little brother with the money for the first year, claiming it was an inheritance from their long dead father. Shortly after that, his luck ran out and he got busted. Instead of telling Hudson the truth, Ford managed to send him a letter saying he was going to take off for a while and good luck in school. Four years later, out on parole, he'd shown back up.

It had taken almost a year for them to patch things up. There was no way in hell Ford was going to tell Hudson the truth after this many years. Besides, they both needed to focus on their newest client and her case, not something that happened over a decade ago.

Chapter 10

By the time Hudson Marks left her parents' home, Tess was as exhausted as the day she buried Jack. Emotionally, physically and mentally. Her mother started to fix dinner as soon as the Marks's left and did her best to convince Tess to stay, but she refused. Tess wanted to go home and think. No distractions, no questions, and no long-faced, sad-eyed stares from loved ones hoping to take all her pain away, but knowing they couldn't.

Harry walked Tess to her car. Giving her a monstrous hug, he kissed the top of her head. "You know you can stay. For dinner, the night, whatever you need."

"I know, Daddy," Tess snuffled, trying hard not to cry. Again. "But I need to think and I'll be able to do that better by myself."

"Come back if you need to."

"I will, I promise."

Tess extricated herself from his arms and climbed into her car. She saw him in her rear view mirror as he stood in the driveway watching her pull away.

"Dammit," she swore, as the wetness on her cheeks grew more pronounced. She was glad Harry couldn't see her losing her shit again. It would just make him feel worse. She felt bad enough, and hated the fact that everyone around her felt almost as sad. Pulling into her assigned parking space at home, Tess jammed the car in park and reached for her phone. She created a new text message to Lilly: My house later?

The response came quick: Sure. U ok?

No.

What's wrong?

The usual. Just come by.

Tess felt bad always running to her sister with every bit of tragedy, but she was the only person she had to rely on. Jack had been her whole life, and she'd never made that many girlfriends. Instead, she and Lilly had been each other's best friend.

Tess climbed wearily out of her car and trudged to the door. Once inside, two anxious cats charged her. "Babies!" she called out, reaching down to pet them both with vigor. She plopped to the floor on her butt and let both felines walk over her lap as she scratched one behind the ears and the other on its exposed tummy.

Memories of the day she and Jack went to the shelter to choose the kittens bubbled into her mind, like a pot of water boiling over on the stove. "He never was a cat person," Tess whispered, as she picked up Spencer and snuggled him against her chest. "But he loved you best. You guys had a bond, Pence." Never liking to be held all that much, the inky, twenty pound feline struggled to get down. "Oh, he loved you too, Timmy," Tess sniffed, reaching for Timothy who didn't mind being cradled in her arms like a baby, as long as his tummy got rubbed.

Tears were unavoidable as images of Jack's face floated through her mind. The harder she cried, the more attention the cats seemed to want. The more she stroked their silky bodies, the faster the tears fell. Flashes of the day Jack proposed. Memories of getting ready for the wedding. The nightmarish recollection of Jack's body on the gurney in the hospital. Realizing that no matter how many doubts she'd had before the wedding, she loved Jack very much and she desperately missed him.

Tess pulled her knees up to her chest and let her forehead rest on them, ignoring the cats. All of the stress and anxiety from the day poured out of her with a strangled moan, causing Timothy and Spencer to move away. Rocking back and forth, Tess's mind whirled and circled with all the information dumped on her. She was wealthy. She didn't have a second family anymore. She had a lawyer. She actually *needed* a lawyer. Jack had kept secrets from her. What else was she going to find out?

As the crying jag abated, Tess hiccupped with every breath, trying to calm herself down. But as she exhaled, the blubbering began again and she growled in frustration. She hated when she couldn't make it stop. She couldn't stand being out of control. She knew she had a right to be as much of a mess as she wanted, whenever she wanted, but what she really wanted was for it to be over, for all of it to go away so she didn't have to try and exert such iron control. If the pain would stop, she could think straight. If she could think straight, she could make decisions and move forward. If she just decided to do it, she could get on with her life again.

But the truth was, the pain wasn't going to stop any time soon. There were only two ways to stop the misery: forgive herself or have Jack back, alive and in her arms. The second was impossible and the first seemed just as hopeless.

Chapter 11

Hudson sat at the metal secretary desk in the waiting room of his office, documents spread out on every inch of its surface. To the right, all of Jack's estate documents. To the left, all of the probate documents filed by David Kingston. In the center, a copy of the autopsy report and a legal pad already a third filled with notes and questions. He was at a standstill until he met with Tess Kingston again, but there was one thing he knew he could handle before the next appointment: calling David Kingston and dropping the bomb that a will did, in fact, exist, and that its sole purpose was to transfer into Jack's trust any assets not already in it and that the probate case he'd opened was about to completely implode. Hudson was anxious to get to it, so he sent Tess a quick text asking if she wanted to be present for the call. Her response, an all caps "NO" and then "go ahead," was all he needed.

Something about the case just didn't sit right with him. Jack had been in too much of a hurry to have his estate plan drawn up. They hadn't been particularly close friends, but he had tried to draw Jack out. After taking down all the details and verifying all of the paperwork Jack provided, Hudson had asked him if there was anything else he should know. Jack had hesitated, no doubt about it, as if he wanted to reveal more. But then a wall had gone up and Hudson spent the remainder of the meeting listening to Jack's assurances that there wasn't anything else. He simply hadn't wanted his parents or brother involved at all.

The hesitancy and urgency had bothered him, but Jack had paid up front with a hefty cash retainer for the work and Hudson had been in no position to turn it down. The rent had been due, as well as a stack of other bills on his desk. Work was work, regardless of his gut feelings.

Reaching for his coffee cup, he saw that it was empty and grumbled. Ford wasn't in yet and he didn't want to have to wait for a fresh pot, so he'd have to make it himself. Hudson hated making the coffee. He inevitably ended up spilling grounds all over himself when he struggled to open the foil packets, or sloshing water onto his pants. Somehow, Ford had made it an art form and his coffee always seemed better.

"I'll do that."

Hudson looked up and found Ford coming through the front door and he smiled in welcome. "I'll let you. Good morning."

"It's morning," Ford replied as he tossed his motorcycle helmet and leather jacket onto the couch. The coffee machine sat on top of a small, four-cube storage unit. He moved in front of Hudson, who stepped aside with relief.

Hudson frowned at his brother's back. Ford was freshly showered and his clothes were clean. He actually looked as though he'd slept the night before. "You're in early. Everything okay?"

"It's all good. What's on the agenda today?" Ford asked as he expertly dumped the coffee grounds into a pristine filter.

"I've got court this afternoon with Josh Baker and then a settlement conference on the Jones matter at five. I need you to call again to see when we can expect the toxicology report for Jack Kingston. I meet with Tess on Saturday."

"You got it."

Hudson went back to the secretary desk to keep reviewing the paperwork lying there as the coffee brewed.

"This is the entire Kingston file. It has a copy of Jack's birth father's trust and all the transfer documents putting the assets into Jack's name. There's also documentation in there signed by Roger Kingston as Jack's legal guardian and adoptive parent. Go through it and see if anything sticks out to you."

"Like what?" Ford fingered through the pages as he listened.

"I'm not sure. But I've been over it about a hundred times since yesterday and I think I'm too close. A fresh set of eyes might not hurt. I don't know exactly what I'm looking for, but if anything seems hinky to you, let me know. While you do that, I'm going to blow a call in to David Kingston. See if I can ruin his day a little bit."

Ford snorted. "Good deal."

Pouring two fresh cups of coffee for both them, Hudson took his with a quick thanks and went back to his private office, leaving Ford to begin his task. Hudson had to admit he was glad Ford looked put together today. His binge drinking had been escalating in the last few weeks, filling Hudson with worry. Ford had connections with a local biker gang, but denied being a member. Hudson wasn't sure if it was true or not, but suspected his brother was more involved than he wanted to admit. Most of Ford's drinking buddies were longtime members of the club. Hudson had even represented a couple of them on drunk driving charges. But even with his problems, Ford showed up to the office every day, handled whatever Hudson needed him to do and he made great coffee. What he did on his own time was his own business, no matter how much it might worry his little brother. Or, so he told himself to feel better.

Hudson looked up David Kingston's office number and dialed, readying himself for whatever might happen. The receptionist who answered placed him on hold and then pleasantly returned to transfer his call.

"David Kingston."

Hudson thought he *sounded* arrogant and he didn't even know the guy. But the way he'd tried to intimidate Tess rubbed Hudson the wrong way and he was predisposed to judge the opposing lawyer badly.

"Mr. Kingston, my name is Hudson Marks. I represent Tess Kingston."

Hudson thought he heard David say "shit" but couldn't be certain.

"I've been expecting your call. Or at least a call from *some* lawyer."

Hudson grinned, enjoying the irritation in David's voice.

"After meeting with Mrs. Kingston—"

"Mrs. Kingston is my *mother*," David snapped.

Hudson raised his eye brows and gave his head a shake in a well-aren't-you-a-hoity-toity-bastard kind of way. "All right. My client thought it would be best if I reached out to you. It's my understanding you've opened a probate estate with regard to Jack Kingston?"

"That's right."

"The documents I got from the probate court indicate that the deceased died intestate."

"Yes."

"Well, it's my duty to inform you that you are misinformed."

"What?" David's voice went up an octave and cracked.

Hudson grinned. "Jack Kingston prepared an entire estate plan."

Silence and then the explosion Hudson was waiting for.

"You must be joking!" David yelled. "How convenient for my ex-sister-in-law to have discovered these documents."

Hudson held the phone away from his ear and cringed. *Hope I don't go deaf,* he thought. "Actually, Mrs. Kingston—"

"*Don't call her that!*"

Hudson found it very difficult to keep from laughing out loud at David Kingston's distress, but he managed to rein it in. "Tess only found out yesterday that the documents exist. I received notification from an insurance company of Jack's death and contacted her. I'll be filing a petition with the probate court–"

"That's fine, you go ahead and file whatever you want. Of course, I'll need copies all documents you *claim* are valid instruments executed by my brother, but in the meanwhile you really need to ask yourself whether it's wise to get involved in this case. Are you aware of what kind of client you have? Did she tell you my brother died *AT THE WEDDING*? I don't know how long you've been practicing, but you can bet the judge will not look kindly on a greedy woman whose sham marriage can be counted in minutes. What leads you to believe the documents you purport to have are even valid? How do you know she didn't go out and have some other lawyer draw these up, that she didn't sign them herself and then try to sucker you into this loser of a case? I'm sure she hasn't paid you anything, and I can guarantee the judge won't award you a thin dime of the assets for filing such a meritless–"

"Mr. Kingston," Hudson took great pleasure in interrupting the jerk, "I know the documents are valid because I drafted them myself. I personally witnessed the signatures. I was friends with Jack in college."

He grinned as he imagined Kingston turning red, or maybe pale white, while his blood pressure careened to Guinness Book heights. There was a pause on the other end. Then Kingston found his tongue again.

"Then you know, *Mister Marks*, that as a material witness you cannot represent any party in this case. Your only role will be to get called as a witness again and again, for hours of testimony, hours during which you will not get paid. You'd better tell your *former* client that she needs a new attorney. Preferably one familiar with the rules regarding attorneys who have turned themselves into material witnesses. Or you can fuck off and forget any of this, and I'll return the favor. Lose her number. It's not worth your time. And send me a copy of the documents you claim you helped draft."

"Mr. Kingston, as a material witness, I am prohibited from representing my client *at trial*, but I can still represent her through the remainder of this case. Which I am sure you know since you are such a knowledgeable attorney. And you can get a copy of the documents from the court, where they'll be, once I file."

That did it, Hudson mused. Silence filled the phone line and he waited patiently for more bluster and bullying. When almost a full minute went by, he tried another tact.

"Look, my client does not want this to turn into a mudslinging affair. She asked me to reach out to you and Jack's family to try and work things out amicably. Maybe we could schedule a meeting to read the documents?" He waited for a response that didn't come. "How about next Monday afternoon? Two o'clock?" He knew full well David's schedule was probably as crammed as his own, but Hudson tossed out the time and date on a whim, knowing it would be rejected. *It's fun fucking with this guy.*

David cleared his throat noisily and Hudson could swear he heard the wheels in the other man's brain spinning. "I don't know if that will be convenient for my parents and I'm in court."

"Okay, how about Tuesday? You pick the time. I'm wide open."

"Tuesday I'm in depositions."

Hudson fought the urge to laugh out loud. He grabbed the coffee cup on his desk and swirled the quickly cooling liquid around in a circle before taking a sip, as he made David wait.

"Well, what about—"

"I'm leaving for court," David interrupted. "I'll put you on with my secretary and you can get my email address from her."

There was a sharp clicking sound and Hudson wasn't sure if David was transferring the call or hanging up on him. When the voice of a pleasant woman came on the line, he had his answer. He took down David's email address and said he would send along some other possible meeting dates and times. He knew damn well a meeting with any of the Kingstons was going to be a huge waste of time, but it was what Tess wanted. She still believed that things could work themselves out.

"They're fucked." Ford appeared in the doorway and leaned against the frame, his one hand shoved deep inside his jeans pocket, the other grasping his cup.

"Most likely." Hudson agreed. "But it's the hassle I'm not looking forward to. And unnecessary anxiety for Tess."

Ford looked at Hudson and raised an eyebrow. "Got a thing for the widow, do ya?"

Hudson frowned and gave his brother a derisive sneer. "No, you ass-hat. Any normal human would feel bad. Her husband dropped dead on her wedding day. Her in-laws have abandoned her, all for the sake of the loot. And now she's going to have to bicker and fight and be exposed to all kinds of scrutiny she doesn't need."

Ford frowned and nodded. "Good point."

Hudson laughed with no guile. "At least this one's going to be able to pay the bill. It'll be nice to send a real statement to a real client and know that the rent'll get paid on time this month. You find anything in the financials yet?"

"I just started, man. Give me a while." Ford stuck the empty cup on his thumb and twirled it about. "I'll let you know if I come up with something."

"Okay. I have an email to send."

Hudson spent the next fifteen minutes typing up dates and times, and emailed it to David Kingston. Glancing at his watch, he saw it was time to leave for his court appearance. Gathering the client file and his briefcase, he stopped to watch Ford reading through documents on Tess's file.

"I probably won't be back to the office today. Do me a favor and start downloading the probate forms I'm going to need. You've seen me do it enough, right?"

"Yeah, I think I can handle it." Ford nodded, not looking at him.

Hudson knew he could. If Ford wanted to, he could be a lawyer himself. Hudson thought his big brother was actually much smarter in a lot of ways, but for whatever reason, Ford had no desire for higher education or bettering himself. It frustrated Hudson because he often thought it would be nice to change the name of the firm to Marks and Marks. But Ford always blew him off when he mentioned the possibility.

"Thanks. I'll be in touch."

* * * * *

With his brother gone to court and the office to himself, Ford was able to better concentrate on the documents he was reading. Too often, Hudson hovered around interrupting his train of thought so he couldn't parse out whatever question was put before him. Ford loved his little brother more than Hudson would ever know, but sometimes he irritated the piss out of him, too.

As he read through the probate file, Ford found himself getting more irritated by the moment. The Kingston family had outright lied in their filings. They claimed Jack was unmarried and without a will. No mention was made of Jack's adoption or where his original wealth had come from. They were doing everything in their power to keep control of Jack's millions. An unfamiliar feeling of protectiveness thumped in his head as he thought of Tess and what the Kingstons were trying to do to her.

He switched over to the financial documents and was shocked to see the extent of the Kingston estate. Sure, Ford had been around here and there when Hudson had worked up the estate plan, but he hadn't paid much attention at the time. It was a cut and dried case and then they had moved on. Now, he was seeing the full value of everything Jack owned and that would be Tess Kingston's.

There were multiple investment accounts: IRA's, 401(k)s, mutual funds and lots of different stocks. Ford noticed it was all the usual stuff, Apple, Boeing, Microsoft. But the amount of property was what astounded him. Houses in the Hamptons, London, and Malibu. Apartment buildings in Los Angeles and New York and acres of property in Canada, Ireland, and Scotland. Ford whistled long and low at the variety of real estate. Tess Kingston was in for a big surprise when she realized just how filthy rich she had become.

Ford switched gears to review the transfer documents, the birth father's original will and trust, and everything else in the file. He didn't see anything out of the ordinary, either, and was disappointed that he wouldn't have any nuggets of wisdom for his brother. It didn't mean they weren't there, but nothing stood out.

Ford refilled his coffee and then pulled a laptop computer out of the drawer in the desk. He flipped it open and logged on to begin downloading probate forms. When he was finished, he put in another call to his contact at the ME's office to get a status update on the toxicology report.

As he sat and thought about the situation, Ford allowed himself to conjure Tess's image in his mind. She was a beautiful girl in her mid-twenties and she should have been experiencing some of the happiest times of her life. Instead, she was a widow embroiled in a nasty estate battle.

Ford didn't like surprises and Tess had done just that. Only knowing her on paper, he thought she was going to be broken and damaged from all she'd been through. Instead, she was way hotter in real life than he expected and a hell of a lot stronger than most people in her spot. When she walked into that kitchen, he immediately recognized her from the post office. Her blonde hair looked soft and it was full of waves, not the crunchy, manufactured curls Ford usually saw on the bar flies where he hung out. Tess wasn't anorexic-thin or flirting with obesity, either. She seemed just the right size for her five-and-a-half-foot frame, fit and curvy. It was her eyes that had really caught him off guard. Electric blue, energetic, contradicting the exhaustion and pain shining through. Clear enough to see the world around her, in spite all of the trauma she'd just experienced in the last few months. She hadn't broken down during the meeting at her parents' house. She looked close a couple of times, but as he watched her, Ford could tell when she pulled it together by the tensing of her jaw and clenching of her fists. She soldiered on.

Usually, Ford just did whatever Hudson wanted him to do. He didn't get emotionally involved or invested in any of the cases they took on. But this one was different. He admitted to himself that she reminded him of the type of woman he used to go for, back when he was a normal guy. More years than he cared to remember ago, he wouldn't have hesitated to pursue a girl who looked like Tess, when he was the captain of the football team and cute blonde girls were the head cheerleaders. But that was before shit got real in his life and he took a different path. Since then, his perception of life and himself had become somewhat altered. Nice, cute, blonde girls weren't in the cards for him anymore.

That didn't mean he couldn't fight hard for this one, though. Ford had plenty of contacts in plenty of places. He wouldn't hesitate to use every single one of them to make sure Tess Kingston ended up with the result she deserved.

Chapter 12

Tess contemplated the pile of paperwork at her feet and reached for the first few pages. She had finally gone through every scrap in Jack's desk and filtered out everything she thought needed saving. A few years' tax returns, a couple of years of bank statements, just in case they still weren't available online for downloading. Other than that, the rest of the utility bills and miscellaneous nonsense Jack had squirreled away was ready for the shredder. She fed a few sheets into it and smirked when the loud whirring noise made the cats flee the room.

Tess's own rummaging had not yielded anything more than Lilly's had. She found nothing pertaining to Jack's secret past. If he had gotten copies of the estate documents, he hadn't kept them at home. If Lilly hadn't found Hudson's card, Tess wasn't sure where she would be right now. She had spent hours reading over the documents her new lawyer had given to her, but little of it made much sense. It was typical legal mumbo jumbo and she was waiting for their meeting on Saturday to get a full explanation.

To keep busy while she waited, Tess had finally decided to tackle the job of cleaning out the office. All of Jack's clothes were now boxed up and ready for donation. She hung on to all of his portfolio books of the graphic and web design work he had done over the years. She also couldn't part with his favorite Detroit Lions football jersey or his pillow.

It was difficult for Tess to see the boxes and bags piled up to be taken away for some other person or family to use. It seemed so strange to give away things Jack had loved or worn. There was just no reason for her to hold on to them, other than sentimentality. Tess was torn between her heart wanting to keep everything Jack had ever touched and her brain that logically spoke of the spirit of giving and donating so someone else could benefit. She knew it was perfectly normal, but it didn't keep her from feeling the conflict anyway.

Only for a minute had Tess considered giving the things to Jack's family for them to sort out and deal with. Perhaps it would have been the kind and thoughtful thing to do. But because they had been so nasty to her, she couldn't find it in her heart to have anything more to do with them until she absolutely had to. Tess knew that confrontation was coming and she wanted to put it off for as long as possible. If giving Jack's things away on her own was a way of doing that, she refused to feel guilty over it. Besides, none of the items in the boxes and bags were from Jack's childhood or held any value to his mother or father. They were things he had acquired in his adult life with Tess and she felt confident that it was her decision to make.

When the entire pile was shredded, Tess gathered the bags of minced paper and combined them all into one giant bag. Tossing it into the corner with the other trash, she would haul it out to the dumpster later. The room was decidedly blank now, with all of Jack's personality stripped from it. Timothy and Spencer hesitantly ventured back in, looking around for the machine that had caused them such fear before. Not seeing it, they both wandered over to her and rubbed against her shins.

"What should we do with this room, I wonder?" she said out loud to the felines. She wasn't disappointed when she didn't receive an answer. "I guess it can be my office now."

Tess had given her notice to Dr. Guildford the day before. She called him and explained the situation about the insurance policy, saying she wouldn't really need to work for a while. Since she was having such a hard time doing a good job for him anymore, she didn't count on him being as upset as he was by the news. Dr. Guildford had argued with her for fifteen minutes that she could still keep her job, just take an extended leave of absence. A million dollars wouldn't last forever. He needed her; she was the best transcriptionist he'd ever had. In the end, Tess had told him no and that she was really honored by his disappointment but that she couldn't in good conscience continue working with him. She agreed to finish the last of her backlogged work, but he would need to find someone else as soon as possible.

Tess decided it was as good a time as any to honor her promise and finish the last of the transcription. She had told herself she would do that before she started thinking about the insurance money and what to do with it. Until it actually hit her bank account, she wasn't really sure she believed it was coming.

In spite of Lilly's insistence that the windfall was the best thing that could ever have happened, Tess wasn't so sure. It was true; she'd never really struggled where money was concerned. Her parents had taken good care of her until she was old enough to work and then she had gotten jobs to pay for the things she wanted. A few times she had gotten in over her head with credit card debt, but those were valuable lessons learned. Now, she was going to have hundreds of thousands of dollars at her disposal and the thought was daunting. Her first impulse wasn't to go out and buy a car or a house or do something stupid. Instead, she was worried about all the tax implications. The coming lawsuit and fight with the Kingstons. What would be left after she paid all the attorneys' fees? Money, to Tess, wasn't a Godsend; it was a curse.

Chapter 13

"Can I help you?"

Lilly Langford stepped inside the small office, a business card in her hand. "Yes, I'm looking for Hudson Marks." She looked around and wasn't impressed. It certainly wasn't a silk stocking kind of firm. Not that it mattered, she was really only interested in knowing what kind of a *person* was representing her sister. Yet, the dingy and somewhat bare office didn't lend a lot of confidence, to her way of thinking.

The handsome, tall guy behind the metal desk stood up and came around to extend his hand. "You've found him."

Lilly took his large hand in hers and gripped it with what she hoped was a decent amount of firmness as she admired his kind eyes and boyishly handsome face. "Nice to meet you. I'm Lilly Langford, Tess's sister."

"Hi!" He looked stunned and did not release her hand right away. Leaning in toward her, his face clouded with concern. "Is everything all right? Is it Tess?"

Lilly relaxed, deciding that he didn't seem to be like the jackass lawyers she saw on television. He certainly was good looking enough to be on some crime show, but she didn't let that blind her. "No, everything is fine. I just wanted to come by and meet the attorney who would be handling her case. She has no idea I'm here."

Hudson motioned for her to take a seat on the couch and she did, while he pulled the rolling chair from behind the desk and positioned it a few feet from her.

"Well," Hudson said with hesitation, "I can't really discuss any specifics of the case with you unless Tess is here…" His voice trailed off, a look of embarrassment flitting across his face.

"I don't expect you to and I don't plan on asking any questions."

Hudson chuckled. "Just sizing me up?"

Lilly smiled and nodded. "Something like that." She made sure to look at him directly, hoping she could convey her concern without coming across as a meddling sister. "I know you met with my folks and Tess already, but I want you to understand a few things. The last six months have been really horrible for my sister. She was just starting to get back to normal when all of this happened. She brought me up to speed about Jack's adoption and inheritance and how shitty the Kingstons have treated her so far. I need to make sure you are the right person to take care of her."

Hudson rubbed his chin with his hand and nodded. "I understand. I'll tell you the same thing I told Tess. I'm only three years out of law school, but I'm confident I can handle it. As far as I'm concerned, it's nothing more than a good old fashioned dog fight. David Kingston might think he's the bigger dog, but I'm pretty scrappy myself."

Lilly laughed and leaned back into the soft leather couch. "That's exactly what I wanted to hear. I don't care if you haven't been a lawyer very long. What matters is that you have the testicular fortitude to stand up to them. I never liked them. Jack was all right, but the rest of his family is a bunch of pretentious assholes."

Hudson laughed with her and she liked the deep, rolling sound that emanated from his chest. He leaned his elbows on his knees.

Looking her in the eye, he sobered. "I haven't met all of them and I've only spoken with David on the phone, but I'm inclined to agree. I promise that I will do everything in my power to make things right for Tess."

"Thank you," Lilly said softly, suddenly realizing how close he was to her. He was pretty broad in the shoulders and gave off a strong male presence with the muscular build that she was certain lurked beneath his button down shirt. Struggling to remain calm and reserved, Lilly tried to think of anything but his nearness.

"Don't thank me yet. We haven't done anything." Hudson straightened and leaned back, crossing one long leg over the other at the knee.

"We? Do you have a partner?" Lilly cringed inwardly at the way her voice sounded a little breathless and hoped he didn't notice.

"Not exactly. My brother works with me. He's sort of my investigator and law clerk all rolled into one." He looked as if he would say more, but the door to the office whooshed open. "Speak of the devil."

Lilly turned to see a slightly older, considerably grungier version of Hudson stride through the door. His face was covered with five o'clock shadow and he wore jeans, motorcycle boots, a white t-shirt, and black leather vest, in direct contradiction to Hudson's professional, navy blue suit, clean shaven face, and tidy hair.

"Good afternoon to you too," Ford muttered as he walked directly to the coffee pot.

"Ford, this is Lilly Langford. Tess's sister."

Lilly took the opportunity to stand up and take a step or two away from Hudson. She put out her hand and Ford swiveled to shake it. His eyes were hidden behind sunglasses so she couldn't get a look at them to see if they were just as opposite as his brother's. She thought he oozed a certain kind of dangerous charisma, but it didn't give her the nervous jerks like Hudson did. Still, she smiled and tried to be open and friendly with him.

"It's nice to meet you, Ford." She kept her own cornball joke about their names to herself, figuring they'd heard them all before anyway.

"Same," he responded as he took the coffee pot to the bathroom to dump it out. When he came back, he didn't seem all that interested in talking with her and busied himself with making a fresh pot.

"Would you like some coffee?" Hudson asked. "Ford makes the best."

"No, that's okay." Lilly shook her head and then took another step toward the door. "I need to get going. I appreciate you taking the time to talk to me about this. Please don't tell Tess that I was here." Hudson took two steps and was beside her, reaching for the door to open it for her.

"It's our secret. When we meet in front of Tess, I'll pretend like it's the first time. We'll probably see a lot of one another in the coming weeks. I'm going to have a lot of questions for Tess and she'll probably need all the support she can get from her family. I'm glad to know she'll have it."

Lilly smiled and nodded as she stepped out into the humid July heat. Coupled with the warmth she felt just by looking at Hudson, she wasn't surprised when sweat popped out on her upper lip right away. "She will. You just make sure you do everything you can, or you'll have *me* to deal with." She winked at him and immediately felt like an idiot. *How cheesy.*

"You bet."

He flashed her one more grin, and Lilly forced herself to walk away before she said any more stupid things. She climbed into her car and headed for her apartment on Little Mack Avenue near the Meijer grocery store, chastising herself the entire way.

"You're such an idiot," Lilly said out loud to her reflection in the rear view mirror as she drove. "Do not get a crush on your sister's lawyer. Do not!"

Chapter 14

Only a few minutes before noon, Tess opened the door to Linda's Place at Shook and Crocker, feeling the rush of air conditioning on her skin. Her arms broke out in gooseflesh. Pushing the strap of her purse higher on her shoulder, she scanned the small restaurant for Hudson Marks. She saw his raised arm at a booth to the left. As she walked to his table, a waitress behind the counter raised a pot of coffee in question and Tess nodded vigorously.

"Good afternoon," Hudson said with a smile as she slid into the booth across from him.

"We still have three minutes." She flipped over the mug on the table and slid it to the edge, hoping it would get filled quickly. Her limbs felt heavy with exhaustion, sleep having eluded her much of the night before.

"Rough night?"

"Yeah." Tess half smiled and sighed. "It's kind of a given."

The waitress appeared and dumped a few creamers on the table while she poured the steaming coffee.

"Would you like to order, or do you need a few minutes?"

"Nothing for me, thanks." Tess grabbed a creamer and opened it.

"Can we have a little while?" Hudson smiled and gave the waitress a wink. She returned it, but said nothing as she left. "Thanks for meeting me here. My office isn't, uh, let's just say it's not the fanciest of places."

Tess smirked and glanced around at the hole-in-the-wall restaurant. "And this is? Don't worry about it. I love this place. The food is awesome."

Hudson's eyebrows perked in surprise. "I'm glad to hear you say that."

Tess watched him sip his coffee over the edge of her own mug. Setting it down, she took a deep breath. "Okay, let's get started."

Hudson tried not to laugh with his mouth full and barely succeeded, to Tess's amusement. "For as tired as you look, you're full of piss and vinegar this morning, aren't you?"

Tess's mirth vanished. She knew she looked like shit, but she didn't need this guy reminding her. Her shoulders slumped self-consciously and she lowered her chin, looking to the side. "Yeah, well, it's either get with the program or stay in bed under the covers for the rest of my life."

Hudson's face was awash with shame, making Tess feel a bit more forgiving.

"I understand." He cleared his throat and took another sip of coffee. "First, before we waste a bunch of time, are you still considering letting the Kingston's keep any or all of the estate?"

Tess chewed on her bottom lip, trying to figure out how to explain her thoughts about it. It was what kept her up most of the night before. "Not really," she finally said. "I gotta tell you, I go back and forth on it. One minute I'm pissed off and want to take every cent away. But then I hear Jack's voice telling me to be a better person. Better than them. And then I get mad again. I don't know what I'll do in the end. I guess I want the satisfaction of knowing they're being called on the carpet for the shitty thing they did to me."

Hudson listened as she yammered and Tess felt glad that he didn't seem to judge her.

"Sounds to me like you want to send a message: don't underestimate me. When it's all over, you can opt to share the inheritance with them."

"Yeah. And I probably will, just so you know. But don't say anything to my parents about it. They'd have a conniption."

Hudson chuckled. "Mum's the word. Then let's get started with an explanation of everything I did for Jack."

Tess tried to pay attention to Hudson as he explained all of the steps he took to set up Jack's estate, but her lack of sleep made it nearly impossible to really grasp everything. All the questions she thought she had vanished as he spoke. His patience put her at ease, though, and she knew he would do whatever was necessary to represent and protect her interests. She figured it was why Jack had chosen him in the first place. Hudson's demeanor exuded confidence and tenacity. She was comfortable believing what he said and following whatever advice he gave. Tess actually felt the relief easing the tension in her shoulders, knowing someone was going to help her figure it all out. She didn't feel so alone.

"So basically, because he left everything to you, it should have been a pretty simple process." Hudson looked around for the waitress and motioned her over. She appeared immediately with a fresh pot of coffee and filled their cups again.

"Would you like to order now?"

Hudson grabbed a menu being held up by the mustard and ketchup bottles. "Yep, I'm starved." When Tess didn't move to take one too, Hudson nodded at her sternly. "I don't like to eat alone."

"All right." Tess pulled a menu but didn't bother to look at it. "I'll have the Farmer's Special, eggs over-medium, rye toast, pancakes instead of hash browns and four strips of bacon."

As the waitress scribbled furiously on her pad to keep up, Hudson's mouth dropped open. "You must be hungry! I'll have exactly the same."

"You'll love it. I told you, the food's great." Tess raised her mug in the air toward Hudson and they toasted with coffee.

"This isn't going to be simple anymore, though, is it?"

"Probably not," Hudson admitted. "Because David opened the probate estate, we have to refute everything that's already been filed. In all likelihood, I see a lawsuit coming. They should probably hire an independent lawyer from here on out."

"Pffft, don't hold your breath. David will be in charge, I guarantee it, whether they hire someone else or not."

Hudson chuckled. "I got that impression, too. Let's just say he wasn't thrilled to hear from me."

"He's an ass." Tess's eyes went wide and then she giggled. "Sorry, I guess that was kinda rude." Rolling her eyes, Tess flapped her hands dismissively. "Jack knew I never really liked David. And after the other day, I sure as hell don't now."

"No worries. Your secret is safe with me." Hudson winked at her. "I tried to schedule an appointment with the family, but David wouldn't commit to a date or time. I don't know if you'll have to go through that or not at this point."

"Gee, that's a bright spot at least." Tess grinned. The longer she spoke with Hudson, the more relaxed she felt. He was giving her reasons to be hopeful and that counted more than any dollars possibly could. "They don't have a leg to stand on, though, right?" Tess's eyebrows crinkled slightly as she thought of fighting with her in-laws in court. "Listening to you, it seems pretty airtight. They'll just fight because they can" It was a statement more than a question, really. She already had her answer from the way they treated her.

"It would seem that way," Hudson admitted. "But they could do all sorts of stupid things. They could say that Jack was unstable. They could say he didn't understand the magnitude or scope of his inheritance. And, of course, they could try to drag your good name through the mud."

Tess snorted. "How do you know I have a good name?"

Hudson smiled and shook his head. "Well, I guess I don't. You haven't given me any reason to think otherwise, yet, so I'm going to go with my gut and say you're a good person."

"Well, thanks." Tess pulled a napkin from the dispenser and began to twist it and tug at the edges, making a pile of confetti in front of her.

"Have you read the estate documents yet?"

"Yes." Tess squirmed. "Sort of. I mean, I don't really understand it. What you say makes more sense than the words on those pages."

"Fair enough." Hudson gave her a sympathetic smile. "Maybe we should do that next, while we eat. I can go over paragraph by paragraph so that you understand exactly what Jack did."

"That makes sense."

"Before we do that, I have to fully disclose a couple of things to you."

Tess's stomach did a flip flop. She didn't like the sound of that. She was beginning to hate surprises.

"Now, don't look at me like that," Hudson laughed. "You look like I just told you I was going to kill your cats or something!"

Tess laughed and relaxed the slightest bit. "That obvious?"

"Yes. All I want you to know is that I'm a pretty new lawyer. I've only been out of school and in practice for about three years. This might turn out to be more complicated than I can handle. If you'd rather find a more experienced attorney now, or even later, I'd understand."

Tess could tell Hudson was holding his breath by the way he straightened up and waited. Her instincts told her that if Jack trusted him, she should. "I don't think I need another lawyer. I'm comfortable with you. Besides, you knew Jack personally and saw what he was like when he made all these decisions. Someone new would have to learn all this stuff from scratch and that doesn't make sense."

Hudson nodded and Tess watched him take in a deep breath of relief. "Okay, I'm good with that."

"If you need to get help, I'm good with that too. Just make sure you stay in charge."

Hudson nodded and then put out his hand toward her. Tess stared at it for a second and then laughed as she shook it.

"It's a deal."

Tess looked into his eyes and was boosted by the kindness she saw there. She pulled her hand away and looked down at her coffee. She thought he held on a little too long and there might have been something else in his eyes besides compassion. It had been *years* since anyone besides Jack had looked at her in that way, she couldn't be sure. *Don't be an idiot.* She scolded herself and then gave her brain a mental shake to forget about it.

The waitress arrived just then with a large tray overflowing with plates and Tess was grateful for the distraction. As she set all the food down between them, Tess spread a fresh napkin daintily on her lap. Hudson helped take dishes and layer them around the table. He then pulled a copy of Jack's will out of his briefcase and spread it open between them.

While they ate, he went over each paragraph with her just like he said he would. By the time he reached the last page, they were both almost finished eating and Tess was feeling much better. The long and short of it was that she was the only heir and that Jack and Hudson had done all the legwork to transfer all of the assets so that everything would be hers and hers alone.

Best of all, the life insurance policy naming her as a beneficiary was a non-probate asset and it would be paid to her, regardless of any ensuing litigation. That made her feel like she'd just won the lottery.

Trying to remember their meeting at her parents' house, Tess thought Hudson might have told her that before. Unfortunately, most of that day was gone in a haze now.

"You'll want to get in touch with a good certified financial planner, too." Hudson wiped his mouth and then tossed the napkin onto the table.

"My parents have a great guy. I'll make sure to use him."

"Good. Even though everything is in the trust's name, I have a list of the different investment companies and the guys in charge so you can get everything transferred."

"How soon will I be able to set up the charity Jack wanted?" Tess asked as she forked the last bite of pancake into her mouth. When she initially thumbed through the will, she hadn't caught the paragraph Jack wrote about having a charity created in his name for the benefit of homeless animals.

"When you get the insurance money you could do anything you want. Unfortunately, you can't touch any of the other assets right now. Not until the probate case is settled and closed."

Tess pursed her lips in a thoughtful pout. "That's okay. I think I can do some pretty good work with a million dollars. It's not like I have anything else to spend it on."

Hudson gaped at her. "Are you kidding me? I know about a million things I could do with a million dollars!"

Tess grinned and leaned forward. "What would you do first?"

"Buy a new truck." Hudson pounded a palm onto the table and the silverware rattled. "Mine is starting to show signs of being on its last legs. But not until I invested at least half of it so it would take care of me for the rest of my life. I'd probably buy a house and a new bike for Ford. I'd donate some."

"Wow! You've thought about this, haven't you?"

"I'd probably take a vacation. I haven't had a real vacation since… well, ever. Seems like I've been working since I was fourteen."

"Nice," Tess said softly. "I guess I'm not that imaginative. When I first found out about the money, all I could think about was taxes and lawyer fees and responsibility."

Hudson nodded sympathetically. "Yeah. I can see that. Your whole perspective on life has probably been skewed because of Jack's death. Think about what you would have done with a lottery win of a million dollars if Jack hadn't died."

"Ooh, that's a good one," Tess breathed, totally caught off guard by the thought. What would they have done with the money? "I guess Jack would have been the one to decide. I mean, he would have asked me what I wanted, but in the end, I would have gone along with whatever he said."

Hudson frowned. "You don't seem like the kind of person who'd sit back and let someone else plan your future."

"Oh no, it's not like that," Tess insisted. "Jack and I always talked about everything. We made decisions together. But he thought outside the box. I don't always do that, so when he would suggest things, they made sense to me. That's why we were so perfect together. He thought of things I couldn't."

Hudson shrugged. "Well, now it's your turn to start thinking outside the box. Don't let anyone else tell you what to do. Figure out how you want your life to go from here, Tess. You're really in a pretty good position. You will have a lot of income and no one to answer to."

"And no one to advise me."

"That's not true. You'll have your parents and sister. And if you vet people carefully, you can choose a lot of good support to surround yourself with. I think your future is looking pretty bright and it's all due to Jack."

"You're probably right."

What Hudson said made perfect sense and the realization slammed into her. Hudson was a lot like Jack. Here he was doing all the thinking so she could understand her situation. It left her feeling a little frustrated. *When am I going to learn to think for myself?*

As Hudson finished the rest of his meal, Tess studied him. He certainly was a handsome guy and smart as hell, but she couldn't decide what his best feature was. *Probably his smile*, she decided. *Ford got the eyes, but Hudson has the smile.* Thinking of Ford made the hair on her arms rise the tiniest bit and her heart flutter as well. There was no classical handsomeness to him; he was all danger and swarthy sex appeal. She brought up the image of their first meeting in her mind and almost shivered with the memory.

"Tell me, how did you and Jack meet?" Tess picked up her coffee for a sip, trying to forget about smiles and eyes.

Hudson shrugged and finished chewing, then swallowed. "We had a couple of undergrad classes together. He was a nice enough guy."

Tess smiled, remembering how many friends Jack had. He had always been an affable guy, talking to anyone about anything. In line at the grocery store, in parking lots. He was always quick with a sociable word to anyone, whether they looked interested or not.

"Frankly, I'm surprised Jack remembered me." Hudson grabbed a piece of bacon and munched on it. "How did you and Jack get together?" He didn't look her in the eye as he asked.

"In the third grade." Tess grinned and set her fork down. "He was the cutest little boy, and even at that age, I thought I'd marry him one day. Of course, everyone just thinks that's the sweetest thing ever. I mean, how could I have known that when I was only eight years old, right?"

"Did he feel the same?"

"Oh hell no!" Tess laughed and some of the tension in her shoulders and neck released with it. "It took him till he was about fourteen before he realized I was a girl. And then it took another year before he asked me out. But I was patient. There was just something good about Jack. He was kind and sweet and loving, from the moment

I met him. As he got older, it reminded me a lot of my dad. Most girls look for some version of their father, and I was lucky enough to find it in Jack. When he gave me a promise ring at my sweet sixteen party, I was just about the happiest girl in the world."

As quickly as the tension had left her, grief replaced it as she recalled all the specialness of her husband. Tess knew one day that it would ease. Hadn't it already begun to fade before all this new drama dropped on her head? She would be able to talk about her life with Jack without wanting to cry or scream or feel like a total fraud. But today wasn't that day. She sniffed and grabbed a napkin to dab at her eyes. "Sorry," she whispered.

"Yeah," Hudson said softly. "I didn't mean to upset you."

"Oh, you didn't. Everything upsets me, but that's just part of it. It can't be helped." Tess crumpled the napkin and set it in the middle of her plate, then shoved the dish aside. "Sometimes I think if I keep talking about him over and over, it'll deaden the pain. So far, that hasn't really happened."

Hudson gave her a sympathetic smile and for once Tess didn't want to bash the face of a person giving her that particular look. It actually offered her some comfort and she was grateful for it. Comfort was in short supply.

"I probably need to make out a will of my own now, huh? Make sure all this money I've come into doesn't fall into the wrong hands."

"That's a very good idea. One I would have suggested at some point." Hudson finished with his food and stacked his plates neatly. "But try not to stress yourself over it. The chances of anything happening to you are so slim, it's laughable."

Tess snorted, but did not laugh. "You could have said the same thing about Jack, too, don't you think?"

Hudson looked abashed. "You have a point. I can draw up some preliminary docs for you that cover the insurance money you'll be getting. We'll have to revise everything when the other case is finished."

"Okay." Tess lifted her cup of coffee to her lips and drained the remaining liquid.

As they waited for the check, Hudson sighed. "There is one other thing I want to bring up, but I'm not sure how you'll react."

"You're good at that." Tess glared at him, but not too sternly. "Just when I'm about to relax behind the plate, you throw me another curve ball."

Hudson grimaced and looked down at his hands, which were laced together and resting on the table. Leaning forward, he lowered his voice. "I'm sorry. It's not the first time I've ever heard that. But I am your lawyer and I need to make sure you're apprised of everything. I know it's a little early to talk strategy for court, but I want to warn you. Things will probably get pretty ugly."

"Is that all? I figured they would." Tess's breath whooshed out of her and she threw up her hands.

"Even if you think you're prepared, it almost always gets worse."

"Well that's encouraging," Tess grumbled.

"I'm sorry, Tess. Money makes people do shitty things."

Chewing on her bottom lip, she shrugged. "How do we get more prepared?"

Hudson stared at her for a moment and just when she was about to become uncomfortable, he spoke. "We start digging. Any dirt we can find to counter whatever they throw at us. Maybe we'll get lucky and this will all get resolved quickly and amicably. However, I doubt that's going to happen."

Tess sighed. "Don't worry. I'm not holding my breath. Navy blue isn't my best color."

Chapter 15

"Let me see it! I want to hold it!" Lilly quivered with excitement, standing next to Tess in the lobby of the insurance company's office.

Tess laughed and handed over the check. Sure enough, it was made payable to her in the amount of one million dollars. She could hardly believe it herself. No scams, no requests to send money to Nigeria. Best of all, David Kingston didn't pop out from behind any planters to yell "Psych!" and whisk the check away.

"Let's get to the bank, quick, before someone changes their mind."

"Before I wake up from this dream," Tess mumbled, as Lilly grabbed her by the arm and hauled her out to the parking lot. Lilly drove, and within ten minutes they were at First State Bank in St. Clair Shores.

"Uh," the bank teller stammered, "we'll need to place a five day hold on this until it clears."

Tess snorted and Lilly giggled. From across the lobby, the bank manager waved to them. Ann had known the Langford girls since they were born. Ruth Langford had worked at First State and trained Ann decades ago. Tess watched as she rose and approached them to say hello.

"How's your mom?" she asked, giving each of them a quick hug.

"She's good," Lilly answered.

"How are you doing, Tess?" Ann's eyes softened but lost none of their happy glint. She was about the most upbeat person Tess had ever met.

"I'm okay, thanks. Just making a deposit."

Lilly outright laughed. "Yeah, right!"

Ann frowned and smiled a little at the same time. "You don't say?"

The bank teller waved the check in her hand and Ann took it from her.

"Just an insurance payment," Tess said softly, her cheeks pinking.

Ann grinned and pulled her in for another hug. "I'm happy for this. Not Jack's death, of course, but this." She gave the check a little wave. "After what you've been through, this has to ease some of your burdens." Ann's words warmed Tess's heart and felt like a cool salve on her scorched soul.

She nodded as Ann handed the check back to the teller. "I kind of thought of it like a curse at first, but I'm finally beginning to believe it could actually be a blessing."

"I'm glad you're seeing it that way." Ann smiled and touched her arm. "I know there's a hold on it, but if you need to write any checks against it, I'll make sure they get honored. Be sure and tell your mom I said hello." With another wave, she left them to finish the transaction.

"It *is* a blessing, lil' sis," Lilly insisted as they left the bank. "Where to next?"

"Hudson's office. He's expecting me so I can sign the retainer and give him a check."

"You got it."

Chapter 16

Ford sipped coffee and surfed the internet. Google Earth was one of the coolest things he'd ever seen. He was able to get crisp, clear pictures of all of the property listed in Jack Kingston's trust. He saved each one to the favorites. He went on to do some searching on Jack's birth father, Benjamin Thatcher. The guy had played football for the University of Alabama and got drafted into the NFL in his junior year. *Pretty cool,* Ford thought as he perused Thatcher's stats. When he finished with football, the guy had managed to break into real estate development: quadrupling the fortune he'd made playing in the pros. It hadn't been hard to figure out who the birth mother was, either, because Thatcher had provided for her pretty handsomely in his estate planning as well. Pamela Campbell was living quietly in Guntersville, Alabama, remarried with three kids. Ford wondered if she knew what had happened to the son she'd given up when she was only sixteen. Honestly, he felt she was a pretty brave woman by making such a huge sacrifice. Sometimes he wished his own mother had done the same thing when he and Hudson were born.

Seemed a damn shame to Ford that Jack hadn't been given the opportunity to meet his birth father. The guy had obviously turned his life around and would probably have been a good influence on his kid.

While he didn't necessarily like to judge, Ford thought the Kingstons were turning out to be a pretty crappy family by not telling their son the truth. Now they were fighting to hang on to Jack's inheritance at the expense of a woman they'd practically raised with their son. How much more selfish and guilty could they be?

Ford couldn't deny that Roger Kingston had done a fairly decent job of maintaining all of the investments left to Jack. He'd obviously watched the stock market carefully to keep the money accumulating. Everything had pretty much stayed on an upward trajectory. When Benjamin Thatcher died in a plane crash nine years ago, the total value of the estate left to Jack had been about five million dollars. Today, it was worth a little more than quadruple that. *No wonder he wants to keep his hands on it.*

The bitch of it was, Tess probably would have let 'em keep it. Judging by her character, what little of it he really knew, she seemed like a kind and honest person. She had known for days she was coming into a million dollars and hadn't done anything careless or wild or stupid. The Kingstons were just being greedy, to his way of thinking. They could have told Tess about everything, offered to share it and then she probably would have declined. *What a bunch of idiots.* It was no wonder Ford always expected the worst of most of the people he met. So far, Tess Kingston was turning out to be the exception to that rule.

Leaning back in his chair, Ford closed his eyes and pictured Tess in his mind. Her arms full of packages that day in the post office. In her parents' dining room, looking beautiful even though she'd been given the shock of her life. They had only seen one another twice, but the lovely widow was burrowing her way into his mind. At first, Ford had fought it, using all the typical arguments about how she was too good for him, but eventually he gave up. What harm would it do to let his mind wander, when that's all it would amount to? A dream, a fantasy, wishful thinking. Nothing would ever happen between them in reality.

The office phone rang, pulling Ford out of his study. He reached to answer it, but Hudson beat him to it. From the inner office, he could hear his brother's professional voice. "Hudson Marks."

"It's David Kingston."

Ford made a face and rolled the chair backwards until he was at Hudson's door. He flipped his middle finger at the phone so his brother could see and Hudson smirked. Ford pulled the door closed and then scooted back to the desk just as Tess Kingston and Lilly Langford breezed through the front door. Ford didn't startle easily, but her appearance within seconds of thinking about her made it seem as though he conjured her out of thin air. If it weren't for the facial features and the sound of their voices, Ford might not have believed they were sisters. Tess was petite and curvy, while her sister was long and lean. But when they laughed, there was no doubt they were related. He couldn't believe how much the sound of them chuckling made his mood lighten.

"Good afternoon, ladies." He stood up to greet them, pressing the laptop closed. He tried not to stare at Tess, but it was difficult. Her eyes seemed to dance with a liveliness he hadn't seen before.

"Hey." Tess waved a hand at him.

Ford thought she looked young and vibrant in the blue dress and leather jacket she wore. She even looked like she'd gotten some good sleep in the last few days; unlike the first time he'd seen her.

"Ford Marks, this is my sister Lilly. This is Hudson's brother."

He forced himself to look at the other woman and respond with a naturalness he didn't feel inside. "Nice to see you again," he mumbled.

Lilly's smile disappeared and Ford felt his stomach drop. *Shit.*

"Again?" Tess asked, looking at him and then back to Lilly.

He fought the urge to slap his forehead and groan. "Uh…"

Lilly rolled her eyes and dropped the hand she had extended out to him. Turning to her sister, she pursed her lips. "I stopped by the other day to meet Hudson," she admitted. "I just wanted to see who was going to be representing you, that's all."

Ford waited for some sort of sibling squabble to bust out right there in the office, but was surprised to hear Tess laugh instead. It was the first time he could remember having heard her do it and it made him want to genuinely smile. It was a breathy, gentle sound that brightened the room and her face. When it tapered off, Tess punched Lilly in the arm and shook her head. He continued to watch her, transfixed. He couldn't remember the last time a woman had held his attention so firmly.

"You're a dork," Tess said. "You could have just told me."

"Well?" Lilly shrugged. "I didn't want to seem like a buttinski."

"But you are." Tess winked and then turned back to Ford, who stood as still as a statue. When her eyes met his, he looked away fast, hoping she wouldn't be able to tell what he was thinking.

A loud voice from the inner office interrupted the moment. Ford turned and looked at the door, making sure he had closed it tightly.

"Uh, Hudson's expecting me. I need to sign the retainer and write him a check." Tess frowned as she listened to Hudson shouting. "I take it he's here."

"Yeah, he's on the phone, if you couldn't tell."

"We noticed." Lilly looked at him like he'd just fallen off the turnip truck.

"Have a seat. I'm sure he'll be finished in a couple of minutes."

Behind him, more shouting erupted from behind the closed door. "You can't get the marriage annulled, you idiot!"

Tess's face went white. "He's on the phone with David, isn't he?"

Ford lowered his head, refusing to look her in the eye. "Yeah."

"He wants to annul my marriage?" she whispered. Lilly put a supportive arm around her shoulders and guided her to the couch. All the former humor from a moment ago was gone in the blink of an eye.

"Sit down, sis."

Ford went to the mini fridge and got a bottle of water. He handed it to Lilly, who twisted the cap off and forced it into Tess's hand. "Yeah. He figures if he can make it like the marriage never existed, then the will is voided too." Ford watched as her face went from stark white to gray and her eyes began to glass over.

"Breathe, Tess," Lilly commanded, rubbing her back. "Take a deep breath through your nose." When she didn't obey, Lilly thumped her on the back gently. "Do it."

Closing her eyes, Tess inhaled and exhaled slowly a couple of times and then took the bottle of water. She used her other hand to press against one of her ears to block out the continued yelling. Ford recognized the sibling bond as very close to his own. Lilly took care of Tess the way he had always taken care of Hudson. Pivoting around, he crossed the room to Hudson's office and opened the door. Leaning in, he frowned and shook his head, mouthing the words, "Tess is here."

"I think this is a discussion better left for another time." Hudson slammed the phone down and shot to his feet. "Shit! Did she hear any of that?"

Ford nodded, but said nothing more. He could tell his brother was still tense with rage by the veins popping out on his neck and the way he clenched and unclenched his fists. Ford felt the same anger, but hid the signs much better. He wanted nothing more than to hop on his bike and ride over to that asshole Kingston's office and punch him in the face. Luckily, no one would ever tell by the way Ford carried himself. His emotions were something he kept tightly under wraps.

"Tell her I'll be right out, okay?" Hudson rolled his shoulders back and flicked his head to the side. Ford heard the tendons crackle and pop. Nodding, he backed out of the room and closed the door again.

"He'll be right out."

Chapter 17

Hudson got control of himself and ran his fingers through his hair. The last thing he wanted Tess to hear was an argument with David Kingston. Stepping into the waiting room, he was blown away by the stricken look on Tess's face. He told her it was going to get ugly, but obviously she hadn't really grasped that possibility. And this was just the beginning. His gut said she was up to the fight. She'd shown remarkable strength up to this point. Maybe this was the impetus she needed to get herself geared up for the long haul. In spite of the discouraging way she had come into the office, Hudson couldn't help but notice how cute she looked in her summery dress. He also couldn't help seeing Lilly beside her. She had on jean shorts and a tank with little skulls and crossbones on it. If he didn't know better, Hudson thought they looked like best girlfriends, instead of sisters, on their way to do some shopping or have lunch. He was very glad that Tess and Lilly were together.

"Hey Tess," he said cheerily, hoping he didn't sound too phony. "Hello, Tess's friend. I'm Hudson Marks."

Lilly shot him a look of pure disgust. "Can it. She knows I was here."

"L, don't." Tess reached for her sister's hand and gave it a squeeze.

Taking a seat beside her on the couch, Hudson clasped his hands together and hung them between his knees. "I'm sorry you had to hear that. It might be good that you did, though. I told you it was going to get ugly."

"Yes, you did," Tess admitted. "I guess I didn't think it would happen this fast."

"Consider the source," Lilly muttered.

"She's right," Hudson agreed. "David Kingston is in full warrior mode at this point. I'm sure he's drafting a counter-suit as we speak so he can be ready when I file all the documents with the probate court this afternoon."

"Why does he want to annul the marriage?" Tess took a small sip of water.

"Because he thinks he can win on a technicality. The reality is, it doesn't matter if you and Jack were legally married or not. He was of sound mind when he drafted his will and he left everything to you."

Tess tried to smile and Hudson appreciated her effort, even if it was an epic failure.

"Look, I know it's pointless to say, but you don't need to worry about any of this right now. At least *try* not to. You're here to sign a retainer and leave a check. After that, you and Lilly should go out and try to have some fun. You're a millionaire now, right?"

Hudson knew instantly he'd said the wrong thing. Tess seemed to deflate even further; her shoulders slumping and making her pull inward. Lilly shot him a furious stare and Ford cringed from across the room. *Fuck*. It was a typical Hudson flub. Ford had always been the smooth one when it came to dealing with people, especially women. Hudson, on the other hand, almost always put his foot in his mouth no matter what the circumstance. It was why he never had a girlfriend for more than a few months at a time. Eventually, he would do or say the wrong thing and they would break up with him. It wasn't that his intentions were bad. He just didn't seem to have the ability to connect with women unless he was representing them as a lawyer.

"Thank you, Hudson," Tess finally said. "I appreciate the thought. Can I just sign the letter and get going please?"

"Of course."

He popped up off the couch and half jogged back to his office. He returned a moment later with a manila file folder. Inside was a two page letter outlining the terms of his representation. "You should read it carefully and then let me know if you have any questions." He handed it to her, along with a pen.

Tess ignored his instructions, took the pen, and flipped to the second page. Finding the spot for her signature, she scribbled it on, snapped the folder closed, and handed it back. Then she tore a check out of her checkbook, signed it, and handed that over as well. Tess tossed the checkbook back into her purse and flipped the pen onto the couch. "Just fill it in. I trust you."

Hudson watched her hoist the bag onto her shoulder and walk out the door, Lilly close on her heels.

Chapter 18

Tess let herself into the apartment and wandered over to the couch. She flopped onto it, dropping her purse on the floor at her feet. Things sure had gone to shit faster than she expected. Leaving the bank, she had sort of felt better. Happy, even. Not just relief, happy or kind of happy, but honest-to-goodness normal happy. There would be money to pay the bills, and thinking about Jack made her feel grateful and hopeful, not guilty. If only she and Lilly had stopped for lunch before going to Hudson's office. If only there had been a line at the bank or something else to hold them up.

It was weird. She wasn't really mad that David Kingston thought an annulment would keep her from getting the inheritance. What really hurt was that if he won that fight, then it would truly be like she and Jack were never married. It was already hard enough for her to believe it was all real. How could anyone think of their marriage as real if their husband dropped dead within a few minutes after walking down the aisle? David had to know she struggled with that, anyway, right? Threatening an annulment was just pouring salt on the wound. Sure, they hadn't always gotten along very well, but was he really, truly this callous? This mean? This hateful?

The answer was yes. For whatever reason, David really hated her now and was going to do anything he could to destroy her, just like he'd threatened that day in his parents' kitchen. Depressed and overwhelmed or not, Tess knew in her heart she wasn't going to let it happen. Yes, she was feeling hurt and betrayed and even somewhat violated after overhearing the conversation between Hudson and David, but already she was feeling the beginnings of a righteously indignant rage growing in her stomach. It wouldn't be long before she was stomping through the apartment, ranting and raving at the cats about the injustice of it all. She'd probably have a few choice words for Jack as well, shaking her fist into the air, as if he were sitting on a cloud somewhere watching her.

But at the moment, she was too tired to work up the fury just yet. Instead, she leaned over and pulled a small notebook out of her purse. There was already a pen stuck inside the spiral wire on the side. Freeing it, she opened to a fresh, blank page.

That was what Tess did when she felt overwhelmed. She made lists. One for the feelings still bouncing around her brain. One for the things she needed to do around the house. One for the things she wanted to spend money on, now that she would have so much of it at her disposal. One for the feelings she had toward the Kingston family. Jack had always teased her about the pieces of paper that filled notebooks from cover to cover, but Tess hadn't minded. She wasn't a writer by any stretch, but keeping track of the jumbled mess of her mind gave her a sense of control.

With a cat on either side of her, Tess sat on the couch, scribbling away. When her cell phone rang, she plucked it out of her purse and nearly dropped it when she saw the number and face displayed on the screen. Emily Kingston was calling.

Tess couldn't decide what to do. Hudson had said not to have any contact with the Kingstons. But her heart yearned to answer and speak with the woman who had been a second mother to her for most of her life. And she wanted to rat David out for the jackass he was being. Tess's finger hovered over the "accept" button too long and the call went to voicemail. She waited to see if Emily would leave a message, but was surprised again when Jack's mother called a second time. Throwing caution to the wind, Tess answered it.

"Hello?"

"Hello, sweetheart," Emily said in a breathless, anxious tone. "I thought maybe you couldn't get to the phone so I took a chance on calling again. I'm so glad you answered."

Unsure of what to say, Tess opted to stay quiet. *Sweetheart? Please!*

"I'm sorry for that terrible scene last week." Emily certainly sounded contrite to Tess. "Roger and David feel awful about the way they treated you."

Tess snorted. *Yeah, right.*

"It's true, Tess. I'm calling to apologize on their behalf," Emily insisted, almost begging.

"If Roger and David really felt bad, they'd be calling," Tess snapped. Immediately she regretted her tone of voice. "I'm sorry, Emily, I didn't mean to be rude."

Finally, she spoke, sounding defeated. "That's all right, dear. You have every right to be upset."

Tess paused, and then gave voice to her feelings. "It's like you guys were accusing me of something, but I'm not even sure what. Why would you do that?"

"It was shock, Tess. We'd only told Jack about his father's death and the money a few weeks before the wedding. Roger and I had no idea he would have gone and made a will so quickly. Jack's father took care of the investments for many years and I think maybe he was upset that he wasn't going to be in charge anymore."

Tess wasn't sure if the explanation was reasonable or not. She never was particularly close to Roger Kingston, in spite of having been in his life for most of hers. He was just the dad in the house who was so very different from her own. She realized then that she never really knew him. And after his attitude, she was pretty sure she didn't want to get to know him.

"I guess I can understand that," Tess admitted. "But still, I don't think we should be around each other for a while. Not until I'm more comfortable." It was obvious to Tess that Emily had no idea what kinds of things David was doing. The situation was going very sideways very quickly.

"But David wants to help you, dear. He can handle all of the probate and investments and whatnot, so you don't have to bother yourself with it."

Tess frowned, suspicious immediately by the decidedly authoritative tone Emily's voice took on. "Well, I have my own lawyer. I don't really need David." Emily paused and Tess could actually hear the dry click as she swallowed.

"When did you have time to find one?" Emily's voice cracked nervously. "I'm sure David would be a much better choice. And what about the fees, dear? How will you pay those while Jack's estate is tied up? Roger always had access to all the money. Perhaps you should ask him about writing a check to tide you over."

Tess rubbed her forehead and scrunched up her nose, confusion coating her brain like a fog rolling in. *Did she forget about the insurance?* Neither Roger nor David was talking to Emily about anything. She was trying to convince her of things that had no truth to them at all. "I got the insurance money and I hired the same attorney who drew up the will. He understands the circumstances and I'm comfortable with him." *Not David.*

"Well, but how could they know anything about it? Roger's handled everything since Jack was sixteen."

Tess held the phone away from her ear and frowned at it, as if Emily could see her puzzlement and growing frustration. "And I'm sure Roger did a great job, but Jack made sure all the beneficiary information was changed to me. I don't see how he needs to do anything anymore." Tess tried to keep her tone civil and calm.

"I see," Emily sighed. "It's just that Roger and I thought you would need his advice, since he made all the decisions for all those years. Investments can be so tricky."

"My guy's pretty good and he's been through all the paperwork. I'm sure he'll do okay," Tess insisted, wishing she'd never answered the phone at all. *Hudson's going to kill me. I'll have to plead insanity.*

Emily sighed again. "Tess, we only want what's best for you. Please don't hold our mistakes against us."

Tess's shoulders slumped with shame. She didn't want to argue or be harsh with Emily because Jack would be disappointed. The thought of disrespecting her husband's mother suddenly left her feeling cold and clammy. "I'm sorry, Emily. Really. I was just starting to feel almost normal and then all of this happened. It's really hard."

"Of course it is, dear. I can't imagine what it must be like, just like you can't feel what we are, having lost a son and brother." Emily sounded earnest enough, but Tess caught a hint of desperation in her voice too. "Why don't you come over for dinner tonight? Let me make your favorite, chicken and cheese enchiladas!"

Tess hesitated. The sudden shift in mood and tone threw her for a loop. Remembering what Hudson had told her, she knew she should keep some distance from Jack's family. Taking the phone call was probably a big enough mistake. "I can't. But thank you."

"Are you sure, dear? I've got all the ingredients right here. It wouldn't take but a minute to put it together. If you're struggling, you should come and talk with Roger and David. They could help you make sense of things. After all, we're your family, not some strange lawyer." Emily was trying too hard and Tess's inner alarms were going off as loudly as tornado sirens.

"I just don't think it's a good idea for me to talk to Roger or David right now."

"Okay," Emily agreed too quickly. "Then maybe you and I could get together, alone. You could tell me what's going on and I could be the go between. We could go out to dinner."

Tess's eyebrows furrowed and she took a deep breath to calm herself. Emily's endless pressure was rubbing her nerves raw. *Remember, she's Jack's mother. Be polite. Be nice. Remember who you are.* "I'm really not comfortable with it."

Tess waited for a response, but she heard nothing. After a few seconds, she pulled the phone away from her ear to look at the display. Maybe the call had dropped? No, it was still connected. "Emily? Are you still there?"

"Yes, of course, dear. I guess we're all just so confused about what's gone on. Don't you think Jack made a hasty decision to have the will made so quickly? How can we be sure he didn't do it out of anger? Was Jack really thinking clearly?"

Tess bounded off the couch and jumped up and down to keep from screaming into the phone. She didn't know what to do. She wanted to hang up. She wanted to yell at Emily. She wanted to go back in time and not answer the phone. This is what she got for not listening to Hudson when he said to have no contact. It was a ploy all along. Emily must have called because David told her to.

After taking a moment to calm herself, Tess said, "Jack may not have told me what was going on before the wedding, but he was fine. He wasn't acting weird or doing anything strange. He was excited to be getting married and he was happy."

"Yes, but he would never let on to you–"

"Jack always told me everything!"

"Well, not everything dear," Emily snapped. "Or else you would have known about his adoption and the will, now wouldn't you?"

Tess's mouth dropped open and she stared in shock at the phone. "I have to go now." She punched her thumb down on the "end" button on her phone before Emily could say anything more. Then she powered the phone off to avoid any more calls.

Tess stood still for at least a minute trying to understand what had just happened. Emily Kingston had never spoken to her in that way in all the years they'd known one another. She had a valid point: Jack had *not* told her everything. He'd held back two gigantic secrets from her and those secrets were now causing her more grief and anxiety. The guilt monster in her brain said she probably deserved it for the disloyal thoughts before the wedding, but it was too late to change any of that.

For the first time since finding out about his adoption and the inheritance, Tess felt angry with Jack. Rage coursed through her veins and she took a moment to stamp her foot like a three year old having a tantrum. "What the hell were you thinking?" she shouted into the apartment, empty except for herself and the two cats. Said felines raised their chins off the couch long enough to look at their mistress before lowering them again and returning to their naps.

"Oh, what do you know?" she hollered at the cats as she paced around the living room. "Jack, I could punch you in the throat right now!" Tess raised a fist and shook it at the ceiling. "Why didn't you tell me right away? Why did you have to hide this?"

Tess picked up a pillow from the couch and punched it, since her husband wasn't available to receive the blow. Then she pressed it to her face and screamed into it for a full ten seconds. With her throat raw and her breathing labored, Tess flopped onto the loveseat across from the couch and groaned. The cats were no longer sleeping, but still had their chins resting on their paws, watching her warily.

Chapter 19

Hudson grabbed his towel from the arm rest as he climbed off the treadmill. He wiped his face and neck and took deep breaths as he cooled off from his five mile run. Usually a hard run would help him focus his thoughts and give him clarity when he was struggling with a case. It hadn't worked this time and he was still as conflicted about the Jack Kingston estate as he had been before he got on the machine. After Tess left his office the day before, Hudson had been making mental notes and doing psychological fact checks about the case well into the evening. An evening he spent alone, as usual.

After a restless night, he'd gotten up early and gone to the office, hoping not to find Ford in another passed out state. His hopes were well founded and the couch was empty. That was a huge relief to him. He didn't need any other stress in his life at the moment and Ford seemed to be cleaning himself up a bit. He wasn't passing out at the office, he looked fairly well rested when he got into the office and hadn't looked hungover in days. Hudson had spent an hour looking through some of the research his brother left for him and worked on completing the probate forms he would need. But the uneasy feeling he had about the entire Kingston matter had grown and clouded his ability to work effectively on any other cases.

Weaving his way between the machines and people working out, Hudson headed toward the locker room, alternately waving at people he knew and nodding at strange women who smiled at him. He felt more mentally exhausted than physically. The locker room was empty and as he reached for the door to his cubby, he could hear his cell phone ringing.

Not recognizing the number, he pinched the phone between his cheek and shoulder as he pulled out his shaving kit and got ready to shower. "Hudson Marks."

"Hi, it's Tess."

"Hey, is anything wrong?" Forgetting his shower, Hudson stood up straight and pressed the phone harder to his ear. Her voice sounded... confused? Unsure? *Uh oh.*

"No, at least I don't think so. I may have made a mistake, though."

Hudson grimaced. "Okay, tell me."

"Emily Kingston called me last night and I answered."

"Shit," Hudson sighed. "I thought I said no contact." *Do I ever have a client who actually listens to my advice? Nope.*

"Yeah, I know." Tess hesitated. "But she was like a second mom to me for a lot of years. After what happened at their house, I wanted to hear what she had to say."

"Which was?" Hudson sat down on a metal bench, tossing his shaving kit back into his gym bag. He kept his voice controlled and even to hide his irritation.

"She was giving me the really hard sell to go with Roger and David for legal and financial advice. When I finally stood up for myself and said no, she wasn't real happy. I couldn't tell if they're not telling her stuff or if they're all acting together to make my life hell. I do think she's hurt and mad about not getting anything in the will."

"How do you feel about that?" Hudson dug around in his bag for the shaving kit again.

"I'm not sure. I was really pissed off before I called you. I mean, the Kingstons never seemed like materialistic or greedy people. But why else would Emily give me such a hard time about it all? And I got really mad at Jack too, though I know it's silly. It's not like he knew he was going to die. He only made out the will because he was mad at his parents for keeping the secret from him, right? I guess it doesn't really matter. Everything and nothing makes much sense anymore."

"I'm sorry it feels that way right now, but I promise I will do the best I can to make it easier for you. Please don't talk to Emily or any other Kingston again, all right?"

"Okay."

"I'm on my way back to my office. If anything else happens, call me."

"Okay. Bye."

Hudson ended the call and returned to the task at hand. He showered quickly and dressed in his old jeans and sweat jacket before leaving the gym to return to his office. To his relief, Ford was waiting for him.

"Hey, boss," Ford greeted when Hudson walked in. He was sitting behind the desk with his feet propped up and the laptop on his thighs.

"You know I hate when you call me that." Hudson threw his gym back on the couch and went to the coffee pot. "What did you find out?"

"Not a ton we didn't already know. Besides, I can tell you rifled through the printouts I left."

Hudson grinned guiltily. "Yeah. Let me fill you in on the latest." While he grabbed a bottle of water from the fridge, he related his phone call from Tess. "Why do you think the mother would call her like that?"

Ford shrugged. "I think Roger and David aren't telling Emily about what's going on and everything they're doing. That could end up hurting them, though. If Emily starts feeling bad, then maybe we could have Tess work on her. Get the mother on our side."

"It's definitely something to consider." Hudson drained half the water and then capped it. "But if she's pissed because she wasn't left anything, then she's not likely to come over to our side."

"Give it a think, but maybe in a day or two, Tess could call her back and see if she can find out what's going on from that end."

"We'll see. In the meantime, I need to get the probate paperwork filed first thing tomorrow. Any word on that tox report yet?"

Ford shook his head and swung his legs off the desk to the floor. "My girl in the ME's office isn't returning my calls. I can't tell if I'm being blown off or if she's really that busy." He closed the laptop and put it in the desk drawer.

Hudson sighed and gave Ford a suspicious look. "You didn't sleep with her and never call, did you?"

Ford flipped him off, but chuckled. "Yeah, I slept with her, but I *did* call again. She was the one who didn't seem interested. Besides, it was a couple of years ago. Maybe I'll take a ride over there and see if I can get some answers."

"Do that."

"What else do you want me digging up?" Ford asked as he stood up and stretched. "I haven't been able to find anything on any of the Kingstons yet."

Hudson finished the water and then crunched the bottle, his knuckles cracking as he did so. "Hold off for now. Go back to working on the other files you have for the time being." He tossed the empty water bottle into the recycle bin across the room.

"You got it."

Hudson went to his office and sat down. Closing his eyes, he conjured an image of Tess and pasted it onto the mental white board in his head. Around her, he threw up pictures of Roger, David, and Jack Kingston. A blank question mark had to suffice for the birth father. More blank squares for the unknown players who might be lurking in the shadows. He tried to draw mental connections between them all, but the lines became tangled in his brain and all he could focus on was Tess's face – her creamy complexion and wide blue eyes. He gave her a smile, so he could view her the way he thought she looked best. Small, even teeth peeking from between her full lips.

"You look like you're thinking about something good."

Ford's voice brought Hudson back to reality and he opened his eyes, hoping he didn't look guilty. "Uh, yeah."

"Maybe we're looking at this the wrong way." Ford leaned against the door frame and crossed his arms over his chest. "I think we should dig into Jack's past a little bit more. Do you think there's any way he might have known about the adoption earlier than he let on or the Kingstons said?"

Hudson shrugged. "Hmm, anything's possible."

"What if he has a history of depression or something? What were his teenage years like? How about his college life? I'm not sure we can get truthful answers from Tess. She loved him and wouldn't be able to see him with an objective eye. She could be protecting him, even if only on a subconscious level."

"Oh come on!" Hudson blurted the words before he could help himself, leaning forward on the desk. "Tess doesn't have a dishonest bone in her body!"

"Take it easy, brother," Ford admonished gently. He was the one giving out suspicious looks now and Hudson felt it. "Is there something you aren't telling me?"

Hudson groaned and ran his hands through his hair, yanking on the ends. "No, no. I'm sorry."

"Be honest with me, do you have a thing for Tess?"

Hudson wanted to shout no, just as vehemently as he had defended her moments before, but didn't. After a few seconds, he found his voice. "No. Not really. I mean, I can't deny she's hot. And I feel really bad for her. This is about the shittiest situation I've ever seen for a girl who's so young, but…" His voice trailed off.

"But what? You hardly know her. You can't be in love with her." Ford glowered as he said it and Hudson felt ashamed of himself for having lost some of his objectivity.

"No. I'm not in love with her." Hudson answered honestly. He *wasn't* in love with Tess, but he certainly was attracted to her. "I guess maybe it's just the case? She's always on my mind."

Ford's glare faded, replaced with a grin. His eyes even twinkled a little from the mirthful expression on his face and that made Hudson feel more like an ass than anything else.

"Don't look at me like that."

"What?"

"Like you're about to start singing 'Tess and Hudson sittin' in a tree.'"

Ford's laughter was like a strong breeze coming through the office to blast away the cobwebby feeling in Hudson's brain and he joined in with a chuckle of his own. There was that connection again, the one brothers shared that was as unexplainable as the Bermuda Triangle.

"How long has it been since you got laid, brother?"

Hudson snorted. "Too long."

"Rebecca? That was the last girlfriend, right?"

"Yeah." Hudson didn't even want to think about her. They'd met at the gym and dated for awhile, but she had wanted marriage and kids and a house – the whole nine yards and it wasn't something he'd been ready for at the time.

"Gotta put yourself back out there, Hud. Otherwise, you'll find yourself mooning over your client and that is not a good idea."

"I know."

Ford leaned down in an attempt to catch Hudson's eye. "I'm serious. If you can't be objective, you won't be able to help Tess."

"You're right. I get it." Hudson looked at his brother and nodded his head. "It's just that—"

"I know. You don't have to say it. Either lock it away until this mess is over, or stop it once and for all. Otherwise, you could fuck it all up. Not just for Tess, but for your license to practice law."

Hudson took a deep breath and nodded again. "Don't worry about me, brother. I'll handle it."

"Good."

"All right then. Do you want me to start looking into Jack?"

"Yes. Do it."

Chapter 20

I'm such a hypocrite. Ford sped along the streets of St. Clair Shores, his motorcycle thrumming between his thighs. He'd given Hudson the what for about not getting hung up on a client, when it was all he could do not to think about Tess. Unless he had a specific task at hand, the image of her face hovered in his vision way more than it had any right to.

And now he felt guilty. What if his brother did want to pursue something with the lovely widow after the case was resolved? Ford hated to admit it, but he would never be able to be in the same room with them at the same time. It would drive him crazy. His logical brain knew that there could never be anything between Tess and him. His rational mind understood that he was just lonely and longing for some female companionship with more substance than the airheads he found at the bars he frequented. His lucid self was firmly grounded in the reality that he was not someone good enough for the likes of Tess Kingston. Besides all of that, Hudson would be a far better match for her than he could ever be.

That didn't stop his gut and heart from wishing it all could be different.

Once again, Ford found himself in a position where he knew eventually he would have to squash any feelings he had for a girl in lieu of what his brother wanted. He was no stranger to the scenario. There had been plenty of times he'd let a girl go because Hudson wanted her or showed even the slightest interest. They'd both been short changed a lot in their lives and Ford always figured it fell to him to see that Hudson got all the opportunities. His little brother had made something of himself. He'd worked hard, gotten through school and started a business. What had Ford done? Jail time. That was about it.

As his mind zoomed down memory lane, his physical self was maneuvering the bike through a particular subdivision. As he watched the house numbers, looking for one in particular, he felt his cell phone vibrate in the right breast pocket of his vest. He pulled it out and smiled.

"What's up, brother?"

"Where are you?" Hudson's voice boomed through the phone. There was loud music in the background.

"Ridin'. What about you?"

Ford came to a stop sign and paused before going through. Idling down, he crept up to Roger and Emily Kingston's house. Lights beamed through the windows from the living room and a room upstairs. Two cars were parked in the driveway.

"At the Goose. Come on over. I'll buy you a burger and a beer."

Ford grinned. The Blue Goose was Hudson's favorite bar, though God only knew why. The clientele tended to be older and the lack of available single women was evident.

"Eh, I don't know." Ford held the cell away from his face so he could open the camera app. He took pictures of both license plates on both cars, then held it back up to his ear. "I'm not really hungry." He pulled away slowly, driving one handed.

"Come on, man. You have to eat," Hudson urged.

"Nah." Ford navigated out of the sub back onto Harper and headed north toward Ten Mile Road. Within minutes he was parked in front of David Kingston's house repeating the same steps as before to get a picture of the license plate, all the while listening to Hudson list off the reasons why big brother should join him.

"Okay, I'm done begging. I'll be here for a while longer if you change your mind."

"Think I'm gonna ride for a little while longer, then head home."

"Shuh," Hudson scoffed. "You'll probably head to that dump where Joe hangs out and get shit faced. Don't drive if you do."

"Yes, baby brother."

Ending the call, Ford rehashed the conversation with Hudson earlier in the day and wondered if his brother really would be able to put his growing feelings for Tess aside while he worked her case. Probably, because his common sense usually outweighed any personal desires he had in life. It's why he never stayed with any one girlfriend for more than a few months. Oh sure, Hud thought it was the way he acted that made women turn away from him, but Ford knew the truth. His brother pushed them away because, deep down, he barely trusted them. While he hadn't directly experienced some of the grisly things from their childhood like Ford, Hudson had still been able to sense that the bulk of the trouble stemmed from their mother's actions. It made him sad to think that his brother might not ever be able to push past it and find a lasting relationship with a girl. Ford decided a long time ago he would deal with having a fucked up life, but loathed the thought Hudson might be bound for the same fate. That's why he would step away, if Hudson chose to pursue Tess. She could possibly be the one to change that fate for his little brother and Ford wasn't about to let that chance go, if he could do anything about it.

But romance would have to wait. Tess needed both Hudson and Ford focused and on point to deal with whatever lay ahead. Usually the brothers were on the same wavelength when it came to gut feelings about cases and Tess's was no different. They both knew something wasn't right, yet they hadn't really been able to pinpoint anything. It was only a theory, but Ford was becoming more convinced that Jack's death wasn't a freak accident. With all that money at stake, it was more likely someone wanted Jack dead. If that turned out to be true and it could be proven the whole game changed. Not only would there be a need to involve the cops, but Tess's life could be in danger. He didn't have a shred of proof, though, and decided he would definitely bounce the idea off his brother. Hudson would tell him if he was being paranoid or crazy.

He wished he knew exactly what it was about Tess Kingston that had him all fired up. At first, Ford figured it was just her looks. Beautiful blond with blue eyes and a really nice body. But the more he learned about her and Jack, the more inspired he felt to help her and make sure she didn't get screwed over. She'd lost her husband all over some dollars, and that was shit Ford didn't cotton to. Even if Jack had made his will out of anger, that didn't mean he wouldn't have gotten over it. Judging by what Hudson had told him about the guy, Ford thought Jack would have made peace with his family and even shared the loot at some point in the future. So why go and kill him? Why not just wait it out? Ford shook his head as the thoughts whirled around his brain.

Looking around, Ford realized he had come to the intersection at Ten Mile and the freeway. He thought about heading west on I-94 to meet up with some buddies at their favorite watering hole to help get Tess Kingston off his mind. Sitting at the traffic light, it was a right turn to get onto the freeway heading to Detroit or a left turn to find his way home.

The light turned green and Ford turned right.

Chapter 21

Tess rinsed the last of the conditioner from her hair and reached to turn off the shower. Stepping over the lip of the bathtub, Timothy appeared immediately to try and lick the drops of water running down her legs. "Git!" she shouted. It wasn't that she minded him wanting a drink, but the tickling sensation drove her nuts. She waggled her right leg at him and off he ran to sit in the doorway, giving her the typical cat stink eye.

Wrapping herself in her bathrobe, Tess yawned. She tied her hair up into a thick, fluffy towel and ambled out to the kitchen to make a pot of coffee. She still had a little more transcription to complete, in spite of having stayed up until nearly three a.m. Knowing she needed to deliver on her promise to finish her backlog weighed heavily on her while the insurance check sat in her bank account.

As she inhaled the thick scent of coffee, she heard her cell phone go off. The bong sound from the Law & Order theme filled the apartment and she chuckled. That was the ringtone she'd chosen for Hudson Marks.

Tess dashed to the bedroom and grabbed the vibrating phone from the bedside table. "Good morning," she said.

"Good morning to you too." Hudson's voice was low. "I'd like to meet with you this morning, if you're available."

"What's wrong?" Tess sat down on the side of the bed and scratched Spencer's chin when he jumped up onto her lap.

"I'd rather not talk over the phone. I could be there in about fifteen minutes."

Glancing down at her robe, Tess felt her cheeks grow a little warm. "Here? Uh, sure. You're kind of scaring me though."

"Don't be scared. I'll see you then."

Tess ended the call and rushed into the walk-in closet to find fresh underwear. What could be so important that Hudson would want to come to her home? And why was he in the area? Was he waiting to see her? Tess felt the familiar knot of worry tie itself in her stomach and tried to calm down with a few deep breaths. She put on underwear, yoga pants and a t-shirt, then moved back into the bathroom to brush her teeth and tie her hair in a messy bun.

By the time she made it back to the kitchen to transfer the fresh coffee into a carafe, the doorbell was ringing. Leaving the kitchen, she shooed the cats away and opened the door. Hudson stood there with his briefcase, looking excited and anxious at the same time. His smile was warm and it eased her fears a little. *He wouldn't be smiling like that if it was bad news, right?*

"Come on in. I was just getting coffee. Want some?"

"Absolutely."

Hudson followed Tess toward the kitchen and took a seat at the dining room table. She brought the carafe and cream and sugar, along with two cups, to the table. "What's so important that you were lurking near my home, waiting for me?"

Hudson accepted a mug from her. "Well, Ford and I have been talking and we really aren't getting anywhere digging up any dirt on the Kingstons. We want to take a different route with it, but I needed to discuss things with you first. That and some other theories we're developing."

Tess bit her lip. "I don't like the sound of that." She lowered herself gently into a chair kitty corner from him and felt as jumpy as a spooked cat.

Hudson sighed and sat back in his chair. "I need to be honest with you. I've had a difficult time staying objective about all this. I knew Jack in college and even if we weren't good friends, I still liked him. Then I met you and I decided that I like you too. I can see why Jack loved and wanted to take care of you."

Tess stared into her cup and a wistful smile played at the corners of her mouth. "Thank you for that." Jack always had taken care of her, from the day they met. He dispatched the schoolyard bullies. He walked her home from school. He was as much of a best friend as her own sister. Surprisingly, Tess felt honored and grateful for those memories instead of lost; knowing Jack wasn't there to do it anymore.

"Ford and I were talking yesterday and I think we should look into Jack's background a little bit more."

Tess's head bobbed up. "Why?"

"Well, we just want to see if maybe there's a possibility he knew about the adoption and inheritance before he says he found out."

"That's silly." Tess shook her head in disbelief. "Jack would never have kept a secret that big for that long. I'm beginning to understand why he didn't tell me before the wedding, but the letter proves he was going to."

"You're right. He was going to say something. Obviously his death prevented that. But don't you find it just a little strange that he died?"

Tess rolled her eyes and then raised a single eyebrow at him. "Now that's a stupid thing to say." She reached out and smacked him on the arm. "Of course I've thought about it. But the ME said it was because of all those energy drinks. I told Jack all the time he shouldn't drink those things but he wouldn't listen. You know, I've been thinking about that a lot. I might take some of the insurance money and see if I could donate it to research on them or do some kind of awareness campaign or something. I think it's really important–"

"Tess, wait. Let's not get off the subject. I could be wrong but Jack's death might not have been an accident."

* * * * *

Tess gasped and nearly dropped her coffee cup. Hudson reached out to steady her hands and lower the porcelain to the table. Her skin was warm against his own. The color drained from her face and he thought she might faint from shock. He felt instantly guilty for blurting it out like that, but she was going off on a tangent and he needed her attention.

"Are you all right?" he asked, grabbing her hands and squeezing. "Put your head between your knees if you think you're going to pass out."

Tess shook her head slowly, taking in a slow breath through her nose. As she exhaled, she turned her head away from Hudson. "I'm okay. I'm all right."

She continued to breathe until he realized his hands still clenched hers.

"Good." Hudson withdrew them back into his own lap. "I'm sorry to startle you. I didn't know any other way but to come out with it. I really hope I'm wrong. I need to ask you a few questions." He rushed on with them before she could say anything, hoping he wasn't moving too fast. "How were you able to have Jack buried so fast? A young, twenty-five year old male, in apparently good health drops dead of a heart attack and no one questioned it?"

"I don't know," Tess admitted. "It's all a blur. There are moments burned in my memory but most of it is just... gone."

"I've read the autopsy report. They blamed heavy consumption of energy drinks. Did you really believe that?" Hudson watched her face for a reaction and wasn't disappointed when pain settled there like a storm cloud rolling in.

Tess began to tremble and wrapped herself in her arms. "I guess. I mean, what was I supposed to believe?" Pulling her knees up to her chest, Tess rested her chin on them. "Who would want to kill him? Everyone loved Jack."

"I know it seemed that way, but there was a lot of money at stake. And the people with the most to gain are the Kingstons. Especially Roger. We need that toxicology report." Hudson paused. "Are you sure you're okay? You're getting pale again."

"I'm fine," Tess sighed. "My head is going to blow up with questions."

Hudson waited patiently and watched with fascination at the myriad of expressions crossing Tess's face. He also knew, without a doubt, Tess was not responsible for Jack's death. There was no way she could be that good of an actress. It was as if he could see the wheels inside her head turning faster and faster. Her eyes were filled with pain and torment, which caused his own heart to twist. Her body was stiff with anxiety. It made his gut clench to see her like that and he wanted to reach to comfort her in some way, but he knew it would be inappropriate. Just that morning, while in the shower, he had resolved to no longer look at her as more than just a client. He was her lawyer, for Christ's sakes. The whole experience was new for him, though. He'd never dealt with a grieving widow, especially one as attractive as Tess. His clientele consisted mostly of blue collar guys popped for DUIs or bar fights, acrimonious divorces, and real estate transactions.

"Should I call your sister? Your parents?" he asked softly, trying to reach through her distress.

Sniffling, she shook her head no.

This was a bad idea. What the hell was I thinking? Hudson wondered if he should leave and wait for her to collect herself. There just wasn't time for it, though. If his suspicions were correct, a clock was ticking and he would need answers. He decided to take a chance and push on, test her strength. If she cracked, he would call her family. If she bucked up and pulled it together, he knew she could handle whatever else there was to come.

Tess pinched the bridge of her nose between her thumb and first finger, then shook her head vigorously. Hudson found the way her blonde hair tried to wiggle its way out of the bun to be very sexy. *Dammit, knock it off!* His voice inside his head was thunderous.

"You think Jack was killed? *Murdered?*"

"I think it's a possibility."

"Tell me why."

Hudson nodded. Ford had sent him some texts the night before with his theory and Hudson had run with it from there, even though there was no proof or evidence to support the conclusion.

As she listened, Tess got up and paced around like a caged cat. "As pissed as I am with them, I can't believe Jack's family would kill him. He would've given them all the money back if he was alive."

"They have motive," Hudson reminded.

"Of course, but so do I. I could be lying to you. I could have known about the will and everything else."

Hudson snorted and took another slug of coffee. "Unlikely. But I see your point."

Tess chewed on her thumb as she gazed out the large French doors. "This is too cloak and dagger for me. This shit doesn't happen in real life, does it? I must have woken up in some bad movie."

Hudson wanted to laugh but held it in. He knew she was joking, but the sadness in her voice was all too serious. "I wish I could tell you that's true, Tess."

"Couldn't it all just be a coincidence? I mean, I don't know you from Adam. You don't know me, or even Jack. Are you reaching?"

Hudson nodded. He was prepared for this. He felt it himself. "It could be my imagination running amok, I'll give you that. But my gut says something's not right."

Tess sat back down and laced her fingers together, leaning her elbows on the table. She rested her chin on her hands and looked at Hudson. He wondered how many times Jack might have seen that very same pose. *So much for looking at her as just a client.* Hudson turned to look into his coffee cup.

"For real, Hudson, I can't even… I just can't."

It was then that a pudgy black cat sidled up beside her chair and jumped into her lap. Hudson instinctively smiled and reached to pet it. Their hands bumped as they each found space to scratch and pet it.

"What a beautiful cat. I've always liked the black ones."

Spencer looked up at Tess and then leaned up to put his front paws on her shoulders. He bumped his nose and head against her chin. "This is Spencer," Tess whispered. "He was Jack's boy."

And just like that, Tess was back to being a client again. Just a client. Watching her nuzzle the cat and knowing he had been "Jack's boy" sealed the deal in Hudson's mind and heart. He figured it would take years before Tess would be ready to move on from the traumatic events of the last few months and he wasn't going to wait around for her. He liked her, she was cute as hell, but he would never be able to separate Tess from Jack or the circumstances under which they met.

"Just make it be over, Hudson. Do whatever you can to make things normal again."

Hudson nodded and stood up. "I'll do my best." Feeling the tremendous pressure of that request on his shoulders, he walked through the living room to the front door where he'd left his briefcase. Tess remained seated at the table, focused on loving the cat still in her lap. Even from across the apartment, he could see the tears falling from her eyes onto the cat's silky coat and the burden settled more heavily.

"I'll talk to you soon," he called to her.

She waved a hand at him but did not speak and Hudson let himself out of the apartment.

Chapter 22

After Hudson left and Spencer abandoned her for his favorite napping spot, Tess paced around the apartment trying to get a handle on the bombshell he had dropped. She racked her brain for any detail she might have missed before the wedding, but there was nothing. She had been so consumed with all her own worries and final details, she honestly couldn't remember anything being out of the ordinary.

Tess tried to imagine Roger, Emily, or David planning a murder and then killing their own son or brother. She couldn't do it. Emily and Roger had been devastated when Jack died. It was obvious at the funeral, with Emily crying constantly and clinging to Tess. Roger had cried too, in the silent way men tended to do. Even David, with all his bluff and bluster, had been sickeningly pale, walking around in a fog of disbelief.

Yes, they had treated her very unkindly that day in their kitchen. Yes, it seemed like they were accusing her of something. Yes, they were lying to try and keep Jack's fortune for themselves. But such a tragic, unexpected death makes people do the craziest things and Tess's heart just wouldn't let a sliver of doubt inside. "Maybe I'm being naïve," she said to the cats, who watched her walk around the apartment like a lost traveler.

After an hour of drinking coffee, pacing and obsessing, Tess could feel her nerves fraying like the ends of the pieces of yarn her cats played with. She needed a distraction, something to do with herself so she could focus on something else. She thought about typing and the small amount of transcription left, but she didn't want to sit still. She wanted to move.

Striding with a purpose to the spare bedroom, Tess flung open the door. The only remaining furniture was the futon and a single two-drawer metal filing cabinet. She'd gotten rid of Jack's rickety pressboard desk, but opted to keep the lateral file for paperwork. She stepped over to the closet and opened the accordion doors to look inside; making sure nothing was left inside. She then went to the file cabinet and began shoving it until it was centered inside the closet. While she was bent over and giving it one final push, Timothy bolted into the room, leapt on her back and up onto the shelf above the hanger rod. "You little shit!" she hollered. His front paws were declawed, but not the back, and they left scratches along the skin on either side of her spine.

He looked down from the shelf and meowed, but it didn't sound like much of an apology to Tess. As she gave him her best pissed off look, she noticed something in the far corner of the ceiling. Cocking her head to the side, she stepped closer for a better look. It seemed like a six by six inch square of the drywall had been cut out and replaced. There was also a circle cut through the middle and some wires were threaded through, going into another circle in the wall. Tess figured it was just wiring for the cable or phones or whatever, but still, she wanted to see for herself. Just to make sure.

Grunting, she pulled the cabinet back out of the closet to create a make-shift ladder. Climbing up, she shooed the cat out of the way and leaned on the shelf. Reaching up, she poked at the square of drywall and shrieked when it came crashing down, followed by a metal lockbox. The box bounced off the shelf and landed on the floor with a heavy thud. She pressed a hand to her chest to try and calm her thumping heart. Her legs felt shaky and she thought she might fall. Tess stared at it for a moment, then jumped down and picked it up. It was the kind of lockbox that needed a key to open it.

"Shit," she mumbled as her breathing returned to normal. "I'm going to have to look up there again."

Tess was deathly afraid of spiders and mice, and she realized that both such creatures could be making homes up in that black hole. But if there was a key for the box, it might just be up there, sitting just inside. She set the box on the futon and raced to the kitchen to grab a flashlight from the junk drawer. Screwing up her courage, she hurried back to get up on the cabinet again. She poked the flashlight's bright yellow beam into the darkness. Breathing a sigh of relief, she saw no legions of tarantulas or rats waiting to attack. Using two fingers, she felt along the edge of the opening, hoping she wouldn't get any splinters, until the familiar coolness of metal met her hot fingertips. She pulled the key down and stared at it. Looking back at the opening, she reached for the piece of drywall still sitting on the shelf. She shoved it back in place and kept mashing at it until it stayed. Praying it wouldn't fall out again, she promised to call her dad and ask him to come put a few nails in it. Just because she hadn't seen any creatures didn't mean they weren't there, waiting for her guard to slip.

Unable to wait to see what was inside the box, Tess hopped down, clicked off the flashlight and tossed it onto the futon. Sitting, she pulled the box onto her lap and unlocked it. She flipped open the lid and almost dropped the box onto her toes. Inside lie piles and piles of rubber-banded cash. She sifted through one and noticed that all the bills were hundreds. She twisted to the side and dumped the entire contents onto the futon. Each pack she held up contained nothing but hundred dollar bills. Underneath all the money, there was a file folder. She pried it out and flipped it open to find a copy of Jack's estate documents and a bunch of other financial documents she'd already been given from Hudson.

"What the hell?" she whispered.

She started to pile the money back into the box when she noticed an envelope taped to the inside of the lid. It was the same gray color as the box, so it hadn't been noticeable right away. She ripped it off and tore it open. A piece of paper fluttered out which she caught and unfolded. An email address and a series of numbers and letters were handwritten on it. Tess recognized the handwriting immediately as Jack's. JXKing0923@hushmail.com.

"*What the hell?*" she repeated. Taking the paper and box with her, she made a beeline for her computer out in the living room. Tess opened a web browser and navigated to the email website. She punched in the address and then the series of numbers and letters, hoping it was the password. It was and she was greeted by an inbox filled with emails dating back to the month before the wedding. She clicked to open the first one that appeared to be from Jack to his father.

To: RKingston1942@gmail.com
From: JXKing0923@hushmail.com
Date: November 18, 2013 8:49 pm
Subject: Revelations

Dad,

I'm sorry for the way I acted at the campsite, but you have to understand how shocking it was to discover that I was adopted and a millionaire all at the same time. I don't give a shit about the money. I'm more pissed because you didn't give me the opportunity to know my birth father. He contacted you when I was 12 for God's sakes. How could you not have told me then? I am still trying to process all of this so I don't want you saying anything to Tess. Tell Mom and David to keep their mouths shut too. I will tell Tess when I'm ready.

Jack

Poor Jack, Tess thought as she scrolled down to see if there was a reply. He probably felt then like she did right now. She was shocked and overwhelmed and completely unable to really understand how or why things had happened the way they had. *If only you'd told me.*

From: RKingston1942@gmail.com
To: JXKing0923@hushmail.com
Date: November 19, 2013 7:12 am
Subject: Re: Revelations

I understand your anger, son. Your mother and I thought we were doing the right thing. We won't say anything to Tess.

Dad

The next couple of emails were more of the same, Jack expressing anger and asking questions about his birth father and mother. Roger's responses seemed kind of curt to Tess. Maybe she was just projecting, but it was as if her father-in-law hadn't wanted to answer the questions at all.

The next email that caught her attention had a subject line reading, "The Money." It took her two tries to click fast enough to get it open.

To: RKingston1942@gmail.com
From: JXKing0923@hushmail.com
Date: November 22, 2013 5:42 pm
Subject: The Money

I've had a couple of days to think about the inheritance my birth father left for me. I'm grateful that you took care of it for all those years, but I'm 25 and I think I should be able to take over. Technically, I was supposed to get control at age 21. I would appreciate it if you could gather together all of the paperwork so I can come by and get it. If there's anything you want to explain to me, we can sit down and talk about it then. Thanks.

Jack

Looking at the date, Tess realized it was just before Jack called Hudson.

> From: RKingston1942@gmail.com
> To: JXKing0923@hushmail.com
> Date: November 23, 2013 6:48 am
> Subject: Re: The Money
>
> It will take me a few days to get everything together. I'll let you know when it's ready.

> From: JXKing0923@hushmail.com
> To: RKingston1942@gmail.com
> Date: November 23, 2013 9:12 am
> Subject: Re: Re: The Money
>
> I'll be by tonight after work. I really don't want to wait that long.

Tess could feel the tension coming off the computer screen in waves. Her stomach began to feel queasy as she counted the number of emails that went back and forth. There were sixteen more and she wasn't sure she could read through them by herself. She didn't know what they held, but she wanted someone with her when whatever truth they held came to light. Pulling her phone out of her pocket, she tapped Lilly's direct contact icon.

"Hey!" Her sister's voice was a balm to her aching soul.

"Hey sis," Tess answered. "I could really use some company again."

"What?" Lilly immediately switched from happiness to concern. "Is everything all right? Are you okay?"

"I'm fine. There's just a lot of shit happening. Can you spare your little sis a few hours to scarf some pizza and drink some beer?"

Lilly never hesitated. "Absolutely. What time do you want me there?"

"What time do you get off work?"

"Five."

"Perfect. It's almost four now. You bring the beer and I'll have the pizza waiting."

"You got it! I'll see you then."

Chapter 23

Ford was still buried beneath the blankets on his bed when his phone chirped with an incoming text. Groaning, he snaked his arm out from under them and reached for the bedside table. His fingers found the slim, cool rectangle and he pulled it to his face. Need to get to Tess's. Pick u up in 10 minutes.

"Aw, hell," he muttered and sat straight up, flinging the bedding in all directions. His head exploded with the fiery stars of a hangover and he dropped the phone so he could put both hands on either temple. Rubbing gently, he slowly opened his eyes and was grateful to be able to see the room around him in a fairly clear fashion.

As he scooted to the end of the bed to stand, the room was filled with the harsh sounds of ringing. Flopping onto his back, he reached for the phone and clicked the answer button. "Yeah."

"Didn't you get my message?" Hudson's voice boomed into Ford's ear and he winced, barely keeping the whine of pain in his throat from coming out.

"Yeah."

"Where are you and where the hell have you been all day?"

"Home."

"Oh for fuck's sake, you're not still in bed are you?" Hudson shouted. "I'll pick you up. Be ready in ten minutes!"

The click of his brother hanging up made Ford flinch and he scowled at the black screen. *Jackass.* Shoving himself off the bed, he stood up slowly and scratched his naked chest, wondering what time he'd finally gotten home. How *had* he'd gotten home? *Must have been a cab, I was way too drunk to ride.* He shuffled across the room to the bathroom where he turned on the shower.

Ford stepped out of his shorts and into the cold needles of water raining down. He didn't bother with the hot tap, he needed to wake up and clear his head. If there was some emergency going on, he needed all his wits to be able to focus on the situation and tune out Hudson's lecture. God, what had he done last night? He should have just met his brother at the Goose or at the very least gone home. Instead, he'd turned to booze to drown out all of the crap in his head. And the bitch of it was, it hadn't really worked. Once again, even in a passed-out state, his mind had produced dreams of Tess, images he didn't dare repeat out loud or even think about.

Ford lathered his face, head and body all in one motion and then forced himself under the frigid spray to rinse, repeating the same thought over and over: *knock it off, knock it off, FOCUS!* The temperature was doing nothing to relieve his hangover or his racing mind, and he hoped he still had some Tylenol in the cabinet. When he stepped over the lip of the tub, he didn't bother with a towel. He made a beeline for the medicine chest in search of pain relief. "Praise be," he mumbled sarcastically as he grabbed the large bottle of extra strength capsules and shook out five. He downed them and stuck his head into the sink to grab a sip of water. As he shook his head back to help the pills down his throat, droplets of water flew all over the walls and mirror. Naked, he went in search of clean clothes.

"You ready?"

Hudson entered the apartment, using the key Ford had been forced to surrender. Baby brother worried too much and insisted he be able to check on Ford whenever he wanted. Rather than argue, he'd given the key to Hudson and this was the first time he'd ever used it. *This must be bad.*

"Almost." Ford sifted through a pile of clothes on the floor, not finding any clean underwear. "Fuck it," he growled as he found a not too stained pair of jeans and pulled them on. Switching to a different mound of laundry, he sniffed at a plain black t-shirt finding it not too offensive. He pulled it over his head and across his chest.

"Come on, man!"

"I'm going!" Ford snapped. He stood in the middle of the room, scanning for his boots.

"They're right there." Hudson glowered at him, pointing to the boots. "What time did you get home?"

"Don't ask." He couldn't have answered anyway.

Ford brushed past him to where he pointed and, sure enough, his boots were lying on their sides, one by the foot and the other next to the side of the bed. He snatched them up and pulled them on without bothering to consider socks. He grabbed a leather vest from a hook on the back of the door and pulled it on. Then he ran his fingers through his hair roughly, to get it out of his eyes.

"What are you waiting for?" he asked Hudson, grabbing his smokes from the resin table that served as his eating space. He walked out the door, knowing Hudson would be close on his heels.

Ford pretended his body didn't ache and his head didn't pound as he clomped down the stairs toward the parking lot where Hudson's truck waited. All at once he threw a prayer of thanks out to the universe when he recognized his motorcycle parked slightly askew in its assigned space. *Shit, I rode home. I was lucky.*

As he climbed into the truck, he lit a cigarette and closed the door. The window was already down and he hung his hand outside in a vain attempt to keep the smoke out of the vehicle.

"You need to quit," Hudson scolded as he hopped in and started the engine.

"Yeah, yeah. Why don't you fill me in, instead of lecturing?"

Hudson scowled and began to drive. "Tess called and said she found something interesting. That's all she would say, but she insisted we both come over as soon as possible."

Ford grimaced but said nothing. He kept silent as Hudson drove and he smoked on the ride from his place at Harper and Crocker in Mt. Clemens to Harrison Township. Tess was born and raised in the Shores, but she and Jack had opted to live in an apartment in the small city just north of their hometown. His brain was beginning to "unfuzz" and he almost smiled, remembering the word his brother had made up for their mother when she was coming off a hangover. He was a little more than ashamed for having tied one on so spectacularly that he didn't remember coming home. Ford tried to recall everything that had happened the night before, but it was all just a blur of beer, shots and multiple bars. At least he hadn't brought someone home this time.

"Wake up," Hudson snapped. He was standing outside the truck, staring back at him through the open door.

"Sorry."

Ford got out of the truck and they both half jogged to the door of Tess's apartment. Before they could knock, it opened wide and Lilly motioned them in.

"Come on in, fellas," she said quietly. "She was fine when I talked to her on the phone earlier, but by the time I got here, she was *pissed off*. Now she's just... I don't know, weird. Up and down. All over the place."

Ford followed Hudson inside to find Tess sitting on the couch with a bottle of beer in her hand. She raised a single hand in a nervous greeting. *This can't be good.*

"Hi guys," she mumbled, taking a sip of beer.

"What's going on?" Hudson's voice was harried.

"More twists and turns," she said with a cold smile that definitely didn't reach her eyes. She took another long pull from the bottle. "Check it out." She pointed to a lockbox sitting on the coffee table. Hudson walked around the table to sit beside Tess on the couch.

Ford stayed where he was just inside the door, wondering how many beers Tess might have downed before their arrival. Her eyes were on their way to a nice glassy finish, and it wouldn't be long before her words were too slurred to understand. He walked around to her corner of the couch and stood there. He reached down stealthily and snatched the bottle out of her hand before she knew what was happening.

"Hey!" she cried.

"I think you've had enough for a minute," he said softly. "At least until you've told us what's going on. Yeah?" He tipped the beer to his own lips and finished what was left, setting the empty down on the coffee table.

Tess glared at him and looked around. "Lilly, get me another one!"

Lilly started to move, but Ford shook his head and she stayed still. He turned back to Tess and squatted down. "Hudson's here now. Your sister's here. Tell us what happened."

Ford caught her eyes and held them with his own. He didn't blink and he didn't move, willing her to focus. After nearly a minute, he could almost see the fog lifting from her face. It was replaced by a look of confusion so profound; Ford felt a stab of guilt in his gut. He hated having to be the bad guy, but if Hudson was going to help her, then she needed to say it all.

Speaking slowly, Tess recounted Hudson's earlier visit and how she found the box now resting on the coffee table. He took that moment to lift the lid.

"Holy shit!" Hudson hollered.

Ford leaned around and peered into the box. "That's a lot of cash," he said, whistling softly.

"Tell me about it," Tess snapped. "I guess Jack hid it for a reason, but don't ask me."

"Did you count it?" Hudson reached over to thumb through one of the rubber banded packets.

"Yep. There's a hundred grand there."

"Show them the emails, sis." Lilly nodded at her and Tess sighed.

"Emails?" Hudson looked from one woman to the other.

Tess pointed to the computer on the desk in the corner. "Have at it."

Ford let his brother practically jump over the coffee table to get to the computer desk in the corner. "What about that laptop of Jack's? Do you still have it?"

Tess looked at him and frowned. "Yeah, but I think it might be broken."

"Let me take a look."

"Okay."

When she returned from the bedroom, it was obvious the unit had been damaged, but it didn't look too bad. While Hudson had his nose glued to the screen at the desk in the corner, Ford took the laptop to the dining room table to have a peek. When he tried to lift the lid, it stuck a little and then made cracking noises as the hinges rebelled. He struck the power button, but nothing happened. "How about the power cord?"

Tess grumbled. "Duh, sorry." She disappeared again into the bedroom and returned with the black cord. "Here you go." Instead of going back to the couch, she sat at the table. Ford could feel her eyes on him as he plugged the laptop in.

"Here goes nothing," he said, looking at her over the top of the machine. He hit the power button again, and with a little bit of a grinding, whirring sound, the machine booted right up. "Well, look at that. I'm not sure how long it will last though. Either the power supply is loose or the hard drive. I'm not much of an expert with laptops."

Tess nodded but looked anxious.

"What's the password?"

"Huh?" Tess blinked at him.

"The logon password," Ford repeated.

"Oh, sheesh, sorry. Tess always knows."

Ford grinned. "Say that again?"

"All one word, all lower case letters, tessalwaysknows."

He tapped out the letters one at a time, some a little harder than others, but eventually the desktop appeared and he was able to pull up the letter from Jack. Working as quickly as he could, Ford opened a web browser and logged into his yahoo mail account. He sent a copy of the letter to himself with a copy to Hudson. When that was finished, he clicked over to see about Jack's browser history. As the page began to load, the laptop died. Unless he took it apart piece by piece, there was no way he was going to revive the thing again.

"Well, that's that." He closed the lid and rested his hands on top of it.

"What's wrong?"

"It's dead. It'll need more skilled hands than mine to get it going again. But I got what I wanted before it turned up its toes. If you want, I can drop it off with a buddy of mine who fixes these things."

"Sure, whatever." She was picking at the cuticles on her fingers and biting her lower lip. Ford tried to look away, but the sight of her small, white teeth on her reddening lip was sexy as hell. *God I'm an ass.*

Forcing his head to turn, he called across to his brother, "How's it going over there?"

"I'll let you know," Hudson murmured. He'd figured out how to print the emails and the little printer on the computer desk was spitting out page after page. Lilly stood in front of it, scanning them as fast as she could get her hands on them.

Now there's a woman for my brother. Ford admired Lilly's concerned face and hand gripping the sheets of paper. She was more of a spitfire, and the type of girl Hudson would need to keep him in line.

Ford chuckled to himself and ushered the thought out of his head.

Tess got up and went to the kitchen. She came back with two bottles and offered him one. Knowing a little more hair of the dog would improve his headache, he gladly accepted. They remained at the table in silence, nursing their beers. Ford wished he could be anywhere else on the planet, yet knew a stack of dynamite couldn't have blown him out of there if Tess was in distress.

After another fifteen minutes, Hudson and Lilly joined them with the stack of pages from the printer. Ford couldn't read the expression on his brother's face, but Lilly looked furious, like she wanted to punch someone in the face.

"So what's in them?" Tess asked, looking from her sister to her lawyer. Ford thought she looked like she didn't *really* want to know, but had no choice but to find out. She had already finished her beer and was almost slurring her words.

"It got pretty nasty toward the end," Hudson admitted. "The long and short of it is this: Jack was angry and wanted control of his own money and destiny. His father tried to talk him out of taking control. He didn't come right out and say he'd kill him or anything, but Roger made it pretty clear that he thought Jack was making a big mistake and that he would regret it."

"Am I mentioned?"

Hudson looked at Lilly and their faces gave away the answer. Ford reached for the pages to thumb through them on his own.

"What do they say?"

Ford sighed and passed them over to Tess.

"I'm a gold digger?" She threw the page to the side. "I'm going to ruin his life?" Ford watched another page hit the pile. "Oh and I'm the worst thing that ever happened to him? What the *fuck*?"

Tess bounded out of the chair and grabbed the sheets of paper. She crumbled and ripped and tore them up, all the while blasting her in-laws with the filthiest language Ford had ever heard come out of a woman so young.

"Tess! Don't!" Lilly shouted. "Hudson's going to need those."

"I can reprint them," Hudson said quietly.

Ford felt the situation was spinning wildly out of control and stood up. He walked around the table and took Tess gently by the arm. "Come on. Let's go outside for some fresh air. I need a smoke."

As he propelled her toward the French doors, he looked back at Hudson and Lilly. "I got this."

Chapter 24

Tess allowed Ford to take her outside but she still wanted to scream. She couldn't believe the hateful, evil things Roger Kingston had written about her. It had started innocently enough with the father counseling the son on how young he was to be getting married. It didn't matter that they had known each other almost all their lives. They were still young enough that they could wait a while. Wait until Jack had a hold on what his net worth meant. Thank God Jack had defended her, otherwise Tess would have wanted to go dig him up just to kill him again.

"That's some pretty heavy shit," Ford said as he lit a cigarette. They stood at the end of the brick patio, staring out inTO the woodsy fields behind the apartment.

"Ya think?" she snapped. "I can't believe Roger wrote those things about me. I never knew about any of it, yet he called me a gold digger. *A fuckin' gold digger!*" Tess stamped her foot at the sheer idiocy of the thought. "I loved Jack. We ate ramen noodles and macaroni and cheese for four years to get through college. We worked part time jobs in the crappiest places. We paid for our own cell phones and didn't ask our parents for squat, but *I'm* a gold digger."

Ford stayed quiet while she ranted and raved. Feeling stung, she continued railing on about all the crazy things she'd seen in Jack's home over the years. "And we can't forget David. He got into a few scrapes himself, which his father took care of for him. I wonder if the money for the restitution came from Jack's inheritance. Oh *man*, I wish I could prove that. I'd sue his ass as quick as hell!"

Tess felt like she could run a hundred miles on the rage-filled adrenaline high she was on. What she really wanted to do was take a ride over to Roger Kingston's house and kick him in the balls. Since she couldn't do that, she continued to curse and bitch about the people who were supposed to have been her in-laws and closest allies, next to her own family. Her alcohol buzz was completely gone.

After a while, she turned to Ford and frowned. "You must think I'm crazy."

Ford only shook his head no as he finished his cigarette and then field stripped it. He put the dead butt into his jeans pocket. "Not at all."

"Well, I *feel* crazy." Tess grabbed her loose hair and pulled it behind her as if to put it into a ponytail. She would have, but she didn't have a hair tie handy. Growling, she let it go and then rubbed her scalp vigorously all over until the blond waves were poofed out all over in odd directions. "Everyone said it would all get easier. That in time, things would go back to normal. Is this shit normal?"

Ford chuckled and shook his head again. "Maybe the new normal."

Tess twisted a piece of hair between her fingers and sighed. She flopped down into one of the chairs at the patio table. "I just want to run away. I could take all that cash in there and disappear."

"Where would you go?" Ford took the seat next to her and stretched his long legs out in front of him and crossed his arms against his chest. Tess admired the toughness of his cool biker pose and even

150

snuck a peek at his face. His eyes were focused in his lap and she was glad.

"What?" she stammered. "Oh, I don't know." Studying his handsome features was distracting her and she tilted her eyes up to gaze at the clear, starry sky. "Does it matter? Anywhere would be better than here, right now."

"What about your family? They'd miss you."

"Don't ruin my fantasy," she grumbled, hating how he was being logical and realistic. Logic and reality were things to avoid.

"Sorry." Ford's face was blank, but Tess could hear the smile in his voice.

"I'm serious. I'm throwing a tantrum here and you aren't supposed to talk me down."

He shrugged and lit a fresh cigarette. "Aren't you a little old to be throwing tantrums?"

"Oh bite me!"

Tess tried to glare at him, but his honesty made her laugh instead. "You're right. I am too old to be acting like a child. I guess twenty-five is the threshold for fits, eh?" She watched him smoke for a minute, transfixed by the movement of his strong hand lifting the cigarette to and from his lips. The light breeze caused his hair to ruffle the slightest bit, and he looked young in the backlight shining from inside the house. "How old are you, Ford?"

As he leaned back to crush the cigarette into a small patch of dirt at the edge of the patio, Ford tilted his head to look her in the eye. "I'm thirty-five."

"Huh." Tess nodded, taking it in. *Not too old*, she thought and then frowned. *Too old for what?* She closed her eyes and let the night air cool her skin as her heart and brain began to settle down. She was actually glad it was Ford who had joined her outside instead of Hudson or Lilly. Her lawyer would have killed her with logic and her sister would have jumped on the rage bandwagon and they would have both been wound up enough to do something truly stupid.

The slight buzz she had from earlier was mostly gone. Standing up, she walked toward the door, fully expecting Ford to follow and he didn't let her down.

"I need another beer," she said as she opened the door.

Ford followed her inside and she saw that Hudson and Lilly were back at the computer, reprinting all of the pages she had destroyed. She went to the kitchen and retrieved a beer for herself. "Anyone else want one?" When no one responded, she shut the door to the fridge and then made her way to the couch. Ford sat down in the easy chair kitty corner from her.

Finally, Hudson and Lilly finished what they were doing and joined them. "Well, it doesn't necessarily say 'I'm going to kill you', but these certainly go a long way to pointing the finger at Roger Kingston," Hudson said as he shoved the pages into his ever present briefcase. "But that's only if the tox report comes back with something suspicious."

"I know I'm pretty damn convinced the Kingstons killed their own son just to keep his money. What a bunch of whack jobs." Lilly's words were dripping with venom.

"You can think anything you want, Lilly," Hudson's tone was stern, "but don't go saying that to just anyone. People are innocent until proven guilty and it's going to take a lot more evidence before we can make accusations like that."

Lilly gave him a peevish look, but said nothing more as she plopped down beside her little sister. Tess's eyebrows lowered as she looked at her sister and her lawyer. There seemed to be some pretty strong feelings there, whenever they went at one another. She felt really lucky to have someone like Lilly watching her back. It wasn't every day that siblings got along as well as they did. Tess knew she could count on her older sister for just about anything, and the coming mess would prove that.

The room was silent as Tess nursed her beer and the others gave her wary looks. Now that the alcohol was dampening her rage, she felt exhausted. The adrenaline dump was taking its toll. As she felt herself going deeper and deeper into her own mind, a single idea popped into her head, making her sit up straight, nearly spilling the beverage in her hand.

"Hudson?" Her voice was shaky. "Am *I* in any danger?"

Before he could respond, Lilly's eyes grew wide. "If they killed Jack, are they going to come after Tess? We should call the police!"

"Don't be ridiculous—" Hudson held up his hands and took a step toward Lilly, who had jumped off the couch.

"Don't tell me what to do!" she shouted back.

"Hey guys," Tess tried to interrupt but found it was way more interesting to watch someone else bring on the crazy.

"You need to get a hold of yourself," Hudson growled, glaring at Lilly.

"And you need to grow some balls!" Lilly spat.

"Hold on, hold on!" Ford threw up his hands. "Just calm down you two. We still don't know for sure if Jack was even murdered! And because he left everything to Tess, it would revert to your family if anything happened to her. It makes no sense to come after her."

"But they're going to fight the will. If they win, then they get everything. They'll want me out of the picture." Tess's hands began to tremble and she put the bottle on the coffee table where it clinked audibly until it settled.

"*If* they win, and I'm sure they won't, what difference would it make to kill you then?" Hudson was thinking logically, even if he seemed riled up because of Lilly's outburst. But Tess knew only rage would drive Roger Kingston to try to murder her. It would be a vengeful act, because of the trouble she had caused him, and she told Hudson that.

"She's right." Lilly's eyes were still shooting daggers at Hudson, but her voice was calmer. She sat back down and threw a protective arm around the younger girl's shoulders and Tess leaned into her. "If they won the lawsuit and got to keep the money, he'd want to kill her as soon as look at her. We *need* to call the police."

Hudson turned to look at Ford who was picking at the sole of his boot. "Let's say for the sake of argument that Jack was killed. The Kingstons certainly look the guiltiest right now, but they don't know you've found the emails or the cash. I think that's what keeps you safe right now." Tess glanced at his serene face and appreciated his calm demeanor.

"What's the update on the report, brother?" Hudson asked. "Did you get a hold of your friend?"

"No. I went by there, but she wasn't in and she's now ignoring my calls and texts."

Tess straightened herself up and reached for the beer bottle again. Draining it, she sighed and rubbed the cool glass against her forehead. "Would it do any good for me to call and ask about it? Maybe they'd respond better to the widow?"

"You can try, but I don't know." Hudson shrugged and leaned back in the other easy chair next to Ford's.

"I don't care what you all think," Lilly huffed. "Tess should go to the police. Show them the emails she found, the letter Jack wrote, tell them everything."

Tess smiled and hugged her sister, basking in the protective vibes coming from her. "What about the money? We haven't even talked about the box of cash."

"I'd take it to the bank." Lilly took the empty bottle from Tess and went to the kitchen with it. When she returned, she had two more.

"No, don't do that," Ford said quietly. "Put it right back where you found it until we know more."

"I agree." Hudson reached over to the box and closed the lid. "Where did you find it?"

"In the ceiling above the closet." Tess rocked her head in the direction of the spare bedroom.

"This thing fire safe?" Hudson asked Ford and he nodded his head. "I'd put it back where you found it. It's cash, so unless you do something stupid like tell the Kingstons you have it, then technically it doesn't exist. You can spend it, but definitely wait for a while and don't use it for any big ticket items. Changing how you spend money will draw attention."

"Can't she just mix it in with the insurance money?" Lilly asked.

"No. That check was for a million even. Not a million and a hundred grand." Hudson sighed. "If anyone ever asks you any questions about a box of money, you don't know anything about it. Okay?"

"Okay."

"And we never had this conversation. Got it?"

"Got it."

"Good. Put it back where you found it, for the time being."

"I'm not going back up there." Tess shivered at the thought of critters moving around.

Hudson and Ford gave her confused looks and Lilly guffawed. "Sis is afraid of spiders. And mice. I'm shocked you even went back for the key."

Tess grinned sheepishly. "I was too curious not to."

"Show me." Ford stood up and waited for Tess to lead him to the secret hiding place. He picked up the box and then followed her into the bedroom. When she pointed out the spot, he hopped up on the cabinet that she hadn't bothered to move in her haste to sate her curiosity. Tess watched as he lightly punched at the loose square of drywall until it fell and he caught it in the palm of his hand. He poked the box back up and then replaced the square more expertly than she had been able to. She didn't scoot out of the way fast enough as he jumped down and he almost knocked her over. Ford's hands snaked out to grasp her by the arms before she could stumble backwards. His strong fingers were firm, but didn't hurt her.

"Hey, careful there," he said when she was firmly back on her feet.

"Sorry." The sound of his low voice made her shiver and she couldn't bring herself to look him in the eye until the feeling backed off.

"Where's the key to the box?" Ford was still only inches from her as he asked his question and Tess stepped backward, pushing her hand into her pocket.

"Right here." She pulled it out and showed it to him.

"Hide it somewhere safe and don't tell anyone but Hudson or Lilly."

"What about you?" Tess's voice was soft and she took a chance to peek into his face. At some point, he had taken a step toward her for the one she took back and the gap between them was only a few inches again. All of a sudden, the room seemed really warm.

"Don't tell me. I'd probably forget." He gave her the same smirky, half smile she was getting used to and she returned it. Moving backward, Ford stretched his arm out and pointed to the door, so she could go out first, back to the living room.

"Obviously he gave Jack all the financial paperwork, otherwise Jack wouldn't have contacted me."

Tess caught Hudson's comment as she and Ford got to the edge of the living room. She put her arm out to stop Ford from entering and she held a finger to her lips.

"That doesn't mean he didn't take Jack out," Lilly argued.

"I'm not going to get into this with you. We can't assume facts not in evidence."

"Oh please." Lilly sniffed and rolled her eyes. "You sound like Sam Waterston."

Hudson chuckled. "Well, maybe I do, but it's true. We can't make any assumptions until we find out what really happened to Jack."

"Can't you get his body exhumed?"

"No!" Hudson gave her a disgusted look. "Well, yes, we could. But that's a whole other mess to contend with. I'd rather not even think about it unless we absolutely have to."

"You better make sure nothing happens to my sister, Hudson Marks," Lilly hissed. "I will hold you personally responsible."

Tess grinned at the sparring lawyer and sibling and then looked at Ford. He was clearly as amused as she was. "Now, now, sis. Settle down," she said. Lilly looked up, her face pinking with guilt at being caught.

"I'm just sayin'."

"Yeah, I hear you. And so did my lawyer. And my lawyer's investigator."

"I think I'll take a beer now." Hudson went to the kitchen and helped himself, but was a gentleman and brought a round back for everyone.

The foursome sat in silence with their own thoughts as they sipped their beers. While she was still angry and confused about everything going on, Tess felt better knowing she was surrounded by people who either loved her or cared enough about her case that they would do whatever they could to help and protect her. She didn't know what she was going to do or what was in store, but she knew she would get through it eventually. She felt the familiar twinge of heartache at the thought of Jack in pain during his last moments and was so grateful he'd never suspected she was having doubts. The emails proved it. While there was a lot of snarky stuff from her father-in-law, Jack's support for her had never wavered. He had been constant in his belief that she loved him and wanted to get married. Tess wasn't sure she could have lived with herself if she thought Jack knew about her doubts. Her own guilt was difficult enough to handle.

"Well, as much as I'd like to sit and get silly with you girls, I think we should get going." Hudson stood up and pulled his keys from his pocket. Ford stood up, too, and shoved his hands into his pockets.

"Okay," Tess replied, unsure if she was ready to let them both go. She felt safe with all of them there.

"You sure you'll be all right?"

Tess was surprised that Ford was the one to ask her. He always managed to keep his face even, but his eyes gave him away every time. She could see the concern for her there. *Yep, he got the eyes for sure.*

"I mean, we could stay, if you want us to," Hudson said, sounding exactly like it was the last thing he wanted to do. Then he looked at Lilly and his expression softened.

"No, I'll be okay." Tess let him off the hook with a wave of her hand.

Ford ignored her words and began to move around the apartment, checking all the locks on the windows. He didn't wait for her permission to go into the bedrooms and do the same. Last, he checked the window in the kitchen above the sink and then closed and locked the French doors. "Turn on the AC if you get hot," he told her when he was back in the living room, standing over her.

Tess wanted to say thank you, but her voice didn't seem to want to come out of her mouth so she just smiled and nodded. She started to get up, but Lilly pushed her back down on to the couch. Her big sister got up instead and walked them to the door.

"I'm going to stay with her tonight."

"Good." Ford gave her a nod, then glanced back at Tess. She got that same warm feeling throughout her limbs and hid the tremor moving across her shoulders by giving him a wave. He smirked and dipped his chin at her before crossing the threshold into the night.

Hudson smiled down at Lilly, noticing flecks of gold in her green eyes. "If you need anything, just call."

Lilly lowered her chin and a soft smile teased the corners of her mouth. "Don't worry. I've got this."

"Good."

Lilly closed the door behind them, locked it and hooked the chain. "I say we order pizza."

"Sounds like a plan."

* * * * *

"That Ford is pretty hot," Lilly whispered.

Hours and many beers later, she and Tess lay on the couch, their heads in the middle and their legs hanging over separate ends. Each had a cat on her stomach to pet and scratch. A half-finished pizza from Hungry Howie's lay in the open box on the coffee table along with several empty beer bottles.

"You think so?" Tess flinched and was glad Lilly couldn't see.

"Yeah. But Hudson's hotter."

Tess laughed out loud, disturbing Spencer enough to make him leap off and scamper to the cat tree. "Maybe you should see if he's on Tinder."

Lilly snorted. "No way. Besides, I think he's got a thing for you."

"What?" Tess sat up and stared at her sister. "No he doesn't. He's my lawyer!"

"That doesn't mean anything. I see the way he looks at you."

"Well, I don't." Tess leaned back down until her head thunked against Lilly's. "Besides, even if he did, he's not my type. Not to mention, I'm a widow."

"Pffft! You don't have a type." Lilly flung a hand back and whopped Tess on the forehead. "You can't fool me. I know you loved Jack, but I can see the way you look at Ford and *not* Hudson. 'Sides, I've known you all your life, little sis."

Tess froze. She knew she needed to protest vehemently, but the words stuck in her throat. Finally, she found her voice. "Okay, so Ford's damn fine to look at, but I do *not* give him any looks." Tess picked at the cuticles on her left hand, staring at her wedding rings, conjuring Jack's face in her mind. His smile, his laugh, the way his eyes brightened when he looked at her. All of those things always brought joy and happiness to her when he was alive, and agonizing torment since his death. But now, she just felt sad. Regular sad. Man-this-sucks, kind of sad. It was as if all the drama surrounding her had caused her heart to go numb to either loving Jack or mourning him.

"How bad do you miss him?" Lilly whispered.

Tess shrugged. "Depends. When I feel guilty. Or when I don't feel guilty. Basically all the time." She groaned realizing the words coming out of her mouth weren't matching the sentences she was forming in her head. Her brain was quoting the script she wrote for everyone else, but it got lost in translation by the time it came out of her mouth.

Lilly sat up and turned to stare at her. "What do you mean guilty? What on earth do you have to feel guilty about?"

Cat's outta the bag now. "Oh nothing, never mind me, I'm drunk."

But Lilly wouldn't leave it alone. She literally poked Tess in the head and shoulders and cheeks until she was forced to sit up as well.

"Out with it. Now's the best time to come clean, when we're both drunk and won't remember it in the morning. You can vent and I can give comfort. We'll both feel better."

Tess tried to giggle, thinking it was the correct response, but she couldn't muster the energy. She was so tired. The grief and the guilt and the anxiety were weighing her down. It felt like someone had put a fat suit on her body and tightened a vice around her brain.

"Okay," she sighed. "Here goes." Breathing deep, she confessed her deepest worry in one long breath. "Before the wedding, I thought about calling it off."

Lilly gave her a long blink. Then another. Then a third before she burst out laughing. "Is that all?"

Tess glared at her and pursed her lips. "What do you mean, is that all? I had doubts, L, real doubts. I wanted to walk away from the wedding."

"Pffft!" Spittle flew of Lilly's lips. "Sorry, my lips are numb." She apologized as she wiped her mouth on the hem of her t-shirt. "Baby sis, everyone goes through that. You had cold feet."

"I'm not so sure," Tess whispered. She wrapped her arms around herself and scrunched up in a ball. "It started right after we got engaged. It's not that I wanted to go out with anyone else, but I started to wonder why we needed to get married at all."

Lilly nodded, wobbling a little while she did. "Kinda like, if it ain't broke, don't fix it?"

"Yeah!" Tess shouted, then clapped a hand over her mouth. "Sorry, that was loud. But yeah, I mean, why change what was working? I wanted to talk to Jack, but I felt so bad about it. It woulda broken his heart."

"Nah, he woulda understood." Lilly patted her leg. "That was Jack. He was so fuckin' perfect."

"Don't I know it?" Tess snorted. "He was *too* perfect. I couldn't even get mad at him. We never even fought. Do you know any couple that doesn't ever argue?"

"Hell no!" Lilly's mouth dropped open in disbelief. "You guys had fights, you told me about 'em all the time."

"Well we didn't. Never once. Every time I bitched to you, it was made up!" Tess figured it didn't matter anymore. If she was going to come clean, she might as well use an extra bucket of Clorox and wipe everything away.

"What the hell do you mean?" Lilly blinked hard.

"I lied. You always made me feel so bad when you'd snark about how perfect we were. So I made up stories about fights that never happened."

Lilly just stared at her, and Tess wondered if she had suddenly stopped speaking English or something.

"Any time I wanted anything, Jack gave it to me. Any time I wanted to do something, Jack went along with it. I even tried to start fights with him, and he would just laugh and laugh. 'It's not important, T. I'm not gonna fight with you. You're what's important to me.' Can you believe that shit?"

Lilly held her stomach as she laughed and Tess railed on about how absolutely perfect Jack had been. Not one single flaw. The epitome of everything good and kind and prince charming like.

Soon, though, she was sobbing as she ranted. Lilly held her and listened, and Tess kept talking until the flow of words trickled to a stop. Snuffling and dabbing at her nose with a greasy napkin, Tess pulled away. "Oh Lilly. I'm the most horrible person in the whole world."

"No you aren't!" Lilly protested. "You're young! You were scared and confused just like most of us. It was all natural. You only feel guilty now because Jack died. Once the wedding was over and you guys got back to everyday life you woulda known you did the right thing."

"But," Tess whispered, "as much as I miss him, I feel a little bit relieved." The conversation and the crying had sobered her up considerably. There was no turning back, though. Now that she had her sister's attention and compassion, Tess couldn't hold anything in.

"How so?" Lilly's eyes were clearer and she wasn't slurring as badly as before.

"Well, Jack died. Now I don't have to ever find out if I actually did make a mistake." Tears welled up in Tess's eyes with the admission. "Now *that* makes me an *awful* person. *I know it does!*"

Lilly grabbed her hands and held them tightly. "No, Tess, it doesn't. Everything in this life happens for a reason, you know I believe that. Whatever lessons there are to be learned from this experience, forgiving yourself is probably going to be the hardest one."

Tess turned away to reach for a cold slice of pizza. She considered it, turning it this way and that, before tossing it back into the box. She grabbed the nearest beer bottle next and shook it a little. To her disappointment, it was empty. "I need to get redrunk."

Lilly snickered. "No you don't. You need to get some sleep now." She stood up from the couch, and pulled Tess up beside her. "Let's go to bed. We can talk more in the morning."

"I thought we weren't going to remember any of this." Tess yawned as they hobbled off to bed, their arms around one another's shoulders.

"Now that I know what's been eating at you," Lilly said softly, "I'm not going to give up until you work through it. That's what sisters are for, you dolt."

Tess smiled and nodded, knowing it was true.

Chapter 25

Tess opened her eyes and groaned. Warm sunshine filled the bedroom, sending daggers of pain into her head. "L?" she croaked, but there was no answer. Flopping over, she saw a note on the bedside table. "Had to work, I'll text you later."

Wanting nothing more than to staple the covers to the sides of the bed so she couldn't get out, and no one else could get in, Tess grunted. Even though she had a cat curled up against either side of her and her head was fuzzy with a hangover, Tess didn't think she could fall back to sleep now that she was awake. She had no idea what time it was, but it had to be late judging by the amount of light in the room. Sucking it up, she yanked herself into a sitting position and rubbed her eyes until they stayed open with less effort. "God, I shouldn't drink like that," she muttered. Timothy meowed at her, but it ended up turning into a wide, feline yawn.

"Oh, how would you know?" she asked, while scratching his head.

Spencer lifted his chin about a millimeter from his paws and gave her a second's notice before closing his eyes again. "Yeah, I can tell you're real sympathetic, Spence."

Giving each feline another pet, she crawled out of bed and shuffled off to the bathroom. One followed her, but the other stayed in the warm bed to snooze. When she was finished, Tess washed her hands and then rinsed the bowl clean of any soap residue. Then she left the cold water tap running in a fast drip so that the cats could have their morning drink. It had driven Jack crazy when she did that, but Tess always figured it was one of the perks of being a spoiled housecat.

Staring into the mirror, she frowned. The worry lines in her forehead looked like they were drawn on with a pencil and the bags under her eyes might as well have been a flashing neon sign saying she was hungover. "No more drinking for me for a while. So not worth it."

At that point, both cats were hanging out on the countertop, leaning into the sink to lap at the drops of water splatting down toward the drain. She stroked their backs, one in each hand, and smiled. If it wasn't for Timmy and Spencer, she knew her life would be a lot lonelier than it was without Jack. At least they kept her company and "talked" with her so she didn't feel like her home was empty. She took a few aspirin from the medicine cabinet and swallowed them with a sip of water cupped in her hands, praying they'd work their magic fast.

Tess wandered out to the kitchen to make coffee and then stopped to stare out the French doors at the beautiful day. The weather app on her phone said it was already past noon and that the day would be sunny and hot. It was the kind of day she and Jack would have spent outside riding bikes or hiking, then throwing dinner on the grill, saving their client work for later. Thinking about that, it made her smile.

When the machine finished brewing, she decided to take her coffee outside onto the small stone patio. The weather was too nice to stay inside and she really wanted to spend some time thinking, hoping it would help to get the fuzziness out of her brain. Knowing the cats would love a foray in the grass, she trapped each one and put on their harnesses so they could join her. Tess grabbed her notebook and coffee and headed outside, leaving the door open so the cats could come along when they wanted to.

Sitting at the table, Tess opened to a clean page but she couldn't really find the words she wanted to write. Instead, memories of Jack flitted in her mind. The day he gave her the promise ring. Their senior class trip to Washington, D.C. The first time he ever beat up the little boy who lived down the street for calling her a name and pushing her down. The day he proposed. They were all good memories, happy ones that made her heart feel light instead of like a stone pressing on the inside of her chest.

Tess wondered why some days she would feel okay and on others, she wanted to go and jump out a window. What was it about her that kept her from just being normal every day? Was this how grief worked for everyone? Maybe she would take some of the insurance money and get herself a therapist. She knew there wasn't any shame in needing someone objective to talk to. With all the crazy shit going on, it might make more sense than unloading on Lilly and her parents all the time. All they wanted to do was reassure her that she was a good person and loved. That was fine, but who would tell her the truth when she was being an idiot? That had been Jack's job. He'd been her very best friend and sounding board. No decision had ever been made without consulting him, no path taken without knowing how he felt first. Tess hadn't always followed his advice or did what he thought she should do, but her bond with him had been complete.

"I miss him, Timmy," she whispered, as the tabby forced his way into her lap. Stroking his soft fur, she sighed. "I know none of this would be happening if he were here, but still. He was always the voice of reason."

The cat meowed as if to answer her, but Tess didn't feel all that comforted. "Yeah, I know. What do you think he'd say if he was standing right here, Tim? Hmm?"

The only sound Tess could hear was the cat's voracious purring.

Jealousy getting the better of him, Spencer stood with his two front paws on her leg, sniffing at Timothy's butt. Without any warning, he nipped at the flanks in his face and Timothy growled. In order to avoid a full out cat fight on her lap, Tess tossed Timothy to the ground and he ran off, Spencer hot on his heels.

Closing her eyes, she let the sun warm her face. Images of the box full of money came to her mind, which then brought on thoughts of the night before. She said a silent prayer that the toxicology report would come back showing no signs of foul play. Tess didn't know what she would do if it turned out Jack was killed. It might just break her spirit for good. Knowing that if she had followed her gut and postponed the wedding Jack might still be alive might be more than she could handle.

Don't be stupid. Tess opened her eyes and looked around. Jack's voice had been so loud in her head, it was as if he was sitting at the table speaking to her. Wrinkling her eyebrows, she concentrated hard, listening for anything else Jack might have to say. The voice didn't sound like it was real, but she heard it in her heart. He would think she was a complete dumbass for sitting around and feeling sorry for herself. He'd also think she was a wuss if she let something like his murder break her. He'd want her to pick herself up, dust off her butt, and get going on figuring out who did it and why. There was no way he would want his death to be in vain. And the only person who would be able to make sure that didn't happen was Tess. She was responsible for making sure that if justice needed to be served for him, it would happen.

"It's time to grow up, Tess."

She said the words out loud to no one, but it might as well have been Jack sitting next to her saying it.

"It's all about positive self-talk, right?" She looked around to make sure there weren't any neighbors around on their patios to overhear her. "I'm smart. I'm capable. I'm *going* to be okay."

Tess stood up and started pacing back and forth. "I did *not* do anything wrong. It's okay to have doubts before you get married. Lilly was right. It was just cold feet." As she walked the short length of the patio back and forth, the cats appeared at the sound of her voice to sit and observe, like an audience to her motivational speech.

"It's been more than six months now and it's okay to feel better. It's okay to want to heal. Whether or not Jack is watching is beside the point. I'm here and alive and I need to get on with my life. No matter how much I wish he were here, I can't bring him back."

Tess slammed her fist into her palm. "I owe it to Jack to go on and live a good life. And I owe it to him to figure out what the hell happened. I can't just sit back and wait for shit."

The more she talked, the better she felt. Her natural optimism and effervescence seem to be returning and Tess could feel the hope building inside her chest, filling her heart. "I have money now. I can do some good things with it. I'm an adult and I will stand on my own two feet. It will be an honor to Jack and his memory to build something he would be proud of."

The stream of consciousness she blurted out was all over the map and Tess didn't care. She wanted to keep saying positive things to build her self-confidence, but she also wanted to be honest with herself. "I'm not always going to feel this good. I'm going to have good days and bad days and that's okay!" She shouted this last bit, causing the cats to cock their heads. "I might still have days when I don't want to get out of bed or cry my eyes out, but those will just be moments in time. They won't define the rest of my life. I won't let them."

Tess tilted her head to the sky and closed her eyes, letting the hot sun soak into her skin. She threw hear arms wide and laughed out loud. "I know there are some more hard times coming, Jack, but I promise not to let them break me. I promise I will do everything I can to do the right thing."

Chapter 26

"You want me to what?"

Hudson held the phone away from his ear. Tess's voice nearly punctured his eardrum. "We want you to reach out to Emily Kingston. Feel her out. See if she's willing to come over to our side against David and Roger."

The silence at the other end of the line was disconcerting to him. He knew that Tess would probably balk at the idea, but Hudson knew he had to ask her to try.

"I don't know. You know how our last conversation ended."

"Yeah, but it's been a few days. We weren't able to find anything in Jack's background and until the toxicology report comes back, we just can't figure out what direction to take. Maybe if you talk to her, we could get a read on what Roger and David are, or aren't, doing."

Tess sighed and Hudson held his breath.

"Okay, how do you want me to do it? Do I call, or go over there?"

"I suppose it's up to you. Whatever you think you can handle best."

"Let me think about it and I'll get back to you."

"Okay, sure."

Tess ended the call without saying goodbye but Hudson couldn't tell if she was upset-angry or upset-scared. He decided not to bug her and wait patiently for her to get back to him. He hollered for Ford, who was in the other room.

"Yeah?" His big brother entered carrying some pages he was still reading.

"She said she'll do it, but will call back once she figures out how."

"I'm not sure it's a good idea," Ford admitted.

Hudson frowned. "It was your idea in the first place. Why the sudden change of heart?"

Ford shook his head. "I don't know. Just a gut feeling. I think keeping her away from that bunch is probably the best thing for her, don't you?"

"Maybe, but we don't have anything else to go on at this point. We have to do something."

Ford rubbed his chin and nodded grudgingly. "I guess."

"I know I asked you an hour ago, but any word from the ME's office?"

Sighing, Ford gave him a nasty look. "Do you think I'm going to keep it to myself?"

"Well don't bite my head off."

"Then stop asking me."

"Fine."

Hudson turned back to his computer screen, ignoring Ford as he left the room. *Dick.*

* * * * *

Jackass. Ford slammed his butt back into the chair at the desk out front. His brother was getting on his last nerve and he felt like taking him outside and beating the crap out of him. But he wouldn't. He knew exactly why Hudson was acting the way he was. He got that way whenever he was nervous or unsure of how to go forward with a case. Ford did his best to ignore the annoying pattern of behavior.

Telling Hudson about his changing feelings was not the wisest thing. The last thing he needed was his brother to figure out that Ford was thinking too much about Tess.

Chapter 27

In spite of her pep talk to herself, Tess sat stiffly at the table, picking her napkin into bits. Emily Kingston had agreed to meet her for lunch at New York Deli and she was now officially three minutes late. That couldn't be a good sign because Emily was never late.

Tess took a sip of her Coke and let the sugary bubbles sit on her tongue for a second before swallowing. She tried not to stare at the door. *A watched pot never boils.* The expression her mother always used frustrated her because it only made her want to watch the entrance more. As a distraction, she pulled out her phone to check for text messages or missed calls. There were none.

Unable to stop the impulse, Tess looked back to the entrance. Instead of seeing her mother-in-law coming in, she saw the last person in the world she expected. Ford Marks stood next to the sign asking patrons to wait to be seated. He was staring right at her. She frowned and raised her shoulders in question. *What are you doing here?* she mouthed.

Ignoring the sign, Ford strode up to her table and gave her his trademark smirk. "Hey. I needed something to eat and figured this was as good a place as any."

"I hope you're getting a carry out," Tess muttered. "I'm nervous enough as it is without having you lurk about."

Ford chuckled. "You'll do fine. Just pretend like I'm not here." He turned around and went back to wait for a hostess to seat him. Tess rolled her eyes and sighed. *Great, now I'm going to be distracted.*

"Who was that?"

Emily was pulling her chair out and sitting down, throwing a suspicious look over her shoulder at Ford.

"Oh, no one," Tess stammered. "I'm glad you could make it."

"I'm sorry I'm late."

"That's okay." She dropped her phone to the table with a thunk and tried to smile. "I'm just glad you came."

"I'll admit, I was a little surprised by your call." Emily's tone was frosty as she spread her napkin onto her lap and reached for the menu. She glanced again across the restaurant where Ford had been seated at a booth.

Tess struggled to think of the right words to ease the awkward moment and to get Emily's attention off of Ford Marks. *You got this. You can do it.* "Well, I wanted to apologize for the way I spoke to you the other day. You've been like a second mom to me and I was ashamed of myself."

Emily remained rigid in her chair for a few seconds and then her shoulders slumped as she dropped her menu. Reaching across the table, she grasped Tess's hand. "I'm sorry too. I was very rude as well."

Tess squeezed back and held on until she felt Emily's grip loosen. "Thanks."

The waitress arrived and they ordered some food Tess wasn't sure she would be able to eat. Between trying to sweet talk Emily and knowing Ford was across the room staring at her, Tess worried that anything she ate would come right back up.

Focusing back to the woman in front of her, she took a deep breath. "I wanted to let you know that we can't let things get ugly."

"Of course not, dear. It's the last thing Roger and I want."

"It's the last thing Jack would want." Tess worried that bringing him up so soon in the conversation might backfire, but she shouldn't have been concerned. Emily smiled sadly at the mention of her son.

"You're right. Jack would be very unhappy about how things have gone."

Tess picked at the cuticle on her thumb and then chewed on the nail a little before speaking again. "Maybe we should all get together and have a meeting so that we can clear the air. Figure out how best to settle the probate stuff so that everyone is happy. Haven't we lost enough?"

Emily's eyes misted over and she dabbed at them with her napkin. "I agree. I don't know what's been going on with Roger and David because they never talk to me anymore. But I'm sure I can convince them to come together to find a reasonable solution."

Tess sighed with relief. "Good. How have you been?"

Emily shrugged. "Oh, you know. Good days and bad, though the good ones seem few and far between. You're looking well, though."

Tess cringed and chewed on her bottom lip. "Well, I do the best I can. The stress since we found out about the will hasn't helped, that's for sure. Why don't David and Roger talk to you anymore?"

"I suppose they don't want to hurt me." Emily straightened the pile of menus that rested between the mustard and ketchup bottles until they were exactly even. "You know men, they handle their grief in different ways."

"Yeah." Tess agreed with her because she didn't really know how men handled grief at all. This was the first major loss in her life and she had no example to learn from. She certainly wasn't looking forward to a day when she suffered another one as big as losing Jack.

As Emily fiddled next with the sugar packets, Tess stole a glance at Ford. He was leaning back in the booth, looking perfectly relaxed as he sipped coffee. He caught her staring and gave her an exaggerated wink. She wanted to flip him off, but knew that gesture would not go unnoticed her, so she stifled the urge.

"So, what will you do with all that insurance money you're getting?"

Tess's eyes went wide, but she recovered before Emily noticed. At least she hoped so. It seemed like a pretty nosy question, but then again, she was suspicious of every word her mother-in-law spoke. It was bound to happen, considering how much animosity there had been already. She tried to look past that and think of how the question might have been meant under different circumstances. "I'm not really sure yet. I'll probably invest most of it. Give some away. Maybe I'll go back to school, do something else. I quit my job."

"You did? Well, it must be nice to feel that secure."

Tess winced. *What's that supposed to mean?* "It isn't really about security. I just didn't have the heart to keep working for Dr. Guildford when I was so messed up. I'll get another job. I don't think I'm the kind of person to just sit around all day."

"No, of course not, dear. I meant no such thing."

The food arrived and Tess was grateful for the interruption. She didn't feel much like eating, but the act of chewing and swallowing kept them from talking for a little while. It also let her sneak peeks at Ford. She could see him eating a hamburger and French fries, and he looked like he was enjoying the show. Tess found herself counting to twenty with every bite until the food was sawdust in her mouth just so she didn't have to speak. *I can't believe I let Hudson talk me into this. What am I doing here? Why am I doing this? Ugh!*

When both their plates were clean and glasses empty, Emily patted the corners of her mouth with the napkin and then laid it on the table. "When shall we arrange our get together? Roger bowls tonight."

Tess tried not to giggle because Emily looked like she'd just smelled something bad at the mention of bowling. "I guess I'll have to check with Hudson to see when he's free."

"Hudson? Who's that?" Emily's mouth turned down at the corners and her eyes narrowed. Then she shot an evil look across the restaurant at Ford. Tess leaned back the tiniest bit. *Oh shit.*

"He's my lawyer." Tess watched the suspicion slowly, too slowly, disappear from the Emily's face.

"Oh, well, that's an interesting name."

"Uh, yeah," Tess agreed, taking a sip of her refilled Coke, and then it hit her. *She thinks I'm seeing someone else, I bet!* Tess almost laughed again, but managed to swallow it at the last second.

"Do you want the meeting to be at his office or somewhere else?"

Pursing her lips, Emily shook her head. "I was under the impression you wanted to sit down and speak with us on an informal basis. Do we really need to involve lawyers?"

Now she really looks like she smelled something bad! "I guess I should have been more clear. I'm sorry, that's my fault. I thought it would be better if the lawyers were involved so that there wasn't any misunderstanding. I guessed David was handling all the legal work for Jack's estate. You guys didn't get someone else did you?"

"Of course not!" Emily snapped. "*We* didn't feel a need to involve any *outsiders* in such a personal, family tragedy."

Tess clenched her fists in her lap to keep from banging them on the table, any amusement she might have been feeling getting totally wiped away. It wasn't exactly her fault that a lawyer got involved, now was it? If they had been straight with Jack from the beginning, then he wouldn't have gotten pissed off and called Hudson. If there had been a little bit of honesty, then Jack wouldn't have kept a secret from them. Tess yearned to say all of this to Emily, but she knew she had to keep her cool. The whole point of the lunch was to try and get Emily on their side, not alienate her even more.

"I didn't really have a choice. David all but kicked me out of your house the day I came to you for help. If you had only talked to me that day, maybe all of this could have been avoided."

Tess watched carefully to see if her words might sway her mother-in-law back into a friendlier place. It seemed to work because Emily's face relaxed and the stony look in her eyes softened. "You're right, Tess. If only things had been handled differently."

Taking a chance, she reached over and took the older woman's hand. "We're on this road now, let's just take it where it leads, all right? I'll have Hudson call David and set it up. Maybe in the end, I won't even need him." *Cross your fingers as you tell that lie, Tess.* "But I need you to talk to David and Roger and ask them to be nice. Would you do that for me?"

Tess hated sounding like a beggar, but she didn't have any choice. Emily was so up and down and back and forth, it was hard to predict what she would say or do.

"Yes, I will. Just have this Hudson person call and I will make sure that there isn't any issue."

"Okay. Thank you."

Tess insisted on paying the bill and they walked out together. She breathed a sigh of relief when Emily didn't pay any more attention to Ford, who still hung out in his booth. As it happened, they were parked right next to each other in the lot. Unsure of how to end things, she went with her gut and gave Emily a quick hug. "I appreciate this. Thank you."

"You're welcome, dear. I'll see you soon."

Tess watched her get into her car and drive away before yanking her cell phone out of her pocket and dialing Hudson.

"Hi, it's Tess."

"Hey! How did it go?"

"I can't say for sure. She's really weird, one minute all snarky and the next as sweet as pie. She did say she would get David to set up the meeting."

"Well, that's something then."

"She said you should call David, but I didn't exactly get a timeline. Maybe wait until later or even tomorrow to give her time to speak with him first."

"No worries."

"Where's Ford?" Tess asked, hoping it didn't sound weird for her to be asking.

"I don't know. He left and said he had some errands to run. Why?"

"I was just curious," Tess fumbled. "I thought I saw his motorcycle go by while I was waiting for Emily. I'll talk to you later."

"Okay, bye."

Tess ended the call and stuffed her phone into the side pocket of her daisy backpack purse. She looked around the parking lot until she found Ford's bike and walked over to it. She leaned against the machine waiting patiently for him to come out of the restaurant. When he finally ambled out the door, she gave in to her earlier urge and flipped him off as he approached.

The sound of his honest laughter was refreshing to her since she'd never heard it before. "What's that for?" he asked as he stepped up beside her.

"For distracting me all through lunch. Why did you come here?"

"Told ya. I needed to eat and we're just right around the corner from the office."

Tess sniffed, totally not believing him. "Were you spying or looking out for me?"

Ford offered a genuine smile, instead of his usual smug look. "Both."

Shaking her head, Tess smiled back. She reached out and gave him a punch on the arm. "Well, thanks. But next time, tell me. I thought I would going to die when you walked in. I don't need any more surprises, okay?"

* * * * *

Ford nodded, thoroughly amused with Tess's irritation. She was even cuter when she was annoyed. He had known showing up might throw her for a loop, but it was a chance he decided to take. He didn't trust Emily Kingston and didn't think throwing Tess into the unknown was a good idea. And he couldn't just tell Hudson he was going to watch over things without giving away some heavily guarded feelings, so Ford had said he was going to run some errands.

He had to admit, Tess handled herself perfectly throughout the lunch. He only wished he'd been able to find out what they'd said. He had hoped to get seated nearer to them, but he couldn't win 'em all.

"Tell me what happened." Ford pulled his cigarettes from his breast pocket and lit one. "How did she seem?"

He listened and smoked as Tess rehashed the conversation for him. By the time she finished talking, Ford was even more impressed. Something had changed in Tess. He wasn't sure he could put his finger on it, but there was definitely more resolve in the way she stood and spoke. It gave him hope that, whatever lay ahead she would come through it okay. Maybe with a few more scars, but whole and okay.

Chapter 28

Tess twitched uncomfortably behind the wheel of her parked car. She sat in the lot of David Kingston's office, waiting for Hudson to arrive for the meeting that had been arranged between her and the Kingston family. True to her word, Emily had convinced David to accept a call from Hudson. Tess still wasn't so sure it was that great of an idea.

Hudson had been ecstatic when he called her about it, but Tess knew better. David had to have something up his sleeve. If she thought they only wanted to talk about money, she would have gladly sat down with the Kingstons in a much less formal atmosphere. She would have told them they could have it all, except for the life insurance policy. The million dollars from that would do nicely to see her through the majority of her life. What did she need with all the other stuff – stocks and property and what not?

But Jack had thought his family might hurt him for those things. It filled her with rage and obstinacy. There was no way in hell she was going to give it back to them if there was any possibility that any one of them had harmed a hair on Jack's head.

Tess had wanted her parents to come to the meeting for moral support, but Hudson had talked her out of it. Things might get acrimonious. Did she really want her mother and father to have to witness that? Of course she didn't. They were already in kill mode because their "baby" was hurting. If Roger Kingston said one wrong thing, Harry Langford was likely to knock him out. And while Ruth Langford was not prone to violence, Tess had no doubt she would scratch Emily Kingston's eyes out if push came to shove.

Glancing around, there was still no sight of Hudson's truck. Tess's leg began to bounce up and down, and she could feel the tension in her shoulders and neck. She began to chip away at the clear coat of polish on her fingernails. A pile of whitish flakes covered her lap when she heard the familiar rumble of a motorcycle as Ford pulled into the parking lot. He slid the bike into the spot next to her and eased it onto the kickstand.

He hadn't even cut the engine before Tess was out of her car and standing beside him, smiling from ear to ear. "Hi," she said, groaning inwardly at the high-pitched, nervous sound of her voice.

"Hey," was his casual reply. He turned off the bike and slipped the keys into his pocket. As he removed his helmet and swiveled to hang it from the hook at the end of the bike, Tess took a deep breath to calm herself. His hair was tousled and the ends were windblown. She watched as he ran his fingers through it, trying to smooth it down.

"What are you doing here?" she asked. *He shaved today.* He was in a pair of khakis and a plain navy blue polo shirt, too. It was a big change from his usual grungy jeans and leathers. *You're doing it again, T. Stop it!*

"Moral support."

"Heh," Tess breathed. "So Hudson gets a backup but I don't?"

Ford smiled. "I'm here for both of you. And to keep an eye on the idiot."

Tess grinned, knowing he meant David. "I'm more worried about Roger than David. He's the one who might keel over from a heart attack over all this."

"Good, one less person to deal with," Ford muttered.

Tess reached out and punched him in the arm. "Hey, that's not nice. We don't know for sure if they're really evil or just mean."

Ford shrugged. Nodding his head in the direction of the driveway, Tess looked up to see Hudson pull in. He hopped out of his truck and strode over to them.

"Hey," he said. Shaking his shoulders and head around, he took in a deep breath and exhaled quickly. "Are we ready for this?"

"No," Ford and Tess said in unison.

"Well, it's too late now. Let's just get it done."

"Lay on, Macduff." Ford extended his hand. Hudson smirked and turned to walk toward the door. Ford waited for Tess to follow so he could take up the rear.

Chapter 29

Hudson spoke politely to the receptionist behind the sliding glass window. She wasn't as friendly, giving him a purse-lipped nod as she picked up her telephone to announce their arrival to the boss. When she hung up the receiver, she did not look at Hudson. "Mr. Kingston will be out in a moment. Have a seat."

"All righty then," Hudson murmured. He turned back to Ford and Tess, giving them a half-hearted smile. "Let's just have a seat, shall we?"

As they cooled their heels, Hudson tried to stifle the anger churning in his gut. The waiting was just a power play on David Kingston's part. *A passive-aggressive power play.* Hudson rolled his eyes mentally while maintaining an outwardly patient demeanor. There was no way in hell he was going to let David get the best of him with such a childish, piss ant move. He stole a glance at Tess and was relieved that she appeared relaxed and calm. She looked crisp and cool in the pale blue top and blue and white flowery skirt she wore. He couldn't take his eyes off her. She was definitely handling things better than he could have hoped for. As the days had gone by, her resolution to find out the truth had solidified and made her stronger. It was as if her grief had taken a back seat to her quest to discover what exactly had happened to Jack.

The longer Hudson looked at Tess, the more beautiful she became. He couldn't help noticing the little birthmark behind her right ear, as she sat on his left. His eyes drifted down and he appreciated the way her bare leg bounced on her knee. When he brought his head back up to study something different, he caught Ford glaring at him.

Oh shit, Hudson thought, whipping his head back to the right. That was the last thing he needed was his brother catching him ogling Tess so openly. *She's just a client, asshole.*

"Mr. Kingston will see you now."

The grumpy receptionist was standing in the waiting area with the door opened wide. Hudson tried not to jump up too quickly, embarrassed that he'd been caught off guard. He straightened his tie and turned to Tess. "After you."

She nodded and walked through the doorway, following the receptionist. Hudson did the same to Ford, inviting him to go next. Ford continued to glare at him. "Keep your eye on the ball, brother," he said softly as he walked past him.

Hudson shook his head and smirked.

They were led to a conference room where David, Emily and Roger Kingston were already seated on one side of an enormous mahogany table. It hadn't escaped Hudson's notice how sumptuous the office was, with its high-end furnishings and fixtures. He felt no shame that his office wasn't as nice; instead, he thought of himself as "Every man's lawyer" where his clients could feel comfortable and not patronized. *Yeah, keep tellin' yourself that.*

Hudson pulled out a chair for Tess to sit, while Ford took the chair to her right. Hudson sat on her left and set his briefcase on the table. "Good afternoon," he said in a pleasant tone. He tried to make eye contact with each of the Kingstons, but only David met his gaze.

"Good afternoon." David's voice was as pinched as the look on his face.

"Thank you for calling the meeting." Hudson reached into his briefcase and took out the thick Kingston file. "This doesn't have to be all that formal."

"Why is *he* here?" David pointed to Ford.

Ford had been reclining in his chair and staring at his clasped hands.

"Moral support," Tess interjected.

"Hmm." David frowned and leaned back in his chair. "Seeing as he is not an interested party, I don't see how his presence is appropriate. I would ask him to leave."

"Well–" Hudson started. *This is going to be bad.*

"No. He stays," Tess insisted. "Roger? Emily? Do you have a problem with this?"

Emily had been staring off into space and her head pivoted in her daughter-in-law's direction. Her eyes narrowed for just a second or two as she looked at Ford. Roger began to object, looking back and forth between his wife and son, but Emily placed a delicate, white hand on his arm. "Let it be, Roger."

The room remained silent for several moments before Hudson cleared his throat. "Okay, that's settled. Why don't we start with taking a look at Jack's will?"

"Oh, we've been reviewing *the will* for some time," David sneered.

Hudson raised his eyebrows. "I see."

"It'll never hold up in court."

Hudson shrugged as if it didn't surprise or bother him that David would feel this way. Secretly, he was angry though. The whole point of Tess reaching out to Emily was to schedule an amicable, non-threatening meeting. Already, David was getting down and dirty.

"I would disagree. Jack was of sound mind when he pass– er died. On what grounds would you have to contest it?"

David sat up a bit straighter in his chair. "Well, any number of things. He made a will without telling anyone. He didn't confide in his fiancé or his family. I would say that smacks of severe paranoia. Obviously there had to be something wrong with him physically and mentally to have taken such actions. What I'd like to know is how you can say he was of sound mind when he signed his will. What do you know that we don't? Anything you'd care to disclose?"

Hudson frowned and felt his stomach flip flop. He looked over at Tess who shrugged, the look on her face one of terror. He caught Ford's eyes and Ford shook his head so slightly Hudson wasn't even sure it moved.

"If there's a point you're trying to make, I think you should make it." Hudson spoke through semi-clenched teeth, trying with great determination to remain cordial and placid.

David's throaty and cynical laugh filled the room. "Is this really necessary? I can't believe you're going to put us through this, Tess."

"Mr. Kingston–" Hudson tried to speak.

"David–" Roger raised a hand to try and gain control, but it was too late.

"No, I'm serious!" David shouted. He would have said more, but the last thing anyone expected was what happened next.

Emily Kingston's head raised up slowly and she glowered at Tess. "You thought you could get away with this?" she screeched, banging her hands on the table. "You thought we wouldn't find out what you did?" Before anyone could stop her, Emily leapt out of her chair and ran around the table towards Tess. Ford was on his feet and hooked her around the waist with one arm lifting her off the floor. She struggled and twisted to get away from him, but Ford held tight. He carried her back to the chair and forced her back into it. When she tried to lunge again, he put his hands on her shoulders to restrain her.

"Get your hands off my wife!" Roger bellowed, jabbing his fists at Ford, who tried to keep one hand on Emily and use the other to fend off Roger.

"Let's get out of here." Hudson grabbed Tess's arm and yanked her up. They bolted for the door but were stopped short.

A plainclothes cop stood in the doorway to the conference room flanked by two uniformed police officers. "Hold it right there."

The room quieted immediately.

"What's going on?" Hudson demanded.

David Kingston found his voice and legs and strode up to Tess. "You must think you're very smart, but you aren't. I have contacts at the medical examiner's office too. You aren't the only one who can get information for a price." He stepped to the table and grabbed some papers of his own, throwing them at her. They bounced off her chest and fell to the floor.

"What the hell are you talking about?" Tess's voice cracked and her face drained of all color. She began to shake and Hudson put an arm around her shoulders to steady her.

"Tess Kingston," the plain clothes cop stated, "I'm requesting that you come to the station to answer some questions about the death of Jack Kingston."

Chapter 30

Tess shivered as she sat in the cold metal room with the large double-sided mirror. She'd seen enough episodes of Law & Order to know that the people behind it were watching her every move. She prayed her quaking didn't look like some kind of guilt to those observers.

Hudson sat beside her, but she didn't feel comforted by his presence. He was as confused as she was and two clueless people didn't bode well for the interrogation coming. The police said she wasn't charged with anything, but the unspoken "yet" hung heavy in the air. What had happened to Jack? What had David been rambling about? She just couldn't fathom what the hell was going on.

The doorknob wiggled and in walked an older man who looked friendly enough. He seemed like the police officer she had been taught to trust as a child, but in her state of agitation she almost cringed at the sight of him. He was probably in his middle fifties with a bushy mustache and little hair left on the rest of his head. His eyes were kind, but piercingly sharp. He sat down across from them and opened a file folder he had in his hand. He plucked two stapled pieces of paper from the stack and looked at it over the top of the half-lensed pair of glasses he wore.

"Good afternoon, Mrs. Kingston. My name is Butch Isham. Detective Carter, the man who brought you in, is my partner." He smiled at her, but it did nothing to put Tess at ease. "The toxicology report on the victim indicates a foreign substance in his blood. What can you tell me about that?"

Hudson spoke before she could. "My client hasn't had an opportunity to review the report, Detective." He leaned forward. "We weren't made aware that it was available. May we have a copy?"

"Sure," Detective Isham said. "Take mine." He pushed the report across the table toward Hudson, who began reading it right away. "The poison used made it look like the victim suffered a heart attack. Do you know of anyone who would want to cause harm to him?"

"Don't answer that!" Hudson growled. "I've advised my client not to say anything at this time. We are only here because you basically ambushed us at David Kingston's office."

"Well, Mr. Kingston gave us the heads up that a meeting was taking place. And I didn't think you wanted to make any statements there."

"Like this is more comfortable," Tess muttered, suffering a withering look from both the detective and her lawyer.

Detective Isham leaned back in his chair. "Did Jack have any enemies?"

"No!" Tess cried. It was a simple enough question and one she thought she could answer honestly enough. But then she wondered about her former in-laws. Could they be considered enemies? *God, I wish I could speak to Hudson* alone.

"What about the large inheritance you received? Were you aware of the victim's financial situation before you got married?"

"No. And I have a letter to prove that."

"Tess!" Hudson hissed.

"Yes, I've heard about the letter. We would appreciate receiving a copy of that. Unfortunately, it doesn't prove anything. You could have written that yourself."

Tess frowned. *I'm the prime suspect. I should have been expecting this.* She looked from the detective to Hudson, feeling her anxiety level rise to new heights. Her palms became clammy and she had to consciously resist the urge to wipe her hands on her lap.

"I can attest to the fact that my client didn't know anything." Hudson folded his hands on the table, over top the report. "It was Mr. Kingston's wish at the time of the drafting of his estate plan that his future wife not be told anything."

"Did you record your meeting with the victim?"

"No."

"Then we don't know for sure he didn't go right home and tell his fiancé at the time."

"I swear I didn't know!" Tess shouted.

"Shut *up!*" Hudson yelled back. She glowered at him, knowing he was only trying to protect her.

"Who did the victim see the day of the wedding, within six to eight hours of the ceremony?"

"If the window is six to eight hours," Hudson mused, "then Jack could have been poisoned within an hour after leaving his apartment. His family didn't know he had made a will and had far more to gain from his death than my client."

Detective Isham smirked in a condescending way. "The Kingston family claims the victim—"

"Stop calling him the victim!" Tess hissed. "His name was Jack!"

Detective Isham glared at her and returned his focus to Hudson. "As I was saying, the Kingstons' statement is that Jack Kingston did not consume any food or drink in their presence."

"How convenient," Hudson muttered.

"The poison could have been in the coffee served to him by his fiancé the morning of the wedding."

"I didn't poison my husband!" Tess yelled, jumping to her feet. Hudson's hand snaked out, grasping her around the wrist.

"Sit down, Tess," he said calmly, but his tight grip said far more. "You have no proof of anything," he continued. "Are you charging my client?"

"Not yet."

"Then we're done here. If you have any more questions, call me directly."

* * * * *

Hudson walked Tess out of the police station with every intention of taking her back to David Kingston's office for her car. Instead, they found Ford sitting on his motorcycle in the parking lot and Lilly in the spot next to him with Tess's car. They both rushed over to begin asking questions.

"What's going on?" Lilly demanded.

"Are you all right?" Ford asked in a softer voice.

"Stop!" Tess pleaded, throwing her hands up to ward them off.

"It's okay, she isn't being charged–" Hudson started.

"Yet," Tess muttered.

Hudson gave her a stern look. "Yet. But we are in the shit now. Lilly, please take Tess home. Ford and I need to get back to the office so we can study the tox report and get to work. I'll call you later to set up a time when we can meet. And if anyone calls you – the police, the Kingstons – I mean, *anyone*, you are not to speak to them. Not under *any* circumstances. Got it?"

"Yes," she whispered.

"I'm serious, Tess. Do *not* speak to *anyone* but me or Ford or your immediate family."

Tess gave him a chastised and anguished look as her sister led her to the car.

"What the hell happened?" Ford growled when the women had driven away.

"David Kingston fucked us. Somehow he managed to get his hands on the report before us and he went to the police."

Hudson started walking toward his truck at a fast clip; Ford close on his heels.

"What did the report show?"

"Just what we thought. Jack was poisoned."

Ford let out a low, long whistle. "Shit."

Chapter 31

Standing under the hot spray of the shower, Tess sighed with pleasure and relief. Her respite was short-lived because she knew she was at risk of spending the rest of her life in a real prison much uglier than the one of widowhood in which she found herself.

"Thanks a lot, Jack," she muttered to the shower loofa in her hand. "If this is some cosmic joke, I'm gonna kick your ass when I see you again."

Tess scrubbed her body until her skin was sore from the exertion. She gave her scalp and hair the same vigorous workout until she felt reasonably confident she was clean. All those nasty questions from that detective made her feel dirty. Polluted somehow. She got out and wrapped up in her oversized terrycloth robe and then threw her hair up into a fluffy towel. Padding along to her bedroom, the kitties followed and joined her when she flopped onto the bed. As she petted them, her mind whirled and swirled.

This was getting too crazy for her. Going back over the events of the day, she was stunned at how she'd been set up. Somehow, David had gotten a hold of the toxicology report and discovered that Jack had been poisoned. Because she was the only person to be alone with Jack the morning of the wedding until he went to his parents, all evidence pointed to her as having been the person to give him the poison.

Poisoned! Jack had been *murdered.* Her stomach clenched and her heart ached. Not her Jack. Not the boy and then man who had been her very best friend for most of her life. Had he suffered? How could anyone think *she* could do such a thing? Visions of tabloid headlines flashed through her mind and Tess grabbed a pillow to hold over her head, trying to make them go away.

Obviously that was a load of crap. She had loved Jack and never would have killed him. No matter how many doubts she had about the wedding and marriage itself, she *never* would have killed him. It was ludicrous. Thankfully, Hudson and Ford believed her. Hudson had seen Jack in his nervous state, there was no way he thought Tess was capable of killing Jack. There was no motive, even if there had been plenty of opportunity. He had promised he would defend her and find a way out of the mess.

Anyone else in her situation would probably break down from the kind of pressure that had just been dumped on her. Not Tess. No, she was raging mad. Not only had her fairy tale ending been stolen from her, but now she was accused of causing it all as well. There was no way in hell she was going to go down for something the Kingstons had *obviously* orchestrated. And all in the name of money.

Tess believed to her core that it had to be Roger or David and the thought of it sickened her. They had more motive than she. They knew about the adoption and the money and the inheritance. And hadn't their actions after his death shown they were trying to keep his money? All those lies in the probate documents. How could the police even *look* at her?

No, it was the Kingstons. Tess was sure of it. And she was going to prove it.

Chapter 32

"Well, at least we know for sure now. And your life won't be in danger," Lilly said, trying to sound glad but failing miserably. The worry in her eyes and the way her voice cracked gave it all away.

"Oh sure, there's that." Tess snorted and stared into her glass of lemonade. She sat on the couch in her parents' living room with them and her sister, waiting for Hudson to arrive. "They sure wouldn't want to kill me now, because then I wouldn't go to jail, framed for the death of their son." Tess was trying to find hope and stay positive, but it was pretty hard. She couldn't have anticipated being suspected of Jack's murder. It was just too far off her radar. She tried to remember all the promises she made to herself that day on the patio. Her confidence was dwindling fast.

"As morbid as it sounds, it's true," Harry Langford admitted. He sipped a beer and stared into the empty, cold fireplace. "I can't believe this is happening to you, Padunkin."

"Neither can I." Tess put the glass on the table, not willing to take another sip. Everything upset her stomach since that horrible day at David's office.

"I have to believe Hudson will find a way out of this," Ruth said softly. She reached out to pat Tess's hand. "He's a very smart young man and he knows you didn't do this."

Tess smiled half-heartedly and accepted the soothing touch from her mother, though it didn't comfort her at all. All she could think about was prison and guards and bars and vicious female inmates beating the shit out of her every single day. Oh, and her family, grieving for her every day she was gone. Tess would never have admitted it out loud to anyone, much less her family, but sometimes she wondered if running away or killing herself might not solve some of the more egregious problems. But then Jack's voice would explode in her head, telling her what an idiot she was for even thinking of something like that.

"Hello everyone," Hudson called out, as he knocked on the front screen door and walked right in, Ford trailing behind him, looking somber and sexy as always. Tess nodded, but did not wave or smile as they entered the living room. Even noticing how handsome Ford was didn't perk her up. She might be determined not to let the Kingstons win, but that didn't relieve the cloud of depression settling over her.

"Hello Hudson, Ford," Ruth greeted. "Iced tea or lemonade?"

"Thanks, Ruth. I'll take some tea," Hudson replied as he sat down on the couch beside her.

"Nothing, thanks." Ford smiled and nodded, then moved to the only chair that was left: her mother's rocking chair in the corner beside the couch.

Hudson pulled a legal pad from his briefcase and a pen from the chest pocket of his short-sleeved button down shirt. Clicking it loudly, he was poised to begin writing. "Okay, Tess. I want you to try and remember everything you can from about three days before the wedding. Tell me everything you did, everywhere you went, anything at all."

Tess sighed and rubbed her forehead with her hand. *We've already been over this a hundred times,* she thought. But she knew it was important. At some point she was going to remember something that would lead them in the right direction. At least that was her hope and prayer.

Lilly and Ruth interjected several times when they were with Tess to run some errand or make some preparation. Harry remained quiet because, as her dad, he'd had little to do with all the "wedding nonsense" as he'd called it, with a twinkle in his eye and a smile in his voice. Those twinkles and smiles were gone now and Tess wanted them back.

Over an hour later, Hudson stopped his barrage of questions and put down the pen, shaking his fingers back and forth. "The poison found by the ME was organic in nature. I've been doing research and it's supposed to imitate a heart attack perfectly, which it did. No one would have thought to look for it, which is why the tox report took so long to come back. I think someone might have requested a deep screen."

"What does that mean exactly?" Harry leaned into the conversation. "Deep screen?"

"A deep screen gets requested when a death is suspicious. Thing about it: Jack was a healthy young male. There was no reason for him to have a heart attack unless he had a previously undiscovered heart condition, which he didn't. The poison being organic means it was most likely plant based and not a chemical. Unless Jack had a drug habit or someone gave him an injection the day of the wedding, he probably ate or drank something that had the poison in it."

Tess shook her head vehemently, unable to believe what she was hearing. "But we were together the night before the wedding, and that morning. Neither one of us ate or drank. Or, if we did, we would have had the same things. Why wouldn't I have died too?"

"Maybe that was the plan?" Ford said this quietly, like dropping a depth charge into the silent sea and waiting for the explosion to roil upward into the atmosphere.

"What?"

Tess couldn't tell who else said the word other than herself because it seemed to come from all sides. Her mother, Lilly, her father. All of them stared at Ford in disbelief.

"If you two had died before the wedding could take place, then Jack's inheritance would have reverted to his family. No fuss, no muss. My guess, *our* guess," Hudson pointed at Ford, "is that whoever poisoned Jack was trying to poison you too. But you didn't eat or drink something that Jack did."

"Those rotten bastards!" Lilly shouted, jumping up from her seat on the couch. She pounded a fist into her palm. "And they managed to convince the cops to look at Tess? What a bunch of holy horseshit!"

"Lilly!" Ruth admonished.

"I don't care, Mom! This is absolutely ridiculous! They have a million times more motive and opportunity, but Tess is the one being investigated. You *have* to do something Hudson. You *gotta* convince the police that Tess isn't involved in this."

"Calm down," Hudson soothed. "I will do everything I can." He picked up his pen and the legal pad, scanning through the notes again. "Again. Tell me everything you can remember, *again*." His eyes burned with determination.

Tess wanted to cry, but refused to allow herself the luxury. Now was not the time to fall apart, especially not if Hudson was willing to fight so hard for her. She would go over the details as many times as he asked. Her entire life depended on it.

Chapter 33

It was long after midnight as Ford flipped through the paperwork in Tess's files for the millionth time, searching for something he had missed. For a week, he and Hudson had been racking their brains, asking questions, gathering names of people to speak to, but they hadn't yielded anything to assist in Tess's defense. Yet.

Hudson had gone home a couple of hours ago, having been at it himself since the predawn hours. That was how they worked best together. Ford was the night owl and his baby brother was the early bird. Between the two of them, they were determined to find the missing pieces of the puzzle to exonerate Tess. The longer he looked, the more frustrated he got. Ford wasn't used to not figuring shit out. It was his best asset. His weird and fucked up brain would often look at things in a way that Hudson didn't. But this one had him stumped.

The toxicology report said that the poison had to be administered within six to eight hours of Jack's death and Tess had been the only person with him in that timeframe, except his parents. She could have given him any type of poison she wanted at any point in time, but they didn't believe that at all. Even though Ford loathed the idea, Hudson had arranged a private polygraph for Tess, which she passed with flying colors. When they'd provided the results to Detective Isham, he'd reminded them that it wasn't proof of anything or admissible in court.

"The poison had to have been meant for both of them."

All Ford's private investigating up to that point had yielded nothing. The license plate search hadn't shown David or Roger's cars in the vicinity of Tess's apartment at any time. The cell phone records didn't show any pings for anyone's phones. He'd combed through all the financial records again and the only thing they could find was Roger Kingston's occasional poor choices for investing the money. But there wasn't anything illegal about it. "He's just a lucky sonofabitch," Ford muttered.

Ford had spoken with everyone in the ME's office to try and figure out if there had been any hanky panky there, but his uncanny sixth sense hadn't picked anything up. The case seemed as airtight as any he'd ever seen, albeit circumstantial.

But still, in his gut, he knew he was missing something.

He got up to make a fresh pot of coffee and movement caught the corner of his eye. His hand went immediately to his gun. Whenever he was in the office late and alone, he carried a pistol even though St. Clair Shores wasn't necessarily a mecca of crime. As he turned to face the glass front door of the office, Ford's eyes went wide when he saw Tess standing there, her hand poised to knock.

Without a word, he withdrew his hand and strode to the door to let her in.

"Hey, I hope I'm not interrupting something," she said as she walked in. She held a large manila envelope and looked scared and thin in her jeans and black hoodie.

She's wasn't sleeping before, but now she's not eating. "Nope." He pulled the door closed behind her and turned the deadbolt. "I was just about to make coffee. Want some?"

"Sure," she said softly as she took a seat at the table with all the paperwork. "Working hard or hardly working?"

Ford snorted. "That's a silly question." He grabbed the glass pot and took it into the bathroom to fill. He poured the water into the machine and slid the pot on the burner, flicking the brew button. Then he joined her at the table. Her hair was loose around her shoulders instead of the ponytail she favored. Her blue eyes looked bigger and wider in her face because of the weight she was losing. The hoodie seemed to swallow her up and she looked much younger than her twenty-five years.

The only noise in the room was the sound of coffee dripping into the pot. The strong smell wafted through the room, swirling around them. Finally, Ford spoke. "What are you doing here?"

Tess shrugged. "I couldn't sleep. Well, I don't sleep anymore. I found some more wedding paperwork, so I thought I'd put it through the mail slot. When I drove by and saw the light on, I figured I would stop in."

Ford said nothing. When the sound of falling liquid stopped, he went to get their coffee. He put cream into hers and left his black.

"Thanks," Tess said, as she took the cup. She blew on the hot coffee before taking a tiny sip. Ford was a bit mesmerized by the sight of her pink lips on the rim of the cup. Other images floated into his head, catching him totally off guard. *Look away, Ford.*

"You know, today would have been my seven month anniversary," Tess whispered.

Oh, holy hell. "I'm sorry," was all he could manage to say, as he drank from his own cup. He expected her to start crying any moment and then he would be stuck. After all the facts he'd learned about her over the last weeks, Ford wanted to comfort her, but he also didn't want to be anywhere near her. She was pulling feelings out of him that he thought were buried too deep to reach.

Instead of crying, she laughed. It was a cynical, bitter sound. "I can't even remember what Jack's arms felt like around me anymore. He used to come up next to me and say, 'Side hug!' and squeeze me until I couldn't breathe, but I can't feel it anymore. Does that make me a bad person?"

Ford shook his head. "No, it doesn't. Most people get to grieve properly when they lose a loved one."

"You're right." Tess pursed her lips. "But I *did* get to grieve. I got six months before the shit started hitting the fan."

Ford was about to tell her that a few months weren't nearly enough time, but she spoke again before he could.

"Want to know a secret?"

He tensed and sat up a little straighter in his chair. "Sure." *Please God, don't let her confess.*

"I was already starting to feel better after about a month," Tess admitted. "I loved Jack with all my heart, but I couldn't help thinking 'shit, Tess, you're only twenty-five.' Like I knew the rest of my life was in front of me, and that maybe this all happened for a reason. Of course, the minute I started admitting that to myself, I fell right back into the whole grief pool and cried for days."

Ford had to admit to himself it did shock him a little. All the stories he'd been hearing about the fairytale romance between Tess and Jack had him convinced they were more deeply in love than Snow White and Prince Charming. He sort of thought Tess would have been one of those women who held onto widowhood and grief for decades before moving on.

"Now *that* makes me a bad person, doesn't it?"

Ford shook his head again, before he could think about it. "I don't think so at all. I think you're young and under a lot of pressure."

"Know why Jack and I were together?" Tess turned the cup around in circles in her hands as if to warm her fingers against the ceramic. "We didn't know anything different and we didn't *want* to know anything different." She took another sip before taking a deep breath. "It was easy. We got along. We liked each other. We fell in love with each other early on. But now that he's gone, I can't help but wonder if we were too young. We never dated anyone else. We never kissed anyone else. We just kept taking all the normal steps in life forward, together, but did we do it because we wanted to? Or because it was easier not to struggle?"

Ford didn't know how to respond. He knew about taking the easy way out. He understood what it was like not to question a situation. He accepted things at face value without bothering to dig deeper. Everything she was saying made perfect sense to him.

Now she did begin to cry a little. Two big, fat tears squeezed out of each of her eyes and rolled lazily down her cheeks, but she did nothing to wipe them away. She took a deep, shuddery breath and tried to smile at him. "I'm sorry. I shouldn't be bothering you with all this."

"It's okay." Ford reached for his cigarettes and stood up. "I need a smoke."

"Okay."

"Join me outside for some air?"

Tess smirked. "Fresh air or second-hand smoke?"

Ford rolled his eyes and shook his head, leading the way outside. They both leaned against the building. Ford smoked while Tess scanned the empty streets.

"Tell me about yourself." She didn't look at him directly at him.

Blowing smoke into the night sky, he chuckled. "There's not much to tell."

"I don't believe that for a second." She did look at him then. "I think there's a lot going on there. Please, talk to me. I'm sick of being in my own head. I'm tired of all my own drama. I want to listen for a while, not talk and talk and talk."

Ford should have seen it coming, probably did see it coming, but didn't want to admit it. It always happened. Whenever someone normal came into his life, whether client or acquaintance, they always seemed to want to know his story. Why he was the black sheep to Hudson's white knight, upstanding lawyer gig. He never told anyone much. Or if he said anything, it was a pack of lies. His history was his own business and no one else's.

But Tess was different. She wanted comfort and friendship in a time of need. Her request was out of innocence, not some ulterior motive. She wasn't trying to worm her way into his heart or life so she could use it later to her own benefit. She just wanted an escape from her problems.

Still, Ford stalled. "I wouldn't even know where to start." He puffed furiously on the cigarette, surrounding himself in a cloud of smoke.

Tess rolled her eyes. "Start anywhere. Just talk to me."

Ford took a last drag and then dropped his cigarette into the long-necked, plastic ashtray Hudson had installed outside the office door. "Hudson wants me to be a lawyer, but it's not for me."

"There you go. Why not?"

"That's Hudson's thing."

Talking was tough. Telling the truth was tougher. Ford hadn't done either in so long, he felt as though he didn't know how.

"Go on," Tess urged.

Sighing, Ford lit another cigarette. He didn't usually chain smoke unless he was nervous or tense, and he found himself feeling both. "Hudson and I come from a pretty screwed-up family. Our dad left when I was five and Hudson was just about a year old. Our mom tried hard enough at first, but she wasn't really cut out for parenthood. When we were young, I was always the good one, taking care of little brother, doing well in school in spite of all the hardship. Real Lifetime movie type of stuff."

"Lifetime movies are stupid." Tess rolled her eyes. "Your upbringing wasn't. How bad was it?"

"Bad," Ford admitted. *Really bad. So bad, I don't know if I can even say it out loud.*

Tess shook her head and her bottom lip came out in a pout. He couldn't explain it, but that simple show of sympathy let the words come tumbling out of his mouth.

"Mom was only fifteen when she had me. Then nineteen when Hudson came along. She was your textbook resentful teen mom who wanted to party and have fun, not be a parent. I barely remember my dad and, obviously, my brother doesn't at all."

"Have you ever tried to find him?"

"Nope. Not interested." Tess said nothing, and Ford pulled another long drag from his smoke. "Frankly, if I saw the guy, I'd probably beat the shit out of him. I don't know if our lives would have been any better or different if he'd stuck around, but just abandoning us earns him an ass-kicking in my book."

"Deservedly so," Tess agreed softly, her voice floating up to him on the late night breeze.

"I gotta tell ya, the time up until kindergarten is pretty much a blur for me. I don't know where Dad was. Working, maybe. Then partying with Mom, I guess. There were always a lot of people hanging around wherever we were living, but I don't remember it being all that bad. Wasn't until I got to go to school that I began to realize our home life wasn't the way things were supposed to be. Other kids had lunch boxes or bags with food in them. I didn't. The adults took over and made sure I had lunch every day and eventually breakfast too. It still amazes me Hudson even lived long enough to go to school. God only knows what was going on at home while I was gone."

Tess was now watching him with compassionate fascination that gave Ford the confidence to keep going.

"It was a good thing my little brother was smart. He was reading by the time he was three and it made it a lot easier to protect him and take care of him when I was around and when I wasn't. He listened to me when I told him what to do. I couldn't give you specific details, but Mom was seriously addicted to drugs and alcohol by the time we were both in school all day. The usual story, we'd get home and she'd be passed out on the couch or in bed."

Tess shook her head ever so slightly and he caught the movement from the corner of his eye as he ditched another smoke.

"I guess all that isn't so bad. But it got a lot worse as I got into high school."

"Did you ever try to get help?" Tess kept her eyes focused on her black and white Chuck Taylors. "Did you have any other family?"

"Nah. What would have been the point? Foster care would have taken over, probably separated us, and I didn't want that happen. Hud was the only good thing in my life. I didn't want to lose him. I knew if I could keep shit together till I turned eighteen, then everything would be okay." The sound of his Zippo smacking closed was like a firecracker to his ears.

Tess sighed. "Was it okay?"

Ford shook his head sadly. "Not for another four years. We lived in section eight housing, so we never had to worry about losing our home. The government sent the check to the landlord so Mom couldn't blow that money on drugs. I got part-time jobs after school, Hud got a paper route, and we managed to keep eating. I thought if we could just keep our heads down and out of her way, then as soon as I got out of high school I'd get a job and we could leave."

How naïve was I? "I didn't have any clue how much worse things would get." Ford stopped then, concentrating on his smoking. He hadn't revealed this much about his past to anyone, *ever*. The ever-present defense mechanism in his brain was screaming for him to shut the hell up, he was going to scare her away. *Away from what?*

"Go on."

Her voice brought him out of his own head. "She was prostituting for drugs. She brought guys home usually while we were in school, but then it started happening at all hours of the day and night. I did my best to hide it from Hudson, but I don't really know how successful I was. We never talked about it and still don't. One time, Hudson wasn't home and some guy comes busting through the door looking for our mother. He was pretty jacked up, on meth, I think, and he came after me with a baseball bat."

Tess gasped, but said nothing more, as her hand shot out to touch his arm.

"I managed to get the bat away from him and gave him a couple of good whacks before my mom showed up and broke it up. She convinced the guy to go, then turned around and blamed me for chasing away her 'john.'" Ford was filled with ancient rage, remembering the look on the guy's face as he came through the door. His skin was pock-marked and he had only a few teeth left. Stringy, greasy hair and nasty clothes that stunk of vomit and urine. He shuddered with the vision. "At least I knew I could handle myself. If Hudson had been there, I don't know what would have happened."

"It's almost like you're more of a dad to him than a brother."

"Yep." Ford tilted his head back and blew a plume of smoke into the air. "I tried to be an example for him. I worked hard in school, got good at sports, tried to show him what to do instead of getting into trouble. I wasn't stupid. I watched enough television to learn right from wrong. Mom sure as hell never taught us that."

Tess snuck a peek up at him. "You definitely are *not* stupid."

Ford snorted. "Yeah, well, I've made my share of stupid mistakes." *Like these*, he thought as he dumped another butt into the ashtray.

The look on her face was one of interest and empathy. Not like most other women, who stared at him like they wanted him to fast forward to the "good parts." The parts that made him sexy and dangerous, waiting for the moment they would find the nugget that made him a conquest. Tess made him want to tell it all, so he could finally get rid of the baggage he carried around every single second of his existence. Well, everything except his time in prison. That was something he hoped never to reveal to anyone. He'd done his time and soon he'd be off parole as well. There was no need to rehash it or hurt people for no reason.

"I'm sorry you went through that. I can't even relate, so I won't try," Tess said, her tone kind and tender without being condescending. "I'm in the minority these days. Most of my friends' parents are divorced and had shitty childhoods. I was pretty lucky."

"At least you recognize it," Ford mumbled. "You don't seem to be suffering from Sense of Entitlement Disorder like most people these days."

"Thanks."

Another cigarette later, Ford could feel the tightness in his chest from the excess nicotine and smoke, and he motioned for her to follow him back inside. Sick and tired of the hard-backed chairs, he settled on the couch instead and wasn't too happy when Tess sat right next to him. He could smell the scent of cherries from what he figured was her shampoo and a slight hint of fabric softener from her clothes, she was that close. Up to this point, the feelings she inspired in him had all been emotional. Her physical nearness now was waking up a whole different side of him. *This is* not *good.*

Putting his arms behind his head for support, Ford leaned back. "I think that's enough of the Ford story for now."

"How much do you think Hudson remembers? Or knows?" Tess asked softly.

Ford shook his head. "Can't say for sure. I kept as much as I could from him." *Especially my prison time.* He knew it was all a part of the public record and if Hudson ever got a mind to, he could search through the databases and discover Ford's secret. But he would just have to cross that bridge if and when he ever came to it.

In the meantime, here he was, in the middle of the night, spilling his guts to a client who made him feel all kinds of things he wasn't prepared for. The decent, caring person that was still deep inside him somewhere wanted to be kind to her and offer up the sort of support she needed. The ex-con, criminal hard-ass on the outside couldn't stop thinking about what she wore beneath the hoodie or what her lips would feel like if he kissed her.

There wasn't much more to talk about, unless he started to spout facts or theories about her case. Ford didn't think that was what she wanted to hear, and he wasn't about give up any more nuggets about his past. He'd gone as far as he could with that.

With the hum of the fluorescent lighting the only background noise, Ford closed his eyes and hoped that Tess would leave soon so he could get back to his own little world inside his head.

Instead, she kept staring at him. Just as he was about to suggest it was time to leave, she placed a hand on his arm. Her fingers were cool on his skin, but not cold, and a kind smile played at the corner of her lips. Ford's spidey sense kicked in, but it was too late to prevent what happened next.

Chapter 34

Tess left her hand on Ford's arm and leaned close to press her lips against his. She could never have explained in a million years why she let herself do it, but it felt right in the moment. She fully expected him to accept the kiss and return it, but that didn't happen. Ford pulled back and she almost fell off the couch. She would have, if he hadn't grabbed her shoulders to hold her steady.

"Tess, don't."

Tilting her head to the side, she looked at him with confusion and hurt. "I'm sorry, I didn't mean to offend you."

"You didn't offend me. I just don't think–"

Tess's heart beat faster with shame and embarrassment. "You're right. I'm sorry." She popped off the couch and almost gave in to the urge to run like hell, but then she twirled around. "Wait a minute. I'm not sorry and you aren't right." Moving back in front of him, she grasped his face between both hands and kissed him again, this time with more force and passion. He still didn't respond, but she could tell he wanted to because his hands came up to the sides of her face as well. At first she thought he would pull her head away, but he didn't. He did kiss back for just a few seconds.

When he broke the contact, he tried to speak. "Tess–"

"Please," she said breathlessly, grabbing a fistful of his t-shirt. She tugged until he stood up. "Don't say anything. I know what I'm doing and I know what I want. Just be with me."

Tess wasn't prepared for what happened next. Jack had been so tender and gentle, almost nervous in spite of their having been together for years. Ford was aggressive, though he didn't hurt her. His hands weren't hesitant; they sought and searched for what they wanted. His mouth was hot against hers, pressing harder, and the blood in her veins boiled over with the trapped moans in her throat; unable to escape with his lips seared against hers.

He pushed her back until she was pinned against the closed door of Hudson's office. His fingers found the zipper of her hoodie and yanked it down roughly, exposing her plain, white cotton bra. He shoved the jacket off her shoulders and Tess shivered with both the unexpected aggression and the coolness of the air against her skin. She wrapped her arms around his neck, encouraging him to go on.

Ford took his right hand off of her long enough to find the doorknob and twist it. They stumbled backwards into the office, but Ford's strong arms kept them upright. He kicked the door closed behind him and then walked her backwards toward the couch Hudson sometimes used for taking naps, their lips never coming apart. Tess felt herself being pushed down onto the soft cushions and then Ford's body was pressed against hers. She ran her hands along his arms excited to feel the muscles there and then let her fingers find their way to the sides of his head and into his hair. She couldn't touch enough, taste enough. There was so much to feel.

Tess opened her mouth and body to him with a level of abandon she'd never felt with Jack. His urgency blotted out all thoughts of Jack. The smell of cigarettes, coffee and leather filled her nose. The weight of his body ignited her passion and the feel of his hands against her breasts fanned the flames.

This is what she wanted, what she needed. A release of all the pent up tension and anxiety. The experience of someone who was not Jack. Something to erase the nightmare that was her life; if only for a moment.

Chapter 35

Ford stared down into Tess's serene face. She had been so quiet for so long and her breathing was so even, he figured she had dozed off. He couldn't believe what they had just done. *I'm such an asshole.*

In spite of feeling guilty, he was tempted to go at it again. It had been a long time since he'd had sex like that. Hot, unbridled, sober. But he knew better. In fact, it wouldn't be long before dawn started creeping up and Hudson would be back to the office.

Reluctantly, Ford stroked the side of Tess's face with his thumb. He ran it along her cheek and chin, and then moved it across her lips. Quicker than lightening, she opened her mouth and playfully nipped at him.

"Gotcha," she whispered and giggled.

He couldn't help but grin. "Yes, you did." Against his better judgment, Ford leaned down and pressed a quick kiss to her lips. "We better get out of here."

"Why?" Tess snuggled up against him and closed her eyes.

"Because Hudson will be in the office sometime between 'fuck it's early' and early." Ford untangled himself from her, taking one last look at Tess in her glorious nakedness. She really did have an incredible body, all curves and smooth, pale skin. Turning away, he found his

213

pants and pulled them on, while he waited for her to find her own clothes. When they were both dressed, he led her out of Hudson's office. Quickly lighting a cigarette, Ford puffed on it several times so that the whole place would be filled with the smell.

"I thought you weren't supposed to smoke inside," Tess teased, as she zipped up her hoodie.

"I'm not supposed to have sex with clients on my brother's couch, either," Ford muttered. He poked his head inside Hudson's office one more time to make sure there wasn't any evidence of their activity and then closed the door. He turned back to Tess and watched her straighten herself and comb her hair with her fingers.

He didn't know what to say. What they had just done was about as irresponsible as it got. She wasn't over her husband and he wasn't in a position to be with any woman, much less one who was as kind and decent as Tess. He knew it was just a spur of the moment thing, but in her fragile state, Ford was afraid Tess would think there was more to it than that.

"Don't look at me like that," Tess warned. "My father won't be showing up with his twelve gauge to make you marry me."

Laughter burst out of his mouth like an unexpected sneeze. His anxiety was eased immediately. "You sure? I mean, I don't want your reputation to be damaged."

Tess returned his laughter and flipped her hair back. "I think I'm the one who did the advantage-taking."

Ford turned out the lights and locked up the office, then escorted Tess to her car which was parked beside his bike. "I need to be straight with you about something."

"Uh oh," Tess sighed. She leaned against her car.

"Hudson can't know about this."

"Duh."

"Not just for the reasons you think."

"Oh?" Tess raised an eyebrow and twirled her hand at him to go on.

"I think he has a thing for you."

Tess frowned. "Yeah, I kind of got that impression. I catch him looking at me sometimes."

"You do?"

"Of course, I'm not blind." Tess smirked.

"Well, I wouldn't want his feelings to get hurt. Especially if he thinks he's got a chance with you." Ford shuffled his feet and shoved his hands into his pockets. "I mean, when all this is over."

"Has he said that?"

"No," Ford said quickly. "He and I don't talk about that kind of stuff. But we don't have to. I know how he thinks."

"Don't worry about it. I won't say a word. But I'll be straight with you about something too."

"What's that?"

"He doesn't have a chance with me. I like Hudson a lot, but he's my lawyer. And maybe one day he could be my friend, too. Just my friend."

Ford realized he was holding his breath and he let it out slowly and carefully. That statement made him feel a lot better and a lot worse at the same time.

* * * * *

"I'll follow you home. Make sure you get there okay." Ford opened her door and Tess smiled. It was a gentlemanly gesture she appreciated, wondering if he would have still done it if they hadn't just hooked up.

"You don't have to do that. I'll be fine."

"It'll make me feel better," Ford insisted.

"All right."

As she pulled out of the parking lot, she heard the motorcycle roar to life. Within moments, the headlight shined behind her, illuminating the inside of her car.

What the hell did I just do?

Tess couldn't tell how she felt about the last couple of hours. Part of her was all tingly and satisfied. Her release had been so profound, she felt as if she could sleep for days. Finally. There was no guilt at finding an outlet for her despair. Well, except that she felt bad for having to involve Ford. But she wasn't the type of person who could just go out and find some random person to sleep with.

Then there was the other part of her. Mortified and racked with guilt for having betrayed her husband who hadn't been in the ground a year. *Slut. Tramp.* She knew she was neither of those things, but being her own worst critic made those labels flash like neon signs on the side of a building.

Driving through the darkened streets of St. Clair Shores, Tess tried to listen for Jack's voice of reprisal, but it was silent. Of course, she didn't hear him cheering for her, either.

Decisiveness had never been one of her strong suits, but Tess figured it was about time she started standing by her choices. She decided once and for all she wasn't going to have any regrets about the time she had just spent with Ford Marks. It would probably be difficult to stick to it, but she was going to try her best. At some point she needed to stop worrying about what Jack would think of the things she did in life. He was gone and she didn't want everything she did to be colored by his influence.

Now that she wasn't in his arms, Tess was able to compare Ford and Jack more objectively. Jack had never been with anyone but her and vice versa, so their knowledge of sex was limited to the things they saw in movies or read about in books. It had been satisfying in a comfortable and familiar way. But being with Ford had unlocked something inside of her. He was aggressive and confident. He took what he wanted, but still gave what she needed. He seemed to know what she needed and wanted, without having to ask or try until he found it. His passion was intuitive and that excited Tess.

As she parked in the assigned spot in front of her building, she was amazed that her breath was short and her body full of electricity. She was nervous to have to see him when he pulled his motorcycle beside her. It had been so long since she had been in a spot like this, nervous about what another boy, or man, thought of her. Trying to figure out what to say, she kind of wanted to invite Ford inside and see where it went. But then she wasn't so sure she wanted things to go any further between them. It would be difficult enough not letting Hudson find out. Staying for a whole night could make that even harder. Tess licked her lips and cleared her throat before getting out of her car.

Ford was holding his helmet in his hands, waiting for her. As she took the two steps toward him, he cut the engine and toed the kickstand into place.

"Well, uh, thanks," she said softly, suddenly unable to look him in the eye. She shoved her hands into the pockets of her hoodie and poked at some rocks with her toe.

"You okay?"

"Yes, I'm fine." She chanced a quick peek at him. His green eyes were like dark emeralds in the dim light.

"You're embarrassed now."

"No!" Tess's head whipped up. "Not at all. I just..." her voice trailed off, not knowing how to say what she wanted to say.

"Just what?"

Tess inhaled deeply. "I'm not embarrassed about what we did." She took a step closer to him so that their bodies just barely touched. "I'm embarrassed because I don't know how to ask for more without sounding like a total tramp."

Ford didn't move. He didn't look away and he didn't say a word. He just stared at her for what felt like an hour. Just as Tess was about to say something, do something, to relieve the awkwardness, Ford leaned over and kissed her. It wasn't rough like before, but Tess felt a wanting there, like he was holding back.

"Come in with me," she murmured against his lips. "Just for a little while longer. Then we'll pretend like it never happened."

Ford's answer was to pull her into his arms. He crushed her against his chest as their lips melted together.

As the sky was changing from full dark to that subtle, slight gray of predawn, Ford took her hand and followed Tess inside.

* * * * *

This is a mistake, Ford thought as he followed Tess inside. *I know I shouldn't be doing this.* But when had he ever made the right choices? Not since Hudson got old enough to take care of himself. Since then, his life had become one long string of chaotic instances and freak occurrences, most of which landed him in some form of trouble or another.

He was about to change his mind and tell Tess that he ought to go, but she turned around and flashed him an angelic smile that unwound him entirely. He pulled her into his arms and clung to her with a ferocity that scared him more than it would have upset her.

Before he knew what he was doing, he had her hoodie and bra off and she was tugging at his pants. They stumbled and staggered their way to her bedroom. In a tangle of limbs and hands, they managed to keep their mouths fused together while still stripping away every last article of clothing.

Pushing her onto the bed, Ford sprawled next to her and proceeded to explore her body with his hands and his mouth. He turned off the voice in his head that told him it wasn't too late to stop. He ignored the gut feeling telling him he was making one of the biggest mistakes in his life. He opened his heart for just a little while and let himself pretend that this was the kind of life he was meant for. A beautiful girl in bed and passion not fueled by alcohol and regrets.

Chapter 36

Hudson dialed Tess's number for the third time since arriving at the office around eight, only to get her voicemail again. Her phone was off and that was odd. Usually it would ring a couple of times and she would answer his calls. Instantly, he was worried. There was always a chance she would run, overwhelmed by the insanity of being suspected of murder, facing a possible life sentence in prison. But Hudson never really thought she would do it. She seemed to have too much confidence in him – way more than he had.

With days flying by and no new evidence coming to him to explain Jack's death, Hudson was getting more concerned. He and Ford worked day and night, around the clock, to figure out what they were missing. Something they weren't seeing. Some avenue gone unexplored. They often argued and bickered, like brothers do, but it was becoming more volatile and belligerent the faster the days ticked by.

And just where was Ford anyway? He had promised to be in the office early. It wasn't like him to break a promise. Hudson dialed his brother's number and it too went directly to voicemail. A sense of foreboding bubbled in his stomach, making the protein bar and smoothie he'd consumed for breakfast jump and jostle. It was almost noon and Hudson didn't want to be worried about both his brother and Tess. If he couldn't reach either, it made him think that something terrible could have happened that he didn't yet know about.

As he was about to try Tess's number again, Ford walked through the door. The first thing Hudson noticed was that he looked... rested. As though he got some real sleep and not just booze-induced unconsciousness. His hair was wet from a fresh shower and his clothes looked reasonably clean.

"Where have you been?" Hudson demanded. His eyebrows furrowed with suspicion and the tone of his voice was clipped.

"Sorry, brother." Ford tossed his leather jacket onto the chair and leaned inside the doorframe. "Late night last night."

"Hmm," Hudson sighed. "Again? Don't become a client, Ford. You need to lay off the booze." He swore he could smell beer from where he sat. *Or maybe I just think I do?*

"You got it, brother. Did you make coffee?"

"About four hours ago. I used the last packet. It's my turn to pick up more."

"Shit." Ford poured two cups of the lukewarm, tar-like substance and then tossed them into the microwave to reheat.

Hudson clicked around on the internet for the time it took Ford to heat the coffee, printing out sheet after sheet. Gathering them from the printer, he moved out to the desk where the rest of Tess's file still sat, spread from one end to the other.

"I've been looking up some information about that poison. Being organic, it could have come from any number of plants. I'm not sure there's any way we'll ever be able to tell exactly what plant produced it."

"That is not what I wanted to hear this morning." Ford handed him a cup, then sat down.

"I found a website that lists a few dozen different flowers that could possibly do it, but I don't know that we have time to look into all of them."

"Uh, I think we'll have to make the time, don't you?"

Hudson's brows furrowed. "I'm doing the best I can here, Ford. I'm not a scientist."

"Then we need to get one, don't we?" Ford's eyes crackled with determination. "I have chemist buddies. Let me have a copy of the tox report and I'll start spreading it around. See who comes up with something first."

Hudson handed over the report. "Go for it. Maybe they can narrow down the list of plants." He felt his brother's resolve boosting his own confidence. He pulled some more yellow sheets of paper out of a file and began sifting through them. "Tess said that they were getting deliveries from people the whole week before the wedding. Flower arrangements, goody baskets with all kinds of food and tea and coffee. The poison had to be in one of those. It's the only thing that makes sense."

Ford nodded. "Probably. It was probably dumb luck that Tess didn't eat or drink the same thing."

"Yeah, *shitty* dumb luck. I know I wouldn't want to live with that kind of survivor's guilt." Hudson ran a hand through his hair and stood up. He came around his desk to pace in and out of the door to his office. "What's worse is that she might have poisoned him after all."

Ford nearly spilled his coffee as he gaped. Hudson put up his hands in defense. "I don't mean she murdered him. But if she gave him the food or drink with the poison in it, even unknowingly, the PA could still try to charge her."

"Jesus," Ford whispered, wiping away the drops of coffee on his jeans.

"Yeah. I'm going to need to go over things with her again. We have to figure out how to trigger her memory somehow."

"I bet she has a list somewhere of the names of florists or the people who sent stuff."

"Yeah, sure, if I could get a hold of her. She's not answering her phone. I've been trying all morning to reach her." Hudson's irritation was evident by the frown on his face. He was about to make another snide remark when he noticed Ford staring into his coffee cup. "Have you spoken to her?"

"Nope." Ford lifted the cup to his mouth to drink. Hudson continued to stare at him.

As much as Ford knew how he thought, Hudson could read his brother's tells just as easily. *He's not telling me something.*

"What's going on, brother?" Hudson sat back down and forced his brother to look at him. "Is something up?"

Sighing, Ford ran a hand through his damp hair. "Tess stopped by last night. She saw the light on and needed someone to talk to."

Hudson waited, but Ford remained mute. "And?"

"What?" Ford got up to get more coffee. "She got here around midnight and left about one. She said she wasn't sleeping, so I bet that's where she is."

"What did she tell you?" Hudson's bad vibe meter was deeply in the red. "Tell me everything she said."

"Nothing, brother. She was sad about Jack and worried about prison. She just needed to vent for a while. I listened and then she went home."

The needle bounced back into safe territory and Hudson relaxed. "Okay. You had me worried there for a second. You looked nervous and I thought maybe she confessed or something."

Ford laughed and sat back down, looking more composed. "No. She most definitely did not confess."

"I'm sure she'll call me back." Hudson turned back to the mess on the table. "In the meantime, I want you to get that report to your chemist pals."

"You got it."

After Ford left, Hudson sat back, chewing on the end of his pen. His brother hadn't been himself this morning and he knew it. Something was going on that he wasn't ready to talk about and it definitely had to do with Tess. Hudson felt a little miffed that Tess had chosen Ford to confide in, rather than him. He knew it was ridiculous to feel jealous, but he couldn't help it. It was hard not to feel protective of her, especially when her whole life was depending on him. *Just a client*, he reminded himself.

Hudson forced himself to shake it off, setting it aside for more introspection later. He needed to keep digging and fast, if he was going to keep his prettiest client ever out of prison.

Chapter 37

"I'm here! What's the big emergency?" Lilly called out as she walked through Tess's front door. She was immediately assailed with the smell of coffee and bacon. Her stomach rumbled, even though she had already eaten a bowl of cheerios.

"In the kitchen!"

Lilly dropped her purse and keys on the couch, quickly following the delicious scents into the kitchen. Tess stood at the stove, fork in hand, poking at the crackling strips of bacon in the frying pan. "Hey, sis."

"Hey, sis." Tess finished what she was doing and then gave Lilly a hug. "Thanks for coming."

"No problem. What's up?"

"Well, let me finish getting breakfast together and then we can talk."

Lilly groaned. "You're going to make me wait that long?"

Tess chuckled and gave her a wink. "You can handle it. What kind of eggs do you want?"

"None for me. I already ate. But I will munch on some of that bacon. I'll set the table."

As Tess continued cooking, Lilly grabbed plates and silverware then took them to the table. She also poured coffee into the carafe, grabbed mugs and cream, and put all that out too. She couldn't stand waiting for whatever news her little sister had, but didn't feel all that nervous about it. If it were something bad, Tess would never have been able to contain herself. She'd have been all over Lilly the minute she walked in the door. *Maybe something good has finally happened.*

Lilly sat down and poured herself a cup of coffee and waited as patiently as she could for Tess to join her. It didn't take long before she appeared, carrying a plate heaped with bacon and another one loaded with scrambled eggs.

"I know you said you didn't want any, but help yourself. There's plenty."

"Just sit down and spit out whatever you have to tell me. I'm on pins and needles here," Lilly groused as she snagged a few pieces of bacon.

"Okay, okay."

Tess didn't say anything right away, though, and Lilly was forced to watch her fill a plate and take a bite.

"What's going *on?*" Lilly demanded.

"Well," Tess said through a mouthful of eggs. "Something happened last night." She washed them down with a sip of coffee.

"*What?*"

Tess's face held a bunch of different expressions. Her eyes were sparkling and bright, much more lively than they'd been in a long time, probably since before Jack died. But her mouth was slightly turned down and the sound of her voice wasn't exactly troubled, but held a hint of worry.

"Last night I hooked up with Ford."

Lilly's eyes exploded open and her chin dropped to her chest. It was the last thing she expected to hear. "You what?!"

"I was in a really low place. I went for a drive and saw him at the office, so I stopped in."

Lilly waited for more. "And?"

"I seduced him," Tess whispered, her face flushing a lovely shade of pink. "I can't believe I did it."

Lilly laughed, relieved that no other tragedy had occurred. "I have to tell you, that's definitely not what I thought you were going to say."

"What did you think I was going to tell you?"

"I don't know, but not that you hooked up with your lawyer's brother."

"I won't lie. I felt a little ashamed of myself at first, but then I decided to get over it. I've spent a lot of time beating myself up over stupid shit and I didn't want to have any regrets."

Lilly grinned. "Good idea. I'm proud of you." She grabbed another piece of bacon and broke half of it off in one bite. "No details, no specifics. How was it?" Lilly loved Tess and they shared a lot of things, but the minutiae of their sex lives was not one of them.

Tess cocked her head to the side and smiled just a little bit. "Different."

"Just different?"

"It was good," Tess said softly. "*Very* good, actually. But it's hard not to compare him to Jack, ya know?"

"I do." Lilly was only four years older than Tess, but still, she had taken way more laps around the dating pool. "You're only 25," Lilly reminded. "And you've been in a very bad place for a while. I don't see anything wrong with it. You needed a release and Ford was it."

"Thanks, sis. I do feel a lot better today."

Lilly nodded and smiled at her little sister. She was going to do everything she could to keep Tess going up. "You look better. Did you get some sleep?"

"Yes, about six hours solid with no nightmares."

"Uh oh," Lilly teased. "You're going to have to ask him to move in until all this is over, if only to keep the bad dreams away." She poked Tess in the arm and gave her an exaggerated wink.

Tess snorted and rolled her eyes. "If only it were that easy. Actually, it's not going to happen again. We both know what a risk it was, and I can't do anything stupid anymore. Not until we figure out who killed Jack and I'm off the hook."

Lilly frowned and crossed her arms over her chest. "Well that sucks. I mean, you two would be a really cute couple. Kind of like beauty and the beast."

Tess raised an eyebrow at her and shook her head. "No way. We would not be good together."

"Why not?"

"Too much baggage. I may only have a couple of suitcases right now, but he's got a moving van full of it. It definitely wouldn't work out."

Lilly pursed her lips, looking unconvinced. *This is something I'll have to dig into with her, I see.* "Well, I wouldn't count him out."

"I already do."

"Yeah right," Lilly grumbled. "I reserve the right to say I told you so." There was something more to the story, but Tess wasn't willing to give it all up. That was okay. Lilly could be patient and wait it out.

"Did you ever do anything like this?"

Lilly munched on another piece of bacon and shrugged. "Yeah. After I divorced the 'toad', I had a couple of dalliances I never told anyone about." She tried to stay casual about it, not make a big deal, but she could feel the heat spreading across her face. It didn't escape her little sister's notice either.

"You're blushing!" Tess tossed a napkin at her.

"Oh stop!" Lilly snatched the paper in midair and fired it back. "It's not something I'm proud of. Neither one of my one-nighters were a tenth as good looking as Ford. But then again, I was wearing beer goggles."

They both started to laugh until neither one of them could get their breath. It took minutes for them to get control to the point where they could speak. "You sound like a guy, L. The kind of guy we call a douchebag."

"Yeah, I know. Like I said, I'm not proud of what I did and I can't think about it too much or take it too seriously, or I'll get depressed. Especially since I haven't had a boyfriend in God knows how long."

Tess frowned. "Is that what's going to happen to me? I'm going to get depressed about this too? I'm already on the brink of a nervous breakdown half the time."

"No, sis, you aren't. You didn't get divorced, you got widowed. There's a big difference. I also never got accused of murder and had all the financial shit to deal with that you do. You can't compare apples to oranges."

That was Tess, always overthinking things and second guessing herself. Sometimes it drove Lilly crazy, but what could she do? Her sister was her sister and all she could do was support her and tell her about her own experiences in life, even if it meant comparing apples to oranges.

"Just take it at face value. You needed someone and Ford was there. Did you ever stop to consider he might have needed you as much as you needed him?"

Tess took a sip of coffee and shook her head. "No, I didn't. He did tell me a little bit about his background. Sounded like he had a real shit childhood."

"There you go. Think of it like two ships passing in the night," Lilly suggested. *For now.*

Tess chuckled, but the ringing of her phone cut it off. She glanced around and saw it vibrating on the coffee table across the room. She darted over to snatch it up. "Shit, it's Hudson. He's been calling all morning."

"Why didn't you answer? Wouldn't talking to your lawyer be a pretty important thing to do right now?" Lilly admonished.

"Ordinarily, I'd say yes," Tess silenced the ringing and tossed the phone back on the table, "but since his brother didn't leave until after ten this morning, I wasn't really in a position to take his calls."

Lilly burst out laughing, rocking back and forth. "Oh, you dog!" She sobered abruptly and looked a little sad. "This sucks. I think Hudson has a little crush on you."

"I know. I think it's just a proximity thing, though. We're together a lot and he's handled so much for me that it's really only a lack of options. If he had a girlfriend or a social life, I don't think he'd look twice at me."

Lilly shrugged and her eyebrows popped up. "Hard to say."

Once again, Tess's phone began to ring. The Law & Order bong repeated itself for a solid thirty seconds.

"You really need to take his call, Tess. How many is that now?"

"I think it's on five. I guess I'm worried he'll hear something in my voice and just know what I did with Ford. That's the last thing I need for him to find out."

"He won't know," Lilly insisted. "Guys are clueless." She wasn't so sure, personally, but wasn't about to let Tess know that. She was here for support and encouragement, so that's what she would do. Nodding her head and twirling her hand, she urged Tess to answer the phone.

* * * * *

"I'm sorry, Hudson. I was sleeping." Tess listened to him upbraid her gently about the importance of being in contact. She didn't mind at all. "Yes, I can come to the office. Now? Well, my sister's here." She glanced over at Lilly, who was waving her arms and standing up to leave. "Maybe she can help. I'll bring her along." Lilly frowned but sat back down. "Yes, okay. We'll see you in about a half-hour."

"Why are you dragging me along?" Lilly demanded.

"Because you're my sister and I need your moral support." Tess flipped her hair back. "And you might be able to help me remember stuff." *And I need a buffer to put between Hudson and me so he won't know I slept with his brother.*

"All right. Hurry up, you said thirty minutes and I know how long you like to be in the bathroom."

Tess got up and walked toward the bedroom. At the last second, she turned and stuck her tongue out at her sister. Some things she would never outgrow.

Chapter 38

Tess kept finding herself distracted and would stare into Hudson's private office, as he perused the receipts and lists from her wedding file for the fiftieth time. She kept remembering what she had been doing just a few hours before, and each time Lilly would smack her in the arm to make her focus.

"I'm not seeing anything new," Hudson said finally, flopping onto the couch in frustration. "What about you?"

"It's all the same stuff I told you before," Tess answered, feeling equally disheartened. "We got a goody basket from Emily and Roger, but we never even opened it. Flowers came from my out of town family who couldn't attend. Three arrangements in all."

"Where the hell is Ford? He's usually good at this kind of stuff."

Tess watched him send a text and she imagined Ford's face when he received the message. *He probably doesn't want to be in the same room with me, any more than I want to be around him.*

As they sat in silence, Hudson waiting for a response from Ford and Lilly sifting through papers and receipts, Tess's mind wandered. Everything in the room reminded her of the night before. She shivered at the images of Ford's hands on her body as they floated through her mind like serene white clouds across a warm summer day. Giving herself a mental shake, she tried to send them away. She conjured storm clouds and pouring rain in her mind to erase the thoughts. Instead, she began fantasizing about what Ford would look like in the downpour.

"I need coffee!" she said suddenly, standing up and pacing around the room. "Should I make some fresh?"

"Shit, we're out." Hudson groaned. He got up and went to the cabinet and opened the door. "I was supposed to pick some up this morning but I forgot."

"Why don't I go get some?" Tess grabbed her purse and shot out the door like a racehorse out of the gate. She needed to get away from the scene of her sexual crime. With her head down, she burrowed into her purse for her keys as she fast-walked toward her car.

"Hey now."

She skidded to a halt to see Ford standing right in front of her, a drink carrier with four Biggby Coffee cups in his hand and a grocery bag in the other. "Shit!"

"Yeah, shit. If you'd have spilled this all over me, I'd have been pissed."

"Sorry!" Tess reached for the bag to ease his burden. "It's not like it would have been on purpose." She smirked at him and he returned it, seeming perfectly at ease with her.

"Course not, but it would have been a waste of good coffee and I couldn't forgive that."

He started to move forward toward the office door, but Tess stopped him. She needed to talk to him for a minute and not in front of the others.

"Is everything okay?" Ford asked.

"Yes," she assured him. "It is, really. I'm just a little nervous about being with you in front of Hudson. I guess I feel a little embarrassed."

He nodded his head and gave her a genuine smile, one of the few she'd ever seen cross his face. "I understand. It could be awkward. But he texted me that Lilly is here too. Did you say anything to her?"

Tess shifted from one foot to the other while avoiding his eyes.

"I can see that you did. She's a cool one, your sister. She'll make sure to keep everything on track. Come on, before the coffee gets cold."

Ford walked her back into the office, holding the door for her to enter first.

"Look what I found! Should we keep him?"

Tess wanted to sink into the floor and disappear. She meant it as a joke, but knew exactly how it sounded to Lilly and Ford. Hudson had no clue, thankfully, and had eyes only for the cup of coffee his brother held out to him.

"Hey Ford," Lilly said casually enough. When Hudson's back was turned, she gave him a pronounced wink and then put her hand over her mouth to keep from laughing. Tess crossed the room in three steps to give her a swift kick in the shin.

"Ladies."

"What's in the bag?" Hudson asked as he blew on the hot beverage and then took a sip.

"More coffee and some brownies. I know they're your favorite."

Tess handed the bag to Hudson, who began foraging inside. When he lifted a square, plastic container of brownies out of the bag, it was like someone threw cold water into her face. She shivered and then almost immediately her entire body became hot and she felt the familiar buzzing just before a faint.

"I remember something," Tess whispered. "*I remember something!*" Lilly jumped out of her chair and rushed to her sister's side. "My coworkers sent me a huge pan of brownies with two mugs and homemade chai tea! Lilly? Do you remember that pretty basket I told you about? It was on the table. Jack ate some of the brownies the morning of the wedding!"

Tess began to shake and her face went white with the memory. It was like she was back in her kitchen on the day of wedding: Jack leaning against the counter, arms crossed, laughing about something. He said he was hungry, then spotted a basket on the counter. His hands rummaging around inside until he found the plate of brownies wrapped in silver cellophane with a gold bow. The crackling and crinkling as he ripped the plastic off and pealed one of the heavy, thick squares from the mound. The cloying smell of chocolate mingling with the smell of coffee throughout the room. Jack loved brownies. They were his favorite. She could clearly see the little brown dots at the corners of his mouth and on his chin.

Both Hudson and Ford were at her side as her knees buckled and she sunk to the floor. They each lifted an arm and helped her to the couch. Ford knelt in front of her and lifted her chin with a finger. "Breathe. Slowly."

Lilly sat beside her and grabbed her hands to massage them. "Lean forward if you think you're going to faint!"

"I'm okay," Tess whispered. "I'm okay." Her face crumpled but she didn't cry. "Why didn't I remember that? *How could I have forgotten?*"

Lilly pulled her sister into her arms and rocked her but still Tess didn't have any tears. She only felt a mixture of relief and dread. Glad that she remember something vital, but unsure of what the revelation would mean. Someone in her *office* had sent that basket. What did that *mean?*

Hudson got her a bottle of water. "Here." He twisted the cap open for her.

Tess took it with a pained smile. "Thank you." She took a sip and then accepted a tissue from Lilly just in case. "Why would anyone from my office want to hurt Jack? It doesn't make any sense."

"Maybe not, but it's something. Ford, you need to question everyone from the office. Give me the names of every person who works for Dr. Guildford."

Tess fired off the names of all the nurses, the office manager, the receptionists, and the other billers. "I've known most of these people for the last six years. I worked as a receptionist there before I became a transcriptionist."

"Most of?" Hudson asked. "Start with who you've known the least."

"There's Mike, the newest nurse. He started about two years ago, I guess. And then there's Julia and Kay. They're the billers who came on about three years ago when Amanda retired. Amanda was with Dr. Guildford for twenty some years."

Hudson scribbled furiously on the page, and Tess despised how mixed up she felt. She was giving him the names of people she liked and respected. She loved her job and the people she did it with and for. How could any of them have been responsible for Jack's death?

"This is great, Tess."

"Is it?" she snapped.

Hudson's head popped up and his face was full of confusion. Within a second, his face flushed red with shame at the realization of what he'd just said.

"I'm sorry, Tess, I didn't mean..."

"These people were my friends. I may very well be ratting out the person or people who killed Jack. How do you think that makes me feel?"

Tears were a definite possibility now, Tess realized, but she bit down hard on her tongue to keep them at bay. Maybe another time, when she was alone and no one could witness it, she would have a breakdown and cry her eyes out while the cats surrounded her and she could let loose all the emotions she was feeling. But not now.

Chapter 39

Dr. Guildford shook his head in disbelief after Ford explained to him who he was, why he was there, and what he wanted.

"Murder? Are you serious?"

"Very, sir." Ford's face was serious and concerned. "Tess will need character witnesses. I'd like to speak with everyone in the office, if that's all right."

"Of course, whatever you need. I don't believe for one second Tess had anything to do with her husband's death. I've known her for many years. She's a lovely girl."

"Yes," Ford agreed, clearing his throat. *You have no idea.* "Your cooperation will be extremely helpful. When can I get started?"

"Now, of course," Dr. Guildford said. "Come with me and we'll talk to my office manager first. She can help you to arrange whatever you need."

Ford was taken to a back office, away from patient rooms, to speak with Daphne Moore, the doctor's long time office manager. She was a tall woman with light brown and graying hair styled in a tidy French twist. She wore a simple navy pantsuit and no makeup. There didn't seem to be any frills about her at all, and she greeted him with a firm handshake and obvious confidence. The word that came to Ford's mind was "handsome." Daphne Moore was a handsome woman – not necessarily beautiful, but attractive. While Dr. Guildford explained why Ford was there, he watched the expressions on Daphne's face go from surprise to confusion to horror. That was definitely a good sign. Her eyes were honest and Ford didn't think he would have any problem getting truthful answers from her.

"Do you mind if I record our conversation?" He pulled his phone out of his pocket and set it on her desk. He also made sure he had his notebook and pen at the ready in case he wanted to make specific notes or questions.

"No, by all means," Daphne said, obviously upset by the circumstances. She rubbed her forehead and then rested her palm against her mouth. "I just can't believe all of this."

"You can only imagine how shocked Tess is." Ford gave her an understanding and sympathetic look. "How long have you known her?"

"Since the day she began working here. I hired her, for heaven's sakes!"

"Had you ever met Jack?"

Daphne nodded. "Yes, on several occasions. When Tess was a receptionist, he often came in to take her to lunch or drive her home. He always came when we had staff parties when significant others were invited. He was such a nice boy and grew into a wonderful man." She smiled sadly. "I was there, at the wedding. I saw him on the floor in the church." Her bottom lip trembled and her eyes welled with the smallest hint of tears. Reaching for a tissue, she sniffed and patted her nose. "I don't think I'll ever forget Tess screaming. It was the most horrible thing I've ever heard."

Ford squirmed in his chair, unable to truly imagine the torment in the sounds Tess must have made, yet feeling a deep sense of sympathy for her. He knew what that kind of anguish was like. He knew what kind of a dark place it came from.

"How many others from the staff attended the wedding?" Ford found his voice and tried to get the interview moving again.

"Just me, actually. Tess invited the entire staff, even though we all knew she couldn't really afford it. They were trying to keep the wedding small. So, we decided that we would all decline the invitation and have a little party here for her, then celebrate after she got back from her honeymoon. In the end, though, I decided I couldn't miss it. I practically watched her grow up."

Ford chewed on the end of his pen and wrote the word "party" in the notebook. "When did you have it?"

Daphne pursed her lips and thought for a second. "It was the Wednesday before the wedding. It was a surprise shower. I called her that morning and asked her to come in to the office for some special project or something, I don't remember what exactly. When she got here, we were all in the kitchen. There were gifts and food and a cake."

"What kind of gifts?"

"Oh, the usual. We got things from her bridal registry, some people gave just a card and some money."

"Was there anything that stuck out? Premade gift baskets? Plants or flowers?"

Daphne's eyes lit up. "Yes! Dr. Guildford asked that we get her several flower arrangements and plants. And there was a gift basket with lots of goodies in it for the day of the wedding. Brownies, cookies, teas, coffee. It was a little bit of a running joke among the women in the office. They all remembered their wedding days and how they hadn't eaten anything. Stories about almost passing out at the altar. We wanted to make sure Tess and Jack had something to eat."

Jackpot! Ford forced himself to sit still and not give Daphne any hint of his relief.

"Where did that particular basket come from?"

"It didn't come from anywhere. Between all of us, everything was homemade. Well, except the coffee and tea. Those came from Biggby,

Tess's favorite. But everyone made something different to put in a basket we got at the dollar store." Daphne eyed him with suspicion. "Why? Does that matter?"

"I can't really disclose too much," Ford explained, "but it might."

Daphne leaned back in her chair and frowned. "I understand."

"I really appreciate your candor, Ms. Moore," Ford told her, as he stopped the recording app. "I think that's all I have for you right now. Could I start speaking to the other employees now?"

"Sure. Do you have any particular order you want them called in? You can use my office."

"No, whoever is free is fine. I don't want to disrupt the day any more than I already have. I just want to ask some general questions about what kind of relationship people had with Tess. She'll need all the character witnesses she can get. I'm here to determine who would make the best ones."

Daphne nodded. "I certainly hope you choose me. There is absolutely no way in hell she had anything to do with Jack's death. I watched those two grow up together. I never saw two people more in love than them."

Ford forced a smile on his face. *I'm getting a little tired of hearing how much in love they were.* He reached to shake her hand as she stood up. "I appreciate that. Hopefully this won't take long." He threw her a charming smile to help her relax.

"Not everyone is in today, though. Mike called off sick this morning and Sarabeth doesn't work today."

Ford jotted the names of the missing employees into the notebook. There was no way they could have known he was coming. "That's fine."

One by one, Daphne sent in each employee at the doctor's office. Sometimes Ford asked the same questions in the same order. Other times he mixed things up. He felt fairly confident that Ms. Moore would make sure there weren't any extraneous conversations between the employees, but he couldn't be positive. He knew his presence was a distraction and tongues wagged no matter what he tried to do to stop it. His biggest concern was that the two missing people would get the heads up about the questioning. If either of them were involved, they might bolt. It wasn't that much of a worry. Ford had his ways of finding people. He just hated to think about the time it would take to do it.

As he left the doctor's office two hours later, Ford was feeling hopeful, but not nearly as confident as he wanted to be. Molly Kincaid had baked the brownies and Madeline Cole had assembled the basket. It did not explain how the poison had gotten into the brownies though. Molly was a kind, sweet woman who had cried real tears upon hearing that Jack's death was suspicious and that Tess was a person of interest. Madeline had been just as affected by the news, but her reaction was one of anger and profanity. Neither woman seemed to have any kind of negative thought about Tess or Jack, or a desire to hurt them in any way.

As he rode back to the office, thoughts of his night with Tess tried to push their way to the front of his brain and he struggled to shut them away. The distraction of those memories was not what he needed then. He had to keep his eye on the prize, which was keeping Tess out of jail and finding the real murderer.

Chapter 40

Mike Andrews walked into Dr. Guildford's office ten minutes early and hung up his coat in the usual spot. After storing his lunch in the fridge, he moved through the halls towards his desk, whistling the theme from Star Trek. He smiled at the other nurses and staff, feeling good. As he approached his cube, he adjusted his scrubs. It was always hard for him to find them to fit his well-muscled chest, arms, and legs. He checked himself in the reflection on a metal c-fold dispenser to make sure his shiny, black hair was still pulled back into a tight ponytail. Giving himself a grin and a wink, he whipped his neck left and right enjoying the pop and crack of the muscles and tendons.

A post-it on the front of his computer screen caught his attention immediately and he pulled it off to read before sitting down. Ms. Moore wanted to see him right away.

Frowning, Mike crumpled the note and tossed it into the garbage. He turned to go straight to Ms. Moore's office, but Sarabeth the biller caught him by the arm as she walked into the room. "Did you hear?"

"What?"

"There was an investigator here asking questions. I was off yesterday so no one will tell me anything. We're both supposed to report to Ms. Moore right away."

"I got a note. Why don't you go first, and then I'll go after, okay?"

Sarabeth looked nervous and her graying hair quivered on her head as she nodded. "Okay."

When she was gone, Mike fished his cell phone out of his pocket. His previously good mood was shattered. He shot off a quick text: We've got a problem.

Chapter 41

David Kingston slammed the phone down and cursed. Once again, the investigating cop on Jack's case hadn't given him squat. He refused to answer any questions and would not tell David what he was doing or where he was going with the case. This was the third time, and the thought of Tess Langford spending more time out and about, instead of in jail, made him want to storm over there and demand answers.

One more time, he would have to make the call to his parents to give them bad news. The last two times he'd done it by phone, but this time he would have to make a trip to the house. There was no way around it. His gut clenched with anxiety at the thought. He hated seeing the looks on their faces whenever he had to confront them about Jack.

Looking at his watch, it was almost five. Might as well knock off early and get this done. Packing up his briefcase, David left his office and told the receptionist he was going home for the evening.

On his way to his parents' house, David stewed over how the scene would go down. His father would rage. His mother would cry. And he would have to do damage control, calming his father and comforting his mother. Frankly, he was getting sick and tired of the whole business. More than once, the idea of having Tess taken out crossed his mind. But then he'd be no better than she. There was no way he was going to risk going to prison for life. Plus, if she died, then all the money would revert to the beneficiaries in the will she no doubt already had prepared.

David knew the police were trying to work up a solid case against Tess, but it was all circumstantial at this point. Yes, Jack had been poisoned and yes, Tess was the only one with Jack for the hours leading up to the wedding. But they still didn't know how she'd given him the poison and her grieving widow act was a good one. She was fooling everyone into believing she had nothing to do with it. David worried that a jury would either find her innocent or be hung and not able to convict her. How would his parents be able to live with something like that?

Pulling into the driveway of his childhood home, David sighed. His mother was puttering with the plants in her flowerbeds and shooing the dogs away from them. *Why does she plant shit she knows could hurt them? Whatever.* His dad sat on the porch reading the Wall Street Journal. They both waved to him and smiled, but he couldn't make himself return the gesture.

"What's wrong now?" Roger asked, as they approached him. He crossed the driveway so that he wouldn't have to shout.

"I got stonewalled again. The police won't tell me a thing."

"Dammit!" Roger roared as Emily's pruning shears clattered to the cement.

"Why?" Emily whined. "Why won't they talk to us?"

"I don't know, Mom."

Just then, a buzzing noise came from the pocket in Emily's gardening apron. With a look of embarrassment, she fumbled for her phone and pulled it out. "Excuse me, won't you?" She stepped away to examine the device. David watched after her, but Roger pulled him away.

"You have to do something, David. Your mother can't go on like this. This needs to get on the fast track, otherwise we'll never be able to fix whatever damage is being done to my investments."

Pulling his gaze away from his mother, who was going into the house and followed by the dogs, David cocked his head to the side. "You mean Jack's investments, don't you?"

Clearing his throat, Roger glanced down at his feet. "Yes, yes, of course. You know what I mean."

David's bottom lip pouted out the slightest bit and he shrugged his shoulders. "Believe me, Dad, I'm as angry about this as you. But there's nothing I can do."

"You need to figure out *what* to do, son. You owe it to your brother!"

David controlled the urge to scream at his father with gargantuan effort. *Don't you think I know that?* He wanted justice for Jack as much as anyone, but the law was the law. There were steps and procedures to follow, no matter who you were. They would have to be patient and let the case develop. David wished he could take some of their pain away and comfort them, but he didn't know how to do it.

The two of them continued to stand on the hot cement in silence. The late afternoon sun was like fire and David could feel himself sweating inside his expensive suit. All he wanted to do was go home and take a shower.

Just then, Emily came out of the house and returned to her husband's side. She no longer wore her apron and had changed clothes. "That was my friend, Moira. She needs some help with a personal problem. Roger, why don't you and David have dinner together? I'm not sure when I'll be back."

"Yeah, sure dear." Roger pecked her on the cheek and Emily walked briskly to her car. She got in and drove away at a faster pace than David thought safe.

"Moira? Who's Moira?" David asked.

Roger shrugged. "Hell if I know. You know your mother. She always has some friend in need or committee meeting. Wanna grill some steaks?"

There goes my shower. But he couldn't leave his dad alone after another disappointment. "Yeah, okay. Whatever you want, Dad." David watched his mother's tail lights disappear down the street.

Chapter 42

"I'm not seeing much here." Hudson scratched his head and sifted through all the notes Ford had taken during his interviews. "Unless we polygraph them all, I don't see which person shows any signs of having something out for Tess."

"There are still two more I have to talk to," Ford said. "Some guy nurse and a woman in billing."

"A guy?"

Ford shrugged.

"Well, I know guys are nurses too. You just don't see them in a private practice. Usually in hospitals." Hudson leaned back and clasped his hands behind his head. "When are you going?"

"I'm on my way there now."

"Good. We need to find something, Ford, anything."

"Doing my best, brother," Ford sighed. "My police contacts are avoiding me. I can't get anyone to talk." He turned away to stare out the plate glass window of the office.

Hudson watched his brother watching traffic. "You want to tell me what's bugging you?"

Ford stiffened but didn't turn back around.

"I know something's going on, Ford. You might as well tell me because I'll figure it out sooner or later."

"Nothing's wrong."

"Bullshit," Hudson spat. "You've been more distant than usual. I can hardly get you in the same room with Tess. You don't pick up the phone or respond to texts like you used to. Spit it out." Hudson got up and crossed the physical distance to his older brother, wishing he could bridge the mental divide as well. He nudged Ford with his shoulder. "Out with it."

Ford sighed, but continued to stare out the window. "Just frustrated, brother. We don't usually have cases like this. I don't like not being able to figure shit out."

Hudson nodded and stuffed his hands in his pockets. "I hear you. You don't know how many times I've wished I hadn't taken Jack Kingston's call. And then I feel guilty thinking that because then where the hell would Tess be now? Everything happens for a reason."

Ford finally looked at Hudson and gave him a grave smile. "You're probably right."

"I know I am. And we *will* figure this out."

Hudson went back to the table and slumped into the chair. He picked up a piece of paper and then put it back down again. Then he shuffled for another. Ford turned to observe him. "I'm going to read every word in this file a million times if I have to. I'm going to think of what we haven't thought of. And you're going to help me."

Ford stepped over to the table and put his fist out. Hudson bumped it with his own.

"Now get going and interview those people."

* * * * *

Ford smoked and rode his bike to Dr. Guildford's office. He knew he dodged a bullet with his brother and felt a little shaky from the close call. No matter what happened in his life, Ford knew that Hudson loved him. He would be there, through everything, even when they fought. He'd been about as close as he'd ever been to spilling the beans about Tess, but his instincts made him clam up at the last second. It wouldn't serve anyone's purpose to have Hudson pissed off. And he'd asked Tess to promise to keep it a secret. Who was he to be a hypocrite?

Hooking up with Tess wasn't something that could lead anywhere, and Hudson would know that as well as Ford did. He knew his brother's counsel would be to stay away from her, that she'd been hurt enough in life. She didn't need some worthless biker guy coming into her life. *Not when she could have the upstanding lawyer*, he thought peevishly. Ford knew damn well Hudson had a little thing for Tess. He smiled sadly, thinking how sibling rivalry was always present, no matter what the circumstance.

Ford climbed off his motorcycle and hung the helmet on the back, cutting off his internal monologue about Tess and Hudson. Shaking his shoulders and taking a deep breath, he ambled to the doc's door and went inside. The waiting room was empty of patients and he was glad for that. At his last visit, he'd gotten quite a few ornery looks from what appeared to be a mostly geriatric patient pool.

Walking to the window, he didn't even have to rap on the glass before the receptionist opened it. "Hi. Ms. Moore is waiting for you. I'll bring you right back."

Ford nodded and within a moment, a door leading into the belly of the office opened and the pretty young girl motioned him forward. He followed her back to Daphne Moore's office. She sat waiting behind her desk, hands folded on the top. She looked grim and displeased. He wasn't prepared for the defensive look in her eyes and hoped he wasn't in for trouble.

"Good afternoon." He greeted her with a firm handshake and strong eye contact which she returned, but there was no warmth in it. He sensed a distinct change in attitude from the day before.

"Yes, well, it was. I'm afraid I can't let you speak with anyone else in the office. Dr. Guildford got in touch with his lawyer and he's concerned about liability." Ford's exhale of frustration was not lost on Ms. Moore. She glowered at him and placed her palms flat on the desk. "I'm sorry this doesn't please you."

"No, it doesn't. What kind of liability?" Ford demanded.

"He didn't tell me." Ford could see the lie in her eyes on that one. "And I'm not at liberty to say more to you than that. The bottom line is you're not allowed to interview any more employees."

"Just to be clear, this was supposed to be for Tess's benefit. Character witnesses, not interviews. What liability could there possibly be?" Ford folded his arms across his chest. "I think I need to speak with the doctor. Now."

"I'm afraid that won't be possible, either. Dr. Guildford left early this morning for a medical conference in Tahiti. He doesn't return for a week."

Ford wanted to growl, but settled for a disgusted sigh instead. Glancing around the office in frustration, he noticed a picture on the credenza behind Ms. Moore's desk. It was a photograph of the staff taken at Christmas time. Everyone was crowded together and smiling for the camera, but the only person not looking directly at the lens was Daphne Moore. Her eyes were firmly fixed on Thomas Guildford.

"That's a nice picture," Ford said, as he leaned across the desk to get a better look.

"Uh, thank you," she said, shifting in her seat, and clearing her throat. She played with the pearl necklace around her neck. "It was taken this past Christmas."

"Tell me, is Dr. Guildford married?" he asked. He watched her drop the necklace with a jolt and then she folded her hands together and squeezed. He could see her fingers getting whiter as the color was choked off from the pressure.

Sitting up straighter, her eyes narrowed with annoyance. "I don't see how that's any of your business, but yes he is."

Ford cocked his head to the side and stepped closer to the desk. "Yeah? How long has he been married?"

"I don't have to answer your questions."

Ford didn't have to be a psychiatrist to see the pain in Ms. Moore's eyes. Softening his demeanor, he took a seat and lounged in the chair, which flustered her even more. It was evident she wanted nothing more than for him to leave immediately. "Well, if the doc took his bride with him to Tahiti, then how much of a medical conference could it be? But if the missus stayed home, then I'm more inclined to believe it was a business trip."

Ms. Moore's eyebrows knitted together in thought, and she slowly nodded. "I see your point. I also realize how unsettling it must be that the doctor changed his mind about being cooperative in less than twenty-four hours." Ms. Moore's eyes clouded over with a veil of peevishness. "Yes, *Mrs.* Guildford accompanied Doctor on the trip."

Ford almost laughed out loud as she spat the words, jealousy practically dripping off her tongue. It was obvious that she carried a torch for the doc and probably had for a long time. Reaching across the desk, he patted her hands. "It's okay. Like I said, this was just to find people to speak on Tess's behalf. There's nothing for anyone to worry about. They've all been talking already, right?"

Ms. Moore sighed and relaxed a little. She unclenched her hands and shook out her fingers. "Yes. There was no way to stop it, once you questioned Parker Lockwood. She's the office gossip. I wish now I'd left her for last."

Ford smiled. "No worries. You can tell the doc I'm through here."

"Please tell Tess we're so sorry about all this."

"Will do."

Ford gave her a two-fingered salute and then left the office while Ms. Moore sat back down and returned to her computer screen. The angle of her doorway prevented her from seeing him take the wrong turn at the end of the hall. Moving in a stealthy manner, he poked his nose here and there into offices and empty patient examination rooms, taking note of how he was received, if anyone saw him. He was counting on the usual looks of surprise, but was hoping he would see something more from Mike the nurse or the other woman he hadn't spoken to, if he happened across them.

When he finally did come upon the one large room where several desks and cubicles were located, he knew he hit pay dirt. It was where the nurses sat to finish their notes and paperwork, the billers had their workstations, and most of the patient records were housed.

Ford leaned his head in the room and immediately almost all eyes were on him. He recognized most of the faces, except for the lady with the grey hair who looked like a deer caught in the headlights. Ford felt around in his brain for his alarm beacon but it didn't go off for her. It shrieked for the one guy in the room refusing to look his way. Mike the nurse was sitting at this desk, typing into a laptop. Not once did he look up to see what had caught everyone else's attention.

"Hi there! Just wanted to thank you all for talking with me yesterday. I left my card with Ms. Moore, so if anyone has any questions, feel free to give me a ring."

Ford waited for the nods of recognition and polite smiles, which came within seconds. And still, Mike Andrews never met his eye.

Chapter 43

Sitting on her patio with a glass of iced tea, Tess had more time on her hands than she knew what to do with, not having a steady job to work. She took Hudson's calls on the first ring so she could help in any way, but other than remembering the brownies, she wasn't doing much good in that department. She tried to keep living like a normal person, even though a huge pile of cash was sitting in her checking account. She hadn't even bothered to make an appointment with the finance guy because she was pretty sure it was all going to be taken away when she got arrested for murder. She talked to her parents and sister multiple times a day, but beyond cleaning the apartment and answering the phone, Tess spent her time bored to the teeth or filled with anxiety as she fantasized about prison life.

In a small way, she knew the time away from most of the world was doing her a little bit of good. As she sipped her tea and watched the cats roam around the grass, firmly harnessed and leashed, she thought about writing in her journal but didn't feel like it right then. She usually did write in it a few times a day, though. She kept making lists and notes about things to do. She wrote about Jack constantly. The day after her hookup with Ford, Tess wrote a five-page entry apologizing to him. She knew technically that she hadn't cheated, but her conscience bothered her just the same. When she read the pages a couple of days later, it made her cry for both Jack and herself. She tore them out of the book and sealed them in an envelope, calling it the last love letter she would write to Jack. Then she put the envelope in the bottom of her jewelry box.

In the days while she prayed and waited for Hudson to find a way out of the mess, Tess talked out loud to Jack, like he was really still there. She never did it in front of anyone, or else everyone would really think she was off her nut, but the sound of her own voice in the empty apartment was comforting. She wasn't crazy enough to believe he would answer, but sometimes she got a sense of what she knew he would say. Not only had he been her boyfriend, fiancé and briefly her husband, he'd been her very best friend in life. Thinking she could still bounce her ideas off of him made her feel better. Those conversations also made her feel less guilty about Ford.

And she did think about Ford. A lot. Probably more than she should. She talked to Lilly about him, too, but her sister was being more of a pain in the ass where that subject was concerned. Lilly kept insisting that she should go for it with Ford, but Tess insisted he had too much of a backstory. She had kind of admitted that she wished it wasn't the case, but she wanted to be realistic about it all. Like her sister. Lilly always looked at things honestly and Tess wanted to be more like that. Ford had walls built up around him to keep people out. It was pretty obvious that his crappy childhood had really messed him up where women were concerned and Tess didn't want to fall into the trap of thinking she could fix him. She had enough shit to deal with, she didn't need a project guy. Sure, he had come clean and told her about his background and that was a point in his favor, but what else was he not telling her, how much more to the story was there?

Tess contented herself with the rolling movie in her head of their passionate night together and nothing more. But every once in a while, Lilly's voice would pop into her head. "Go for more," it would say.

"Take a chance." Tess kept pushing those thoughts away. Ford had been a buoy in her ocean of grief. She reached for him and he pulled her in. He had mountains of baggage in his past and she was in no position to help anyone sort through their suitcases. She had her own to unpack.

The cats were finished with the explorations and were now winding themselves around the legs of her chair. Tess finished the last of her tea and went to the door to slide it open. Timothy and Spencer tried to race inside, but scared the hell out of themselves when the patio chair tried to follow them. Tess laughed and set the glass on the table. "Come here, you goofuses." She grabbed Timmy and hooked her fingers into one of the loops of his harness and unclasped the leash, then did the same to Spencer. She carried them inside and set them down. Off they went to bathe the outdoors off themselves.

From the kitchen, she heard her phone begin to ring. *Law & Order strikes again.* "Hello, good lawyer," she said, after swiping to accept the call.

"Good afternoon. You sound chipper."

"Doing my best. What's up?"

"Ford thinks he's onto something."

Tess's heart skipped a beat. "Really? What?"

"The male nurse at Dr. Guildford's office seemed suspicious. What can you tell me about him?"

Gnawing on her thumbnail, Tess thought for a moment. "Not much. I never really saw him. Whenever I'd bring work into the office or come to pick up my check, he was with patients or at lunch or sometimes not there at all. I saw him at office parties or meetings and he seemed fine. You don't think he put the poison in the brownies do you?"

"We don't know," Hudson admitted. "But Ford thought he was off and I trust my brother's instincts."

"Me too."

"Do you think he might have had a secret thing for you? A crush maybe? If he was the one who did the poisoning, could it have been because he wanted Jack out of the way?"

"No!" Tess shook her head and frowned. "Not at all. Like I said, we never had that much contact. Plus, he would talk about his girlfriend all the time to the other girls in the office. I only know that because they would tell me. He doted on her and all the other girls always wished their spouses would fawn over them that way."

"Damn," Hudson muttered. "That would have been a good path to take. Well, Ford is going to try and catch him outside the office to question him because Dr. Guildford had a sudden change of heart. Apparently, he's worried and he won't let us talk to anyone else on the premises."

Tess frowned. "That's weird. Doc's known me for years. That seems more suspicious to me than anything else."

"I'll make a note of it for Ford. Unfortunately, he's left for some medical conference this morning and won't be back for a week."

"Let me guess. Tahiti, right?"

"How did you know that?"

"He goes there every year right about this time. Calls it a medical conference so he can write it off. He takes a couple of classes online so he can sorta make it legit." Tess snorted.

Hudson chuckled. "Well, I know lawyers who do the same thing, so I won't judge. But if he does this every year, I'm not sure we have anything to worry about with him. He's only freaked out because he thinks he might get sued by one of his employees. Don't let your fear get the best of you, okay?"

"All right." Tess sighed. "Is Ford there?"

"No, he's out following Mike."

"Okay. Tell him I said thanks when you see him again."

"I will."

Hudson was silent for a moment and Tess asked if he was still there.

"Yeah, I'm still here. Look, I need to ask you something."

Tess tensed up. The tone of Hudson's voice changed and he no longer sounded... lawyerly to her. "Yes?"

"I think something's going on with Ford. He's been different lately and I'm worried about him. He hasn't said anything to you has he? I mean, not that he would, but he's funny like that."

Tess was scared to answer too quickly or not fast enough. "No, he hasn't spoken to me about anything except the case."

"Okay. It's just me then. The whole brother thing, I guess."

"Yeah, it must be. I don't know him very well..." Tess trailed off, hoping the conversation would come to an end. The last thing she wanted to discuss with Hudson was his brother. *Ugh, please be the end of the call!*

"I'll give you a call when I know more."

"I'll be here."

Tess ended the call and put her phone back on the charger. She retrieved her glass from outside and refilled it, all the time racking her brain for any information about Mike. Everything she'd told Hudson was true. She hardly ever saw him and he wouldn't have been on her radar, anyway. The first time they met, he'd shaken her hand and been polite. Tess had thought he was okay. Not too tall, not too short. Plain brown hair and eyes. He was unremarkable then and left no real imprint on her memories now.

She sure was thinking about Mike Andrews now, though. Ford was out following him around and that worried her. What if Mike was the one who put the poison in the brownies? What if he went after Ford?

Chapter 44

Ford sat in Hudson's truck about a block away from Dr. Guildford's office, waiting for the staff to close up shop for the day. Closing in on six o'clock, he counted heads as employees emptied out of the building like rats off a sinking ship. He was lying in wait for one particular rodent.

Mike Andrews was the second to last person to exit, followed by Daphne Moore. He stood beside the office manager as she locked the door and set the alarm. They walked side by side to cars in the parking lot. He waved goodbye to several others and then got into a red Prius. Ford watched as he pulled out his cell phone and called someone. The conversation seemed animated and from his vantage point, Ford thought Mike looked irritated. There was a lot of talking with his hands, a couple of smacks to the steering wheel and then one massive fist slam on the dashboard.

When he finally began to pull out of the lot, Ford put the truck in gear, preparing to follow him. Mike putted his way through St. Clair Shores, then into Roseville, ending up in the south end of Warren. He parked in the driveway of a fairly run down house and got out. He unlocked the door and went inside.

Once he was gone, Ford pulled the tuck up in front of the house, leaving the tinted windows up to hide his face. Using his phone, he took pictures of the Prius and the front of the house, including the address. He waited a while before getting out of the truck and sneaking up to the Prius, where he placed a sensor underneath the driver's side back wheel well so he could track the car if necessary. Then he drove back to the office.

As Ford downloaded the photos to the computer and texted the license plate information to his contact at the police department to research, he closed his eyes and rubbed his face. He was exhausted from running constantly and not sleeping at night. Never having been much of a dreamer in the past, he sure was having nightmares now. Some involved Tess in prison. Some were about his brother and Tess in bed together. But the worst of them involved Jack's killer going after her. It was driving him crazy to the point where he was beginning to regret ever having spent the night with Tess. Ford hated the idea of regretting it because he had needed a release just as much as she had. But the aftermath was draining him emotionally and mentally. He was struggling to keep focus. He found himself losing his patience and control when people didn't give him what he wanted, all because he was feeling more concern for his client than he should.

When all the photos were uploaded, Ford scrolled through them. The folder contained all of the photos he had taken since the case began. A splash of yellow caught his eye from one photo to another. Clicking to look at the previous shot, it was Roger and Emily's home. In the front of the house, the flowerbeds were in full bloom with some kind of exotic looking yellow plants. That was nothing out of the ordinary. What was unusual was that Mike Andrews's house had the exact same blooms surrounding the front of his home.

Ford grabbed his helmet and ran out of the office to his motorcycle. It was now well after eight o'clock and he raced through the streets toward the Kingston house. Leaving his bike in the parking lot of a sandwich shop at the corner, Ford walked the half a block to stand in front of the house next to the Kingston's. There were no lights on and the driveway was empty of cars. Walking slowly and quietly, Ford crept across the lawn to the flowerbeds. Grabbing a handful of the yellow plants, he yanked them out by the roots, and hid them inside his jacket as he jogged back to his bike.

Ford stored the flowers in his saddlebag and fifteen minutes later he was on the street and idling as quietly as he could until he was in front of Mike Andrews's house. Frowning, Ford noticed that there were lights on inside. It was going to be tricky to get up close enough to the house to grab some of the flowers without being noticed or tipping off a neighbor. Two doors down, one of the houses was boarded up, so Ford took a chance parking in front of it. Scanning the area, he noticed that most houses were dark. Taking a chance, he sprinted to the front yard of Mike's house and grabbed a couple of plants then raced back to his bike. No dogs barked and no one noticed him.

Back at the office, he carefully placed the flowers from Mike's house into a Ziploc bag and labeled it, then did the same with the blossoms from the Kingston house. First thing in the morning, he would take the bags to the best chemistry buddy he had so he could determine if they were exactly the same. They sure looked identical to his untrained eye. But if his suspicions were correct, and he had no doubt they were, Ford felt confident he had the murder weapon in his hands.

Chapter 45

Ford pushed the motorcycle up to ninety miles per hour as he raced along I-696 on his way back to the office from his buddy Boyle's place. He hadn't understood a quarter of what Boyle said, but the way he explained it, Ford felt more hopeful than he had in days. The plants were a perfect match and Boyle was convinced that they could have been the flowers responsible for creating the poison that killed Jack. He was going to do some more tests, but when Ford got jumpy and wanted to go back to the office, Boyle had turned him loose.

Ford hated obeying the speed limits in the city proper, but did so. The last thing he wanted was to catch a ticket and further delay his arrival. As he pulled into the lot, he squealed the tires in his haste. Walking through the door, Hudson was sitting on the outer couch looking like he hadn't slept in days.

"Where have you been?" he asked, his voice tired and surly. Ford thought it was probably how his own voice sounded much of the time, sealing their kinship yet again.

"I have been out solving the case."

Hudson's eyes bugged out. "What?"

"Well, sort of."

Ford explained what had happened when he was looking through his surveillance photos. He couldn't help but feel proud of himself that he'd finally been able to find something to make the case turn a corner.

Instead of getting a high five or words of praise, Hudson groaned.

"What's wrong?"

"Well, this could be great news, except that you used a known drug dealer to do your dirty work. There's no way this will stand up in court. We need to get the plants to a reputable lab as soon as possible. Did you bring them back?"

"No," Ford growled. "I left them with Boyle. It doesn't matter at this stage if it stands up in court because Tess hasn't been charged. All we need to do is give the police somewhere else to look."

"I see your point." Hudson sighed and hauled himself up off the couch. "But it's another added step if they don't believe us. Just tell Boyle not to destroy those plants entirely in case we need to send more samples somewhere else."

"Fine."

Ford wanted to grumble some more but decided against it. Hudson was right, although he still could have given up an atta boy or thank you. He sat down behind the secretary desk and pulled out his phone to send a text to Boyle.

Looking up, Hudson stood over him. "Thanks, brother. You did good."

Ford shrugged. "You're welcome."

While Hudson worked in his office, Ford remained at the front desk looking through Tess's file again. While they most certainly had the murder weapon and a solid suspect in Mike Andrews, they still had to zero in on a motive. Why would Mike the nurse want to put poison into the brownies? Could Molly Kincaid have been a part of it all, since she baked the brownies? If it wasn't some secret crush on Tess and a plot to get Jack out of the way, then what? Did he know Jack before he died? Did he somehow have anything to do with the adoption and inheritance? Since the flowers were at the Kingston house too, there had to be a connection. Did Mike know Roger or David and, if so, how?

Ford grabbed a pencil and began doodling on a legal pad. He drew circles all over the page and put the names of the players inside. Tess, David and Roger Kingston, Mike Andrews, Jack. He drew arrows back and forth between them all, jotting notes about connections between each person and every other person. The logical conclusion pointed to David or Roger. Or both. They could have done research on the plants to figure out a way to create the poison. Then, they could have looked for a connection to Tess. Maybe Andrews didn't have a crush on Tess, maybe they paid him off to do it. If they hadn't known about Jack's will, poisoning him would have been the easiest way to keep his money in the family.

Hudson broke his concentration, as he came back into the room. "What are you doing?"

"Not sure." Ford kept underlining and drawing lines. "It's a good thing we got the weapon or poison, but things still don't make sense. Jack's money is the only motive anyone has. The only people to benefit from Jack's death, had he not made a will, were the Kingstons. It has to be them."

"But why are the flowers at Mike's house too? Coincidence?" Hudson leaned in closer to read the notes and scribbles on the page.

"I don't know. My gut's all over the place."

Ford tossed the pencil down and rubbed his forehead with his hand. "David and Roger are both huge assholes, but I can't believe they would actually kill their brother and son. You saw them that day at David's office. They looked as sick as anyone who's lost a loved one. I don't think either of them is that good of an actor."

Hudson sat down on the corner of the desk and laced his fingers together behind his head. "Maybe we're underestimating them."

Ford shrugged, but then shook his head. "Think about it. They adopted that kid and raised him as their own. You can't just turn that off, can you?"

"I don't know. I wouldn't think so. Money does crazy shit to people."

Ford nodded. "Yes, it does."

"We have to talk to Andrews."

"I can't get near him at work. And he knows what I look like."

Hudson pursed his lips. "Maybe we could have Tess reach out–"

"No!" The shout that erupted from Ford surprised even him.

Hudson frowned. "Easy there, brother."

Ford willed himself to calm down. "It's too dangerous. If he *is* involved, it might spook him to see her."

"But that's exactly what we need!"

"No, if we let on that we know anything, he might bolt. Then we're screwed. Besides, I don't think Tess would agree to it, anyway."

"Agree to what?" Tess asked.

Chapter 46

On a whim, Tess had decided to drive over to Hudson's office. She couldn't stand being in the apartment a minute longer. Even her beloved cats were driving her crazy with their incessant need for attention. She stood in the doorway to Hudson's inner office, and her breath stopped when her eyes met Ford's. He actually looked happy to see her and almost smiled. She could tell he stopped himself at the last moment by the way the smile died and then faded away.

"What are you doing here?" Hudson turned around to see her.

"I needed to get out of the house. What are you guys talking about?"

Hudson pulled a chair from the other room so she could sit next to Ford. Tess was glad he didn't notice when Ford shoved his own chair back a little bit, creating more distance between them.

"Do you want some coffee or water?" Hudson asked as she sat down.

"Water would be great."

Hudson turned to the minifridge to get her drink and she looked quickly at Ford. He was staring at his folded hands resting in his lap. Tess smiled, but he didn't see it. She wished she could be alone with him for five minutes. Unfortunately, Hudson was there and handing her a bottle of Aquafina.

"So what's going on?"

Hudson looked at Ford and then smiled at her. Tess didn't know whether to feel hopeful or sick.

"We have some good news. We may have traced the poison back to some plants that Ford found in the Kingstons and Andrews' front yards."

Hope soared through Tess's body. "That's great! Right?"

"Yes. We're having it confirmed with an expert. Ford and I want to speak with Andrews, but we can't do it on the work premises. And we think if he sees Ford, he might bolt."

"Okay." Tess crinkled her brow as she listened, wondering what they wanted her to do. She didn't have to wait long for an answer.

"My thought was to have you reach out to Andrews for a meeting or something, and then we feed you some questions to ask. You could wear a wire and a camera so we could get a sense of his answers."

"And my thought is you should stay out of it," Ford said quietly, still not looking at her.

"Well that's not going to happen," Tess retorted. "If there's any chance we can get me out of this mess, I'm all in. You just tell me everything you want me to do."

Hudson quivered with excitement. "Good, now that it's settled, let's work out the logistics."

Ford glared at Hudson and it wasn't lost on Tess. *Now that's interesting*, she thought. *I really need to get him alone.*

"Maybe you could show up to the doc's office on Monday and ask him out to lunch or something?" Hudson suggested.

"Under what pretense?" Ford interrupted.

Hudson glared at him.

"He's right." Tess gave them both a sympathetic look. "But it just so happens I have the perfect excuse to stop into the office."

The men stared at her, waiting for more. "Well?" Hudson asked after a few seconds. "You gonna tell us or make us play charades?"

Tess gave him a sour face, but then smiled. "I finally finished the last of the transcription I had. Usually I email it, but I could hand deliver it just to say goodbye to everyone."

"Brilliant!" Hudson shouted. "Then, while you're there, you can think of a way to get near him or talk to him. Maybe invite a bunch of them to lunch? Or drinks after work?"

Tess shrugged. "That might work. Those gals love to go to the Blue Goose Inn on Jefferson on Tuesdays for Mexican. Maybe he'll come along, but I can't guarantee it." The hope she felt earlier dampened just a little. She couldn't remember Mike ever having joined them before.

"Is there anyone there you're particularly close with?" Ford asked. "Maybe you could tell her to make sure he comes or something?"

"I could try, but I'm not sure I trust anyone. Especially now that you've been there asking questions. They'll be suspicious of me." *Great, more funny looks. First a widow and now a murderer.*

"All we can do is try. Head over there Monday around lunch time and see what you can do. Then give me or Ford a call and let us know how it went. I'll have my brother get started on getting the surveillance equipment together so you can be wired up."

"What if they want to go to lunch right then?" Tess asked. "I could use my phone to record stuff, I guess."

"If that happens, be prepared. Otherwise, set it up for whatever night and then we'll make sure you have everything you need. And we'll be listening."

Chapter 47

Lilly wasn't keen on Tess going alone to the doctor's office. When she found out about the half-baked plan Hudson had convinced her sister to carry out, she had insisted on joining Tess on the mission. If this Mike person was really involved and capable of murder, then Lilly wasn't about to let her only sister walk into a situation without some form of backup.

Sure enough, when they got to Dr. Guildford's office just before lunch time, most of the staff was milling around, wondering where they would go and what they would do. When they saw Tess, they all surrounded her with supportive hugs and good wishes, leaving only polite nods and smiles for Lilly. She watched carefully to see if she got any sense of unease from the staff, but her internal radar wasn't cut out for that kind of thing. Still, she kept her eyes and ears open just in case.

Lilly knew that Hudson was hoping the staff would be open to a night out for drinks after work so that he and Ford could follow along and listen in on whatever happened. But she knew that the abrupt appearance of Tess on the premises would likely encourage them to want to spend time with her right then, and not wait for another night. When Tess tried to suggest the Blue Goose for the next night, it was Molly Kincaid who insisted they all go out for lunch right then. El

Charro was just down the street and they could all go there. Luckily, Molly cornered and convinced everyone to go, even Mike Andrews. Lilly expected him to be reluctant, but he seemed as excited as everyone else. She didn't like the looks of him from the moment she saw him, with his excessive muscles and hipster ponytail.

Not knowing what else to do, Tess agreed and she and Lilly went out to the car to head off for the restaurant, promising to save enough spaces at the tiny eatery on Harper. "I told you this would happen," Lilly admonished as they walked up to the car. "I'll drive and you text Hudson and Ford. Let them know what's going on."

"Okay. Don't sound so worried. It's broad daylight on a Monday. What do you think's going to happen?" Tess blew off her sister's concern and Lilly wanted to smack her upside the head for it.

"And you don't take things seriously enough. The fact is, we don't *know* what might or might not happen. You need to be on guard, sis."

"*Okay*, sis."

Lilly drove them to the restaurant and parked in the closest spot she could get to the door. Tess was busy sending text messages when cars carrying the staff of Dr. Guildford's office began to arrive, taking all the surrounding spaces. Mike Andrews's little red Prius pulled in on the driver's side in the only handicap space available. Lilly gave him a stern look as she exited her car and he shrugged his enormous shoulders.

"I had knee surgery a couple of months ago. I have a temporary tag."

Lilly nodded but didn't say anything. He hadn't been limping earlier and he wasn't now, but the red temporary handicap flyer was displayed predominantly from his rearview mirror.

All through the meal, her former coworkers peppered Tess with questions about everything under the sun while Lilly sat quietly beside her, eating her lunch. Tess did a good job of answering the questions and playing the part of grief-stricken widow and stunned suspect in her husband's homicide. It wasn't really that big of a stretch. Her phone was recording everything going on, just as Hudson had told her to do. Lilly kept her eye on Mike Andrews but he did nothing to set himself apart from the group. He didn't ask any questions of his own though, but just listened and ate. He laughed when appropriate and shot Tess looks of sympathy when it was the right thing to do. Still, Lilly had glommed onto him because there was no one else she could put in her cross hairs besides Roger and David Kingston.

When almost an hour had gone by, Daphne Moore announced that it was time to get back to the office. There were groans from some of the nurses, but they knew they had patients to see. A hoard of bodies dressed in scrubs floated toward the door with Tess and Lilly behind them. Outside in the parking lot, Tess received hugs from everyone and they all filtered into their cars, departing in a line. Only the red Prius remained.

"Where's Mike?" Lilly whispered, looking around to survey the area.

"I don't know." Tess was busy looking at her phone, which had blown up with messages from Hudson.

Lilly frowned. "Get in the car. We'll head over to Hudson's." She stepped off the curb and opened the car door. As she stepped around to sit down, the door was shoved hard, catching her head in between it and the frame of the car. Bright white spots of light filled her vision and she slumped to the ground. Her last thought was *Fuck*!

Chapter 48

Mike Andrews grabbed Tess by the arms from behind and wheeled her toward his car before she even knew what was happening. Her phone clattered to the pavement and she yelled, "Hey!" as it shattered and the pieces scattered all over the place.

He arced an arm around and punched her squarely in the side of the head. She slumped and stopped struggling, and he was able to dump her into the passenger side of his car.

Running around to the driver's side, he hopped in and started the vehicle. He peeled out of the parking lot and headed north on Harper Avenue.

Chapter 49

"Something's not right."

Ford paced back and forth in the office, staring at his phone. "Tess isn't responding to any of my texts. She said they were finishing lunch and would be here within ten minutes." *This is not good.*

"Maybe she and Lilly stopped for coffee or something." Hudson was watching his phone too, waiting for a message from his client. He didn't sound convinced.

Just then, Lilly burst through the office door, blood pouring down the side of her head. She staggered toward Hudson, who caught her in his arms before she went to the floor. "He took her," she whimpered. "Mike Andrews took her."

"*God dammit!*" Ford roared. He knew the whole thing had been a mistake. He hadn't wanted Tess involved in anything like this and he could have beaten the shit out of his brother for coming up with the stupid plan to begin with. "Call 9-1-1!" he yelled as he ran out of the office. He pulled up the app on his phone to see if he could find Mike Andrews as he ran to his motorcycle, grateful as hell that he'd put the tracking device on the Prius. Hopping on, the engine screamed to life. Ford pulled his blue tooth earphones out of his saddlebag and turned on the device. With shaky hands, he paired it to his phone and made sure they were working.

Anxious to get on the road, he forced himself to follow all the necessary steps it took to get his phone into voice activation mode. He wouldn't have two hands available to manipulate it as he drove the bike. He tested the necessary apps for texting and calling by shouting commands to open, close, and operate them. Satisfied that he could keep in contact with Hudson by text and voice, Ford gunned the engine and took off. His phone beeped and a bubble popped up with the location of the car. He was on I-94 West heading toward the Port Huron area.

Zooming down Harper toward the freeway on-ramp, Ford clenched his teeth and forced himself to take deep breaths. The last thing Tess needed was for him to let his rage get the best of him. *Focus. Stay calm. You will catch up. You will find them.* He repeated the words in his head over and over, even though his vision was clouded with fear and anger.

It wasn't just a crush or some nostalgic infatuation anymore. Ford couldn't lie anymore. He was falling in love with Tess. The thought of her being taken by force and suffering only God knew what at the hands of the possible killer just about made him crash the bike as he whizzed between cars, racing along I-94 West.

Chapter 50

Lilly refused to let Hudson take her to the hospital. He wanted her head looked at and felt it might need a stitch or two, but there was no way in hell she was leaving his office. Police officers milled back and forth, alternately stopping to ask her questions. She answered them as best she could, but couldn't focus on anything but the fact that her sister was missing, taken by a lunatic who probably had a hand in killing her brother-in-law.

"Ma'am," said the latest uniformed cop, "you really should be looked at."

"I'm *fine*," she snarled. "Don't worry about me, go and find my *sister!*"

Hudson arrived by her side and shooed him away. Sitting down beside her, he put his arm around her shoulders. "I'm so sorry, Lilly. This is all my fault."

"You're goddamn right it is," she snapped. "This isn't some television crime drama. This is *real life*, asshole."

Hudson took her recriminations in silence and she was glad. Had he said anything to defend himself, she would have punched him in the throat. Logically, she knew he hadn't intended for Tess to be hurt or in any danger, but it didn't matter now. She *was* in danger and Lilly wasn't there to protect her.

"Can I get you anything?" he asked softly, his arm still around her and Lilly took a moment to realize how much she appreciated the weight of it there.

"My sister."

Hudson sighed. "They're doing everything they can. Ford's tracking him and they're tracking Ford. We'll find her."

"They better. And she better not have a scratch on her or else Mike Andrews won't see the next sunrise." The hard edge in her voice even gave *her* a slight chill. Hudson felt her shiver and squeezed a little tighter.

"I haven't called your parents yet. Do you want me to?"

Lilly hesitated. That was the most difficult decision she could be faced with. "I don't know. Part of me wants to not worry them, but when they find out I didn't call them, I'm going to be toast." Turning her face toward his, Lilly realized they were within kissing distance and it shocked her. She tried to pull back, but Hudson refused to let her go. "What would you do?"

Hudson shook his head and pulled on her so that her head rested on his shoulder. "I don't know, Lilly. I don't have any parents who worry about me, so I don't know what that's like. They seem like strong people, though. I'd probably call them."

Lilly sighed and reached into her pocket for her cell phone. "Okay. I'll do it. Just promise you'll stand between me and my dad so he doesn't kill me."

Hudson gave a weak chuckle. "You got it."

Chapter 51

Tess's head ached worse than the night Lilly got drunk with her after finding the hoard of cash and emails. She reached up to rub her temple where a nice lump was beginning to rise and her memory flooded back like an overflowing bathtub. Gasping, she sat up straight and looked around. Mike Andrews was driving with one hand and pointing a gun at her with the other.

"Don't do anything stupid," he warned, glancing from the road to her and back again.

Tess wanted to say she wouldn't, but her mouth was too dry. Her tongue felt like it was the size of a loaf of bread and it stuck to the roof of her mouth. She had trouble swallowing and wanted a drink of water almost as badly as she wanted to wish herself away from the situation.

"You had to come around asking questions, didn't you?" Mike spat. "You couldn't just leave well enough alone."

"I don't understand," Tess croaked.

"You know damn well what I mean." Mike waved the gun at her. "You wanted all that money for yourself. If you had just taken the insurance money and shut up, then none of this would be happening."

Tess's brain swam with confusion. *How did he know about all that?* She tried to think, but her head was fuzzy with pain and she really wanted to close her eyes and go to sleep.

"Don't go to sleep on me, bitch!" Mike hollered. He reached across and smashed the gun across her face. Tess cried out as the pain exploded in her cheek and she felt blood begin to flow. "You might have a concussion. And there's someone who wants to see you before you die."

"People don't die from concussions," Tess sobbed, tears filling her eyes and mingling with the blood on her cheek. She heard his words, but their meaning didn't quite cut through the clouds in her mind.

Mike ignored her and kept driving.

Chapter 52

Ford scanned traffic for every red car, whether it was Prius or not. While he maneuvered the bike through the cars on the road, he reached around in his saddlebag and lifted the lid. His Colt .45 was right where he left it, loaded but with the safety on. He hoped he didn't have to use it, but would not hesitate to do so if it meant keeping Tess alive and unharmed.

The beacon on his phone told him Andrews was still heading west on I-94, but Ford couldn't zoom in while he tried to drive and the app would not respond to his constant shouts for it to do so. He took incoming calls from Hudson constantly, assuring him he was still in pursuit. More than once, his brother tried to convince him to let the police handle it, but Ford refused. He should have done more to stop Hudson from involving Tess and he felt responsible for getting her back.

Checking the tracker on the phone again, Ford saw the car had stayed on I-94 until it turned into I-69. Twisting the throttle, he pushed the bike past a hundred miles an hour, grateful that the afternoon traffic was not heavy yet as rush hour approached. He looked at his gas tank and saw it was still at half a tank. *Thank God I filled up this morning.*

An incoming call from Hudson splashed across the screen.

"Yeah!" he shouted.

"Where are you?" Hudson demanded.

"Still on 94. I'm coming up on 69!" Ford felt his throat explode with pain from having to yell to be heard.

"Any idea where he might be taking her?"

"No!"

"There's a BOLO out on the Prius, but they haven't gotten any hits."

"I'm doing the best I can, Hudson!"

His brother sighed. "I know, Ford. I know. Just be careful. Don't do anything stupid!" Then he hung up.

Ford shook his head and then opened his mouth and howled like a wounded animal. His frustration was reaching a fever pitch and he wanted to lean on the throttle of the bike even more than he already was. The lone voice of reason kept him from doing it because his driving was already reckless and bordering on dangerous. He wouldn't be able to save Tess if he crashed and killed himself.

Watching the screen of his phone and the road, he watched the red dot shift the slightest bit. He got off the freeway! Checking behind him, Ford whipped to the right and exited the highway the first chance he got. He turned right at the stoplight and pulled into a gas station. After examining the tracker app for closer details, he texted Hudson. He got off at Pinegrove Ave. Still following. Will be in touch.

Chapter 53

Mike Andrews drove slowly down the dirt and gravel road deeper into the woods. Tess had no idea where she was, having never been good with geography or direction. Lilly told her all the time she'd get lost if she went outside the front door without the GPS going.

If only I had my phone, she lamented. *Lilly was right. I never take anything seriously or pay attention. And look where it's gotten me.* Tess tried to pay attention for landmarks as she watched outside the window, but every tree and rock looked the same. The only thing in her favor was that the sun still shone brightly in the afternoon sky and she knew that they were headed west.

She had tried to get Mike to talk to her a couple of times, but he only grunted at her or swore at her to shut up. After a while, she gave up, scared shitless he would get frustrated and just shoot her in the car. Clamming up, she tried to think her way through the mess she was in, but there wasn't anything to think about. It didn't matter what questions she wanted to ask. It didn't matter how Mike knew about the money or Jack or anything. He was intent on taking her somewhere secluded and killing her. Unless she could overpower him or get away somehow, the answers to the questions really didn't matter at all.

The trees on either side of the road got thicker, causing the light from the day to dissipate the farther they traveled. The dirt road disappeared and became two muddy ruts. Still, they moved forward. Tess began to hope the Prius would get stuck and then she would try to make a break for it. She wasn't the athlete Lilly was, but she felt pretty confident that running for her life would give her a bit of an adrenaline boost.

Her hopes were dashed, though, when they came upon a dilapidated cabin sitting off to the side of the path. It looked a hundred years old to her with the wood sides pockmarked and gray from years of exposure. The roof was nothing but dirty, rusty sheets of metal. The porch on the front had sunk down so far it looked like you needed a rope to pull yourself up to the door. Mike stopped the car about ten feet from the rickety steps leading to the porch. "Get out." He waved the gun at her. When she didn't move fast enough to suit him, he reached in with his free hand and grabbed her by the hair. He pulled her from the car and slammed her to the ground. Sharp edged rocks dug into the skin on her knees and she cried out in pain. Before she could get to her feet, he cocked the hammer of the gun. "And don't try to run. If you do, I *will* shoot you."

Tess nodded, her entire body trembling. *So much for making a run for it.* She wasn't sure her legs would allow her to stand, much less try to run away. It took a couple of tries before she finally managed to stand back up. Mike shoved her forward toward the cabin and she almost went face first into the stairs. Using her hands, Tess half crawled and half climbed across the slanted porch. Mike jammed the barrel of the gun into her back as he propelled her through the warped front door.

The interior wasn't as shabby as the outside. It was clean and freshly painted, with throw rugs on the floor, old but clean furniture, and lamps on every table surface. "What is this place?" she asked, timidly looking around.

Mike ignored her and then kicked her in the butt. Tess's arms swung in circles and she tripped over the corner of the rug, landing on her knees, her torso bouncing against the sofa cushions of a couch. She scrambled up and sat on the couch quickly. He approached her with a roll of duct tape and proceeded to bind her wrists.

"Ow!" she hissed.

Mike snorted and walked away toward the back of the cabin where the kitchen was. He took out his cell phone and began texting.

Well, there's obviously cell coverage up here, she thought. Tess wished she was as clever and strong as the characters she often watched on television. They always seemed to find a tool or weapon to get free and then they would beat the crap out of their captors. Slumping down in her seat, she knew that wasn't in the cards for her.

Chapter 54

Ford sat on his parked motorcycle at the top of the path about a quarter of a mile higher than where the cabin in the woods sat. The Prius was parked outside. *Thank God for tracking apps.*

Ford knew without a doubt he should wait for the cops and let them handle things. He had no right to go storming into a situation he knew little about when there was a gunman involved and an innocent woman, especially with his record. But the stubborn, hard headed part of him would not sit back to wait and watch. If Mike Andrews caught sight of the police, he might go off half-cocked and kill Tess immediately. And if he didn't, Ford didn't think a hostage situation would end in a positive way for anyone. He decided to sneak down for a closer look.

Moving as quietly as possible through the brush, he was all set to dart out from behind a tree and make a break for another one only twenty yards from the cabin, but was forced to duck down and hide behind a rock. Headlights bathed the dusky path in bright candescent light as another car approached the cabin. It was still early afternoon, but all the trees surrounding the property kept the sunlight from getting through. Ford's eyes widened in complete shock when he saw the make and model. Moments later, the vehicle stopped next to the Prius and Emily Kingston exited the car.

Chapter 55

The cabin door opened and Emily Kingston walked inside. Tess gasped and felt the room begin to swirl. Little dots of white light peppered her vision like snow falling in winter.

"Oh, don't faint now, dear. It would be very anticlimactic, don't you think?"

Emily's cool voice was like cold water splashing on Tess's face. She sounded calculating and mean, nothing like the woman she'd known most of her life.

"You killed Jack." The words felt like ashes on Tess's tongue.

"Yes, I did."

Emily looked trim and unruffled in a chambray linen blazer and khaki slacks. Her hair was freshly cut and styled. Her makeup was flawless. She looked to Tess like she was about to go out to lunch with some friends or shopping for the day, as though she didn't have a care in the world. The outfit was probably her version of camping gear in such a rustic setting. The nonchalant way she admitted to killing her son made stinging, bitter bile rise in the back of Tess's throat. The same white spots danced across her eyes again, but she bit down hard on her tongue to kill them.

"How could you do such a thing?" she whispered. "He was your son."

"Yes, he was," Emily snarled, crossing the room in four long steps to stand in front of her. "And I loved him with all my heart. But then you came along."

Tess's lip curled with confusion. "I didn't do anything."

"You bullied your way into his circle of friends when you were in elementary school," Emily accused as she paced in front of her. "Then you flaunted your budding little body in front of him when you reached middle school." Emily sniffed with disgust.

"What are you talking about?" *This woman's a whack job!*

"And then you spread your legs for him in high school, making certain that I'd lost him forever!" Emily's voice cracked and she turned away.

"That's a lie!" Tess argued. "Jack and I never slept together until after we went to college. I didn't do anything to take him away from you."

Emily sniffed and threw her a skeptical smirk. "Don't be coy. You stole my son. Once you came into the picture, Jack hardly spent time with me or listened to a word I said."

Tess's eyes hurt, they were spread so wide open with disbelief. "You *poisoned* him!"

Emily snorted. "You're right. I did kill my son. The problem, my dear, is that the poison was meant for *you!* You were supposed to eat those brownies!" Emily screamed, spittle flying from her mouth. "That wedding was *NEVER supposed to happen!*"

Tess moaned as Emily approached her like a spider stalking a fly. Of course the idea that the poison was really meant for her was in her mind, but it hadn't ever really taken root. But now the seed bloomed in her head and she was filled with shock and fear and regrets.

While Emily ranted and raved, Mike Andrews had stayed in the background, not saying a word. Now he moved forward to pull Emily into his arms. "Shhh, baby, it's okay." He leaned in and gave her a soft kiss on the lips.

Tess's mouth hung open as she watched the tender moment. "You're such a liar!" she shouted, breaking into their private moment. "You wanted *both* of us to die! That's the only way the money could have stayed with your family!"

"Don't say anything more to her, babe," Mike growled, circling Emily's thin frame even more protectively.

"Oh what does it matter?" Emily scoffed. "She's going to die anyway."

"You can't kill me. They'll know it was you. The police will arrest you both and you'll go to prison."

"Unlikely," Emily argued. "Who would believe you over me? I've made very certain that the police think it was you who poisoned Jack. My grieving mother act is much more convincing than your weeping widow. No, Mike will put a bullet in your brain and then bury you out in the woods, while I purchase tickets for the two of us to go to Morocco."

"That's the thing, Emily. I do have proof it was you."

Emily stopped clutching with Mike and pushed him away. "What did you say?"

"Those are some pretty yellow flowers in your front yard. And I think I saw the same ones in the pictures Hudson has of Mike's house. Seems to me, I remember you telling the dogs to get out of those flowers more than once because they would send them to doggy heaven, or some other bullshit. Why would you and Mike have the same flowers growing in front of both your houses?"

Emily's makeup couldn't hide the way her face paled by the second. Feeling bolder, Tess kept going, even though it might get her a bullet to the brain. She was pretty sure she was a dead girl anyway. *Might as well get some digs in while I can.*

"You know, Hudson Marks is a real good lawyer and a smart guy. He's handy with the internet and a search engine too. I betcha those flowers are just as deadly to humans as they are to dogs, aren't they?"

"Shut up, you bitch!" Mike roared, backhanding Tess across the face.

Blood pooled in her mouth and she spat it at him, wondering at the same time where she got the ovaries to do such a thing. "Fuck off!"

Emily found her voice then, as she placed a restraining hand on Mike's arm. "Don't be ridiculous. You don't know what you're talking about. Most plants or flowers are harmful if ingested." Emily fiddled nervously with her bangs, swiping some loose hair behind her ear.

"Maybe so," Tess growled. "But how many of them exactly mimic a heart attack? I'm kind of guessing Hudson could make the connection between the poison found in Jack's body and those flowers in about four key words on Google."

Emily took a step backward as if Tess's words were the slap the young widow's bound hands so wanted to deliver.

Tess stared in horror as Emily's arm rose, arcing toward her face. Instinctively, Tess turned away, unable to use her arms to deflect the blow. Emily's small fist had the advantage of anger and momentum. It caught Tess on the side of the head and a shimmering of stars exploded before her eyes. She slumped a little to the side, her head filled with buzzing.

Emily bent over, but did not try to hit her again. Instead, she shook a finger in her face as if Tess were a small child who had just done something naughty. "I don't care what you think you know. You will be dead before anyone can listen to a word you say."

Emily straightened up and then turned on her heel to march toward the door.

"You won't get away with this," Tess called after her.

Chapter 56

"Are you fucking crazy?!" Ford whispered hoarsely into the phone, trying to keep his voice under control. "They're going to *kill* her and then make a run for it!"

"Settle down son," Detective Isham replied calmly. "That's not going to happen."

"You aren't here, are you? I'm hearing a lot of shouting going on in there, most of it between Emily and Tess. But that asshole Andrews is there too and he's got a fucking gun!"

"Ford, listen to me—"

"I'm through listening!"

"FORD!" Detective Isham's voice boomed through the phone so loudly, Ford was worried the occupants of the cabin would hear it and he clamped the cell to his ear with both hands to muffle it. "Are you listening to me now?"

"I'm listening." Ford gritted his teeth and bit down on the side of his tongue, trying to get himself under control.

"I want you to get back on your motorcycle and go back out to the lead-in of the path. Meet the local sheriff's deputies. Give them the status of the situation. I'm already on my way to you and should be there in about 15 minutes."

"Tess doesn't have fifteen minutes," Ford growled.

"She does, I promise. There are things you don't know and I don't have time to get into it now. You have to trust me." Detective Isham's voice was mild and smooth. "I know about your history, Ford, the time you did in Jackson. I also know your brother is unaware of where you were while he was in school. I won't say anything to him as long as you work with me and not against me. Am I clear?"

Fuck! Ford wanted to crawl through the phone and choke the life out of the cop on the other end. "Clear." Crouching low, he made a beeline for his bike. When he got there, he knew he would have to push it for at least a hundred yards before he could safely start the engine.

"Are you still there?"

"Yeah."

"Get out to the main road as fast as you can. The cavalry is coming."

Ford ended the call and wanted to throw the phone out into the field so he'd never have to talk to Butch Isham again, but he fought the urge and pocketed the device instead. Grabbing the handlebars, he pushed hard to get the machine moving and then jogged alongside as it gained momentum. It didn't take long to get a safe distance away so he could start it, but he had to drive slowly so as not to gun the engine and giving away his presence.

Just as he reached the lead in, four cop cars screeched to a halt in front of him. Fully expecting to be arrested on the spot, Ford raised his arms in the air in full surrender mode, a holdover instinct from prison.

A tall, broad-shouldered officer approached him. "Put your arms down, Marks. We know who you are. I'm Sheriff Walker. What's the situation?"

Ford climbed off the bike and gave the officer all the information he had. As he finished with the last of the details, a S.W.A.T. van pulled up with another unmarked sedan. Butch Isham climbed out of that and jogged over to join the conference at the side of the road.

Ford's legs felt a little wobbly with the relief coursing through him. The serious looks on all the faces around him and the immense amount of man– and firepower displayed gave him the hope that everything would be okay.

Chapter 57

"We need to kill her now, baby." Mike paced back and forth across the room, running his free hand through his hair while his other hand waved the pistol around.

"Soon, darling," Emily soothed. "Let's wait until it's dark so no one will see when you bury her body."

Tess listened to them, feeling her hopes sink a little more with every word. Her whole head and face throbbed in time with her racing heart and she could feel the blood drying on her chin. She couldn't believe this was happening. Never in a million years would she have ever thought her life would be ending in a cabin in the woods at the age of twenty-five. *And I thought being widowed five minutes after getting married was the shit.* A maniacal giggle tried to force its way out of her mouth, but she swallowed it and then let herself flop over onto the couch. Her movement caught Mike's attention but he turned away when he saw she was still tied up.

Tess felt tears come into her eyes and she let them drip out and onto the scratchy cushion she lay on. *I'm sorry, Jack. I was supposed to get justice for you. I'm sorry it was your mom that did this. I think we're going to be together again soon.* She could feel her nose beginning to run and sniffled loudly.

"Shut up!" Mike yelled, stamping his foot and firing the gun into the ceiling. He then pointed it inches from her face. Tess could feel the sizzling heat from the barrel.

"Darling, calm down," Emily said softly as she went to him and wrapped her arms around his neck. Tess scrunched her eyes shut, trying not to hear their noisy kissing.

Oh Jack, I hope you can't see this. I hope you haven't seen any of this. It would break your heart. I hope you'll forgive me about the thing with Ford, too.

Ford. Just thinking about him brought his face into her mind. The way it had a little bit of five o'clock shadow before lunch. The green, penetrating eyes that knew what you were thinking before you did. The sultry, dangerous look about him that was everything Jack had never been. Tess began to weep in earnest. For all her bluster about not wanting to pursue anything with him, she realized now she was never going to get the chance to change her mind. She could think all the apologies to Jack she wanted. She could mentally count all the things she wished she had done or said to everyone she loved. She could pray to whatever God was up in heaven to forgive her for any sins she was guilty of. But she would never be able to speak the words she wanted Ford to know. *I wish we'd gotten to know one another better. I wish I could have been more than just a client to you. I wish—*

The sound of glass shattering and wood splintering interrupted her thoughts and Tess's eyes flew open. She stared mutely at the S.W.A.T. team busting in through the door and windows. Emily let out a blood curdling scream and gave Mike a gigantic shove, sending him pin wheeling toward the nearest cop who riddled his body with bullets.

"He kidnapped us both!" Emily shrieked. She shuffled over to Tess and tried to cover the girl in a protective way. Tess saw the gun in her mother-in-law's hand and opened her mouth to scream a warning. Using every ounce of strength she could find, she lunged up and bumped Emily away, then landed hard on her shoulder next to Mike's dead body. Waiting to get shot, Tess squeezed her eyes closed and balled herself up tightly in a fetal position.

Thunderous, roaring voices filled the room and her head until Tess couldn't even hear her own thoughts. Gunfire erupted around her and she felt a stabbing pain pierce her leg as she felt many, heavy-booted feet clomping around her. Beneath all the male voices, Tess could hear Emily's nasally, tearful protests. Daring to open an eye, she watched as the evil woman was physically dragged from the room, her hands shackled behind her in handcuffs.

She dropped her head to the floor and began breathing heavily, until she was sobbing with relief. *Thank you God, thank you God, thank you God* was all she could manage to think or feel until a familiar pair of motorcycle boots appeared like magic in her line of sight. She couldn't find any more strength to lift her head, but moved her eyes to see if it was really true.

"Ford," she whispered.

"Shhh." He held a knife in his hand and he hacked away at the duct tape binding her hands.

She tried to reach for him, but her hands wouldn't work. She didn't have to, because he was already pulling her into his arms and burying his face into her hair. "You're okay. You're safe. I've got you."

Tess wanted to say thank you, but she was already sobbing again as she clutched him tighter and pressed her face against his chest.

Chapter 58

Ford rocked Tess as he held her, not caring how much she cried or how wet he got from those tears. He wasn't about to let her go, now that she was safe in his arms again. It wasn't until he felt them begin to relax and a warmth spreading on his leg that he pulled away from her. Tess had passed out and he saw the blood spreading from a wound in her leg.

"We need some help over here!" he bellowed and one of the other cops yelled for the paramedics.

Ford was shoved out of the way by the large male medic and the female professional stepped over him like he wasn't even there. He watched as they got to work on the gunshot wound in Tess's thigh, expertly cutting away her pants leg and assessing the damage. Their hands whipped back and forth across her body and in their bags for the tools of their trade.

Oh Jesus, please let her be okay! He got to his feet and shifted from one foot to the other as his heart tried to climb out of his throat. Ford could feel the sweat pouring out of his body as another set of EMTs brought in a stretcher and then loaded Tess on it. She was carried out to the waiting ambulance and it sped off into the dark, lights flashing and sirens wailing.

Ford turned around in different directions, searching frantically for Detective Isham. He was standing next to the car where Emily Kingston sat in the backseat, her head hung low. He sprinted over to the detective and grabbed him by the shoulders.

"I need my bike! Someone needs to take me back to my bike!" Ford panted. "What hospital are they going to?"

"Calm down, son." Detective Isham took him to the patrol car that was first out to the path leading back to the main road. "Officer, can you take Mr. Marks back to his motorcycle and then escort him to the hospital?"

"Yes, sir."

Ford hopped into the car and slammed the door shut. Detective Isham was about to say something to him, but he couldn't get the words out. The deputy already had the car in gear and was accelerating down the road.

"Go!" Ford encouraged, and the deputy gave him a sneer.

"Don't tell me how to drive, fella."

Ford clenched his teeth shut but said nothing more. He couldn't afford to piss the guy off and slow things down any more. All he wanted was to get to the hospital. All he wanted was Tess.

Chapter 59

Tess gazed dreamily at the faces of her family hovering around her and gave them all a dope-filled grin. "Hi guys!" Her words were slightly slurred, and it was clear to Lilly that her sister was not in any pain.

"Hey, sis," she sniffed, swiping at the tears streaming down her face. "You sure gave us a scare."

"Bah, I'm okay." Tess tossed her IV riddled hand over the railing of the bed and waggled it. "Don't cry." Lilly laced their fingers together and squeezed. "You look terrible."

"Thanks." Lilly chuckled and continued to snuffle.

Tess flopped her head in the other direction to find her parents on the other side of the bed. "Hey guys, yer here."

"Of course we are, sweetheart," Ruth whispered, leaning in to kiss the top of her forehead. She brushed at the tangled mess of blond curls at her temple. "We're right here and we're not going anywhere."

Tess giggled, another goofy grin spreading across her face. "I got shot. Did you know that?"

Harry Langford, who looked about a decade older, burst out laughing. "Yes, we know. Thanks for telling us, Padunkin. We thought you were just here for the food."

Tess squinted at him for a second and then the joke made its way into her fuzzy brain, past all the medicine. She snorted and giggled again. "Thas a good one, Daddy." She struggled to sit up a little straighter, and several pairs of hands reached out to push her gently back onto the bed. "Stoppit, I wanna go home."

"Here we go," Lilly muttered. "Tess, Tess, look at me." She watched as her sister tried to focus and see clearly.

"Whut."

"You can't go home, sis. You have to stay tonight. The doctors just want to watch you."

"Don't wanna. You can watch me."

"No, I can't, the doctor has to," Lilly insisted. She pressed a little harder on Tess's shoulder, not worried about hurting her. The gunshot wound was to her upper thigh and luckily nothing too serious.

Tess didn't look so comfortable anymore, and even though she didn't struggle, she looked pissed off, like a child about to throw a tantrum. "I wanna go home. I want mah kittehs and watch TV. And a cookie. Can I have a cookie?"

Lilly smiled and leaned in close to her baby sister. "If you promise to stay, I'll bring you all the cookies you want."

Snuggling back down on the pillows, Tess nodded her head. "Okay. Oreos. Losof 'em." Her eyelids began to droop.

"Okay, sweetie." *Whew, crisis averted.*

A nurse walked into the room just then to check on Tess's vital signs. "Who're yew?" she mumbled. She came awake the slightest bit.

"I'm Gale."

"Gale who?"

"Gale, your nurse." She deftly strapped on a blood pressure cuff and began the process.

"Ow," Tess sighed.

"Almost done." Gale smiled at her and within seconds, removed the cuff and noted the results on the chart. "How are you feelin', kid?"

"Fantabulous." Tess tried to give a thumbs up, but got trapped in the tubing again. Lilly stifled the giggle in her throat.

"You having any pain?" Gale picked up her wrist to check the pulse.

"Nope. I wanna go home." Tess tried to pull away and glared at Gale, but the seasoned nurse held firm and looked her in the eye.

"That's not going to happen. I need you to lie still, okay?"

"But–"

"No buts. Don't make me sit on you all night. I have other patients, ya know." Gale smirked and gave her a wink.

Lilly was amazed when Tess giggle-snorted again and stopped fussing. "Gotta listen to the nurse, sis. They make the rules."

"Fine." Tess pointed at Gale. "You jus' make sure I get that cookie."

"You got it, kid."

Gale patted her on the shoulder and smiled kindly at the rest of the family before casually exiting the room.

Her minor set-to with Gale the nurse forgotten, Tess closed her eyes and yawned. Within seconds, she was sleeping peacefully and snoring through her open mouth. Lilly watched her for another couple of minutes before deciding it was safe to leave. She gathered her mom and dad and ushered them into the hallway, where Hudson and Ford Marks were waiting patiently.

"How is she?" they asked in unison. The brothers scowled at one another, then shuffled their feet in embarrassment.

Lilly chuckled. "She'll be fine. The bullet went right through and she didn't need surgery."

Ruth threw herself into Ford's arms and noisily kissed his cheek. "Thank you for finding my daughter," she whispered into his ear. Lilly struggled not to tear up again, watching her mother squeeze the very unsqueezable Ford Marks.

"You're welcome, Mrs. Langford."

"Are you all right?" Ruth asked, when she pulled away, studying his face.

"I'm okay." He took her hands in his and squeezed. "Really, I'm fine." Lilly didn't think he looked fine. He still seemed scared and anxious. He won't be okay till he sees her.

Lilly cleared her throat and turned to her folks. "Detective Isham's waiting downstairs for you guys. He'll take you home. Go on and go, get some rest. I'll stay with Tess."

"Don't be silly," Ruth scolded. "She's my daughter. You think I'm going to leave her here by herself?"

"That's exactly what you're going to do," Lilly insisted gently. "You guys are exhausted. I'll be fine; we'll be fine. Please. Go home. I'll call you in the morning, I promise."

She knew her mother was about to argue, but for once her father stepped in and took control. Usually, he let Ruth have her way in all things child related, but this time he followed his eldest daughter's lead. "She's right, honey. It's all over now. Let's go home and get some sleep. We can come back first thing tomorrow."

Not ready to let go just yet, Ruth opened and closed her mouth several times before grabbing Lilly for a hug. "All right. Fine. But we'll probably see you before you can even call."

"Okay, Mom." Lilly gave her a tight squeeze before breaking the embrace.

When her parents finally left and they were out of sight, she slumped against the wall and dropped her head into her hands. Hudson rushed to her side and put his hand on her arm. "What's wrong? Lilly?"

"Nothing, nothing," she sighed, flapping her hands at him. "I'm just tired." She found a reserve of energy from somewhere inside and stood up straight. She shook her shoulders and snapped her head from side to side. She looked at Ford and wondered how he was still standing. He looked as used up as she felt with dried blood all over his pants. "I'm sorry they wouldn't let you see her in the ER, Ford. The whole 'not family' thing."

Ford shook his head and put his hands out. "Don't worry about it. They told me she was all right and that was good enough."

Oh, he's lying through his teeth. If I don't let him in that room soon, he's going to go insane.

"Can we see her for a minute?" Hudson asked, glancing through the doorway.

"She's asleep, but I guess it'd be okay for a minute." Lilly nodded at Ford, but then grabbed Hudson by the arm to keep him from going in, too. "Let your brother go first."

Hudson gave her a strange look, but stopped his forward motion as Ford practically ran into the room. "What's going on?"

"Come sit with me for a minute." Lilly took his hand and pulled him down the hall to a little nook with chairs. She pushed him into one and then sat in another beside him. "I think there's something you need to know."

Maybe it wasn't her place to tell Hudson about the budding feelings between Ford and Tess, but Lilly knew the situation had changed. She figured it was better if she explained things to Hudson first before he could misunderstand.

"I don't really know how to tell you this," she began, "but Ford and Tess have a little, uh, thing going."

Hudson shook his head and his eyebrows lowered. "What? No. What are you talking about?"

Taking a deep breath, Lilly told him about the night her sister and Ford hooked up and how both of them were into each other, but weren't really ready to admit it yet. With everything that had happened in the last day, Lilly knew that was going to change. "I don't tell you this to cause trouble or hurt your feelings, Hudson. I just wanted you to be prepared for whatever happens next."

"Prepared? How can I be prepared if I don't even understand what you're talking about!"

Lilly sighed and rubbed her forehead. "I think you understand perfectly. They each had a little crush and then they hooked up. They tried to deny how much they liked one another, but what happened today is either going to bring them closer or push them apart for good. I think from this point on, we need to stay out of it and let whatever is going to happen, happen naturally."

Hudson stood up and paced around in the little alcove. "Why wouldn't Ford just tell me?"

"I don't know," Lilly admitted. "Maye he thought you had a thing for Tess and he didn't want to hurt your feelings?"

"Jesus," Hudson breathed. "We did have a talk about that a while ago. He told me I needed to focus on her like she was a client, nothing more. I'd say that was pretty hypocritical, wouldn't you? I mean, if he wanted her, he should have said something. But she's his client too, I mean, like–" Hudson stammered, his thoughts all over the place. Lilly felt sorry for him and began to second guess her decision to say anything to him.

"Look, I shouldn't have said anything to you."

Taking a deep breath, Hudson sat back down and looked into her eyes. "No, you did the right thing. Something's been off for a while with Ford and I would never have guessed Tess was the reason. I'm glad I know."

Lilly played with the cuticles on her fingers, suddenly feeling a little shy. "Do you have a thing for Tess?" she asked softly.

Hudson didn't answer right away. "No. In the beginning, I guess I was a little infatuated with her, but I decided a while ago that I had to think of her like a client and nothing else. I kind of thought she wasn't over Jack yet. Not to mention I could lose my license if I got involved with a client."

"Oh, she'll never get over Jack. He's going to be in her heart for the rest of her life. But she's a smart girl. Strong. She was already moving into accepting what happened before this whole mess started."

Hudson stared at his hands as he leaned over and dangled them between his knees. "Well, I knew Jack a little. I knew I'd never be able to really see her without seeing Jack too. Does that make sense?"

"Yep. Perfect." Lilly smiled and leaned her head on her hand. "That's how you know it wasn't meant to be with Tess. So you can't be jealous."

"Yeah," Hudson agreed. "I'm not jealous. If they want to be together, that's fine with me. I just wish he'd talked to me about it. I'm his brother, for Christ's sake. Why didn't he think he could trust me?"

Lilly almost couldn't focus on the words he was saying because she was so relieved to hear Hudson say he wasn't jealous or angry. "I don't think it's about trusting you, or you trusting him. I think Ford's got issues with trusting *himself*."

Hudson shrugged. "I don't know, maybe. We didn't exactly have the best role models growing up." He looked sideways at Lilly and gave her a rueful grin. "He thinks I don't know about a lot of what happened when we were kids, but I know more than he thinks."

Lilly screwed up her courage and reached to take one of Hudson's hands in her own. "It sounds to me like you two need to have some honest conversations."

"Shit," Hudson scoffed. "Why start now? All that's in the past." He surprised her by not letting go, their fingers remaining intertwined as they sat beside one another.

"Not if it's going to negatively affect your future." Lilly's left eyebrow rose in a skeptical way. "You can save all that for another time, though. For right now, just let the two of them do whatever they need to do. Okay?"

"Yeah, sure."

* * * * *

Hudson watched as Ford sat on the edge of the bed, holding Tess's hand and stroking her fingers. He was whispering to her, but he couldn't hear what his brother was saying. *Maybe that's a good thing. I probably shouldn't even be spying like this.*

Hudson was torn. He wanted to go in and punch his brother in the face for keeping secrets. He also wanted to see his brother happy. And the way he looked at Tess, it was obvious she made him happy in spite of himself.

Chapter 60

Ford didn't want to leave the hospital, but Ruth Langford unceremoniously evicted him, saying that if she saw him again before he'd gotten at least six hours of sleep and a shower, she would personally kick his butt. She and Harry had arrived to find him sitting in the chair he'd pulled next to Tess's bed and slumped with his head next to their daughter's lap, sound asleep.

Not wanting to argue with the mother of the woman he was now in love with, Ford had accepted his banishment, promising to come back later. He still hadn't spoken to Tess about his feelings because the pain meds had kept her asleep the entire night. It didn't matter. There would be plenty of time for the two of them to hash things out.

As he drove back to his place, he had plenty of time to think about everything that had happened the day before. The hour-plus drive should have let him reflect and process, but all he could remember was the feel of Tess's arms around his neck when he had finally been able to get to her.

Ford did as he was told and went home to get a shower, but he ignored Ruth's demand that he get some sleep. Who needed sleep when there was coffee to be had? Dressed in fresh clothes and with the first cup of coffee in his stomach, he decided to go to the office to catch up with his brother. He'd been sending texts and had tried to call a couple of times, but Hudson wasn't responding. After all the drama of the last few weeks, Ford's trouble radar was taking a rest and he didn't think anything of it.

When he arrived at the office, the door was open, the lights were on and the smell of fresh coffee was thick in the air. "Hey!" he called out as he entered and dropped his helmet and vest on the couch.

Hudson came out of his office to lean on the doorframe with his arms crossed against his chest. "Hey. How are you?"

"Okay. I'm good. How come you didn't call me back?" Ford got a cup of coffee and stepped closer to his brother. "What's up?"

Without any warning at all, Hudson's fist came out of nowhere and landed squarely on Ford's jaw, sending him stumbling backwards and the coffee cup spiraling through the air splashing liquid everywhere.

"What the *fuck*?!" he yelled, rubbing his jaw and charging at his brother.

"Whoa! Whoa!" Hudson put his hands up, palms out. "Truce!"

"Truce? You fuckin' hit me!" Ford ignored his little brother's surrender and clocked him back, his right fist connecting with Hudson's stomach.

"Ooof!" was all the sound he could make as the air whooshed out of his mouth.

"You don't ever get a free shot, little brother," Ford growled. "Now we're even." He grabbed some napkins from the coffee stand and threw them down on the spilled coffee, then bent over to retrieve the cup which thankfully had not broken. "Now what the hell was that for?" he asked.

Hudson was still leaning on the door frame, but in a slightly bent posture as he rubbed his gut. "For lying to me," he said hoarsely, trying to get his breath.

"Lying?"

"About Tess!"

"Aw, shit." Ford shoved the cup next to the coffee maker and shuffled over to the couch, where he flopped down, throwing his head back to bang against the wall. "Shit, shit, shit. How did you find out?"

Hudson joined him and then slapped a hand on his brother's leg. "Lilly told me."

"Oh for God's sakes!" Ford sighed.

"What? You didn't think Tess would tell her sister? You're dumber than I thought." Hudson chuckled and assumed the same pose as his brother, so they both were staring at the ceiling. "She told me last night at the hospital, though I probably could have figured it out for myself, the way you charged into her room and wouldn't leave her side."

Ford didn't know what to say, so he said nothing.

"It's all right, brother," Hudson said after a while. "I'm not mad at you."

"Could have fooled me. That was a hell of a punch."

Hudson chuckled and nudged him with his shoulder. "You should have just told me. I would have been okay with it."

"Bullshit," Ford spat. "I told you to get your head out of your ass where Tess was concerned. You woulda told me the same thing."

"Maybe. But when it was all over, I would have told you to do whatever made you happy." Hudson lifted his head and stared at his brother. "You know that."

"I guess." Ford rubbed his jaw some more and wiggled it around to relieve the soreness. "This is all new territory for me, brother. I don't know what the hell I'm doing. It's been a long time since I've felt like this."

"Don't worry about it. You'll figure everything out. But you have to promise me one thing."

Ford turned to meet his brother's eyes. "What's that?"

"No more secrets, man. Just be honest with me. Talk to me. Okay?"

Ford didn't answer right away. He wasn't sure he could make that kind of promise, even to his baby brother. There was still a lot of shit in his past he didn't want Hudson to know. If he promised to be honest, he'd just be lying. And a hypocrite. Again.

"Is it a deal?" Hudson pressed. "No more lying. Just shoot straight with me."

"Okay," Ford finally agreed. "From this point forward, no more secrets."

That would have to do. It was the only thing he could say to ease his conscience and satisfy Hudson's demands.

* * * * *

Hudson ignored his brother's fidgeting and twitching as they drove back to the hospital in St. Clair County where Tess was recovering. He was already pushing the truck past 90 miles an hour, what more did Ford want? Hudson had to admit, though, it was pretty amusing to see his brother as nervous as a groom on his wedding day.

When they got to the entrance to the hospital, Ford opened the door and began climbing out before Hudson could bring the vehicle to a stop. "Hey! Don't be an ass!"

"See you upstairs!" Ford called over his shoulder as he bolted inside.

Hudson parked and then walked into the hospital, well behind his brother. He punched the button the elevator and waited for one to arrive. When the doors whooshed open, Lilly came out before he could take a step inside.

"Hey!" she said, before nearly bumping right into him.

"Hey. How is Tess?"

"Much better." Lilly's eyes were bright with relief and she looked much less stressed than from the night before. "Walk me to my car? I need to get home."

"Sure," Hudson agreed, following her back toward the door. "I thought you left last night, since Ford was going to stay."

"No, I didn't want to go. I slept in that alcove where you and I had our little talk." Lilly closed one eye and shrugged her shoulders. "I know, I'm an idiot."

"Nah. Just a big sister. You and Ford have that protective thing down pat."

"It's a gift." Lilly chuckled and nudged him in the arm with her shoulder. "Or a curse. I guess it depends on how you look at it."

They walked in silence for a while until they reached her car. Instead of getting in, she leaned against the side and squinted up into the sunshine. The day was bright and hot with hardly any clouds in the sky. When Hudson looked at her as she enjoyed the sun on her face, he was struck by just how beautiful she was. Now that she wasn't in "big sister" mode, the lines in her forehead and around her eyes were almost gone. The corners of her mouth weren't being dragged down by stress anymore and Hudson could see that Lilly and Tess shared identical smiles. *Why didn't I see this before?*

"You know," he said, "I'm the only one who hasn't seen your sister yet. She's going to think I dropped her case."

Lilly's laugh was clear and true, and her smiling with it made her look happy and full of joy. "No, I don't think you have to worry about that. She asked about you this morning. But now that Ford's here, I don't think she'll care anymore." Lilly gave him an exaggerated wink.

"You're probably right. But that's okay."

"Did you and your brother talk about things today?" Lilly asked, all serious again. Even though she had changed the subject, she still held on to the radiant happiness Hudson had finally noticed.

"Uh, yeah. You could say that." He snickered and told her about their dust up at the office. "I think I'll have to skip the crunches for a while."

"Men are dumb," Lilly muttered. "I swear."

"Yeah, well. Not all siblings can be as perfect as you and Tess." He smirked and then winked at her, not really able to stop looking at the way her hair shifted lightly with the slow summer breeze.

"I guess you and Ford will just have to take lessons, then." Lilly batted her eyes cheekily. "I'm glad you worked it out anyway."

"For now. You have to admit though, it's going to be fun watching the two of them while they figure it all out."

Lilly nodded in agreement and her laughter filled the air around them again. "Yep. And we have front row seats for it."

Chapter 61

With the pain medicine wearing off, Tess could feel the throbbing in her leg getting worse. She wouldn't ask for any more, though, because the last thing she needed was to become an addict. The pain would go away eventually and she would just gut it out until it did.

More than anything, she wanted to go home. The constant fussing from her parents and sister was getting on her nerves faster than she would have expected. Okay, yeah, she got shot. And beat up. But she was fine now. The injuries weren't serious and Emily was in custody. Mike Andrews was dead. For the first time in a very long time, Tess felt like everything was going to be all right. The knot of anxiety that was constantly in the pit of her stomach and back of her mind was gone. It disappeared the second she saw the handcuffs around Emily Kingston's wrists. Now she just wanted to go home and recover there.

And think about Ford. And Jack. And what the hell she was going to do next. When she thought she was going to die and there were only moments left, her final thoughts hadn't been for her parents or sister, or even just Jack. Tess had thought of Ford and how many regrets she had about him and what went on between them.

When Jack died, it had crushed her heart. She had been lost and alone and hadn't thought she could go on living without him for a

any regrets. She had been honest and true
er heart in spite of any of the worries or
edding. Not a day had gone by in their
tell each other how much they loved one
any secrets or half-truths. Tess couldn't
her and think, oh I wish I'd done this or

ot exploring a possible future with Ford
he'd spent the night with her because
adn't seen him yet that day and was
d show up sooner or later and she was
for it when he did.

Tess made Lilly leave. Told her to get the hell out and not come
back, that she would see her sister at home. Then she politely asked
her parents to go to the cafeteria to get some breakfast, or better yet,
leave the hospital totally and find a restaurant where they could eat.
She wanted to rest and they were keeping her from doing that. Lilly
knew exactly what was going on, but had the good sense not to let on
in front of the folks.

With her eyes closed and the room finally silent, Tess replayed
moments from the night before. The sight of Ford's boots and the feel
of his arms around her. Total and complete relief washing over her like
a hot shower after a strenuous workout. His lips on her forehead and
temples before she lost consciousness. She really wished they hadn't
doped her up so much last night. She would have wanted to see him
one more time.

"I would have kissed him," she whispered to what she thought
was an empty room.

"Kissed who?"

Tess's eyes flew open and there he was, standing at the foot of the
bed with his trademark smirk firmly in place. *It's like magic. Whenever I*

think about him, he just shows up. Not letting her brain get the better of her, Tess grinned and answered immediately. "You."

Ford didn't wait for more confirmation than that. He was next to her in two giant steps and grabbing her face in his hands. His lips were hot against hers and Tess pressed against him, burying her fingers into his hair. The kisses said more than any words either of them could speak. When he finally let her up for some air, Tess hugged him tightly, ignoring the pain in her thigh.

"Thank you," she whispered in to his ear.

Pulling back, he frowned. "For what?" His eyes searched hers for the meaning behind the statement.

"You saved my life."

Smiling he leaned his forehead against hers. "No, that was the police. I was just there."

"Pffft, if you hadn't followed me, I'd probably be dead right now."

Ford tried to shake his head, but Tess scowled at him. "Okay, you're welcome."

That's better.

Tess wanted to say more, wished she could explain everything she was feeling and thinking in just the right way at that exact moment, but it was all too new for her. She didn't know how to do it and was afraid if she did it the wrong way, it would scare him off. Instead, she kept her mouth shut for a little while, happy to feel his arms around her and to lean in for a kiss from time to time.

When she finally thought she had a good opening line to start "the talk", Ford beat her to it with the last thing she expected to hear.

"Hudson knows about us."

Tess leaned back and let her arms drop to her sides. "Uh oh. Is that a good thing or a bad thing?"

Ford grabbed her hands in his and grinned. "It's okay, he's okay with it. I'm sorry, I didn't mean to freak you out."

Tess blew out the breath she didn't even realize she was holding. It hadn't even occurred to her to worry about Hudson or any possible fallout between the brothers if she and Ford decided to... to date? Was that what they were going to do? "Geeze, you scared the shit out of me, saying it like that."

Chuckling, Ford brought one of her hands to his lips and kissed it. "I'm sorry. I'm not exactly the smoothest guy in the world. I think you're going to have to help me out with stuff like that."

Returning the favor, Tess kissed Ford's hand back. "And you think I'm the voice of experience here? I didn't even think about Hudson. I was more worried about making sure we were okay."

"Scoot over."

Tess shifted carefully to the side so he could lean back in the bed and pull her into his arms.

"I know it seems a little late, but I was wondering if you'd be interested in having dinner with me some time. You know, after you get home and healed up."

Tess laughed and nodded her head, giving him a soft, quick kiss. "I would love that."

Epilogue

Tess knelt at Jack's grave and pulled out the dead stems of the last bouquet of flowers she had placed there. Putting fresh blooms in the holder, she smiled and ran her hand down the chiseled marble face of the tombstone. Until last week, his marker was of the flat, in-ground variety with only his name and the dates of his birth and death. Today, the new monument had been installed and Tess felt proud to see it standing over Jack's final resting place like a beacon of protection.

"Jack Xavier Kingston. Gone too soon, but forever in my heart."

"It's lovely, Tess." Lilly came up behind her and knelt down. "I think you picked out a really nice one."

"Thanks. He sure deserves it."

"Yes he does. Except for you, he got nothing but shit in life, it seems."

Tess shrugged. "Well, not totally, but I know what you mean. I'm glad he's not here to see all this." She shivered and cupped her elbows while she crossed her arms in front of her.

Emily Kingston was sitting in jail, charged with the murder of her youngest son. She swore she wouldn't plead guilty and would go to trial, but Tess hoped eventually she would give up. What was the point? With Tess's testimony, she would absolutely get convicted. Why waste all that time and taxpayer money? In the end, it didn't really matter. She was going to prison no matter what and Tess would be more than willing to take the stand and hang her out to dry.

Roger Kingston was also being prosecuted, but not for murder. That was all on Emily. Roger, though, was being charged with all kinds of fraud and perjury counts. When the toxicology report had come back with evidence of foul play, the police had started an investigation long before anyone had even known about it. Detective Isham had been watching the Kingston family and doing whatever cops do to nail people for crimes. It had been as much of a surprise to him as anyone else when Emily turned out to be the murderer. She had met Mike Andrews as a patient of Dr. Guildford and together they had cooked up a way to keep all of Jack's inheritance for themselves. Unfortunately, Jack wasn't supposed to die, but Tess was. Logically, Tess understood most of what happened, but emotionally she just didn't care anymore. Her ex-in-laws were both going to prison, one for the rest of her life and the other for a good portion of the rest of his life.

The only person who remained unscathed as far as criminal charges went was David Kingston. His father had been the one to sign all of the probate documents and make all the false claims. David had only followed his "client's" instructions. No charges would be brought against him. Instead, he would be left to wonder what the hell happened to his family. Both of his parents in prison and his brother dead. He would be alone and who knew what would happen to him. Sometimes Tess felt sorry for him, but the one and only time she tried to reach out to him, he had blamed her for everything that happened, promising that he would one day get to the real truth and see her punished. That rejection was all the permission Tess needed to finally be done with the Kingston family once and for all.

"Come on. It's time to go." Lilly stood up and touched her sister lightly on the shoulder.

"Yeah. I did what I needed to do."

Tess leaned forward and pressed a brief kiss to the front of the gravestone. "Love you, J." Then she put her hands on top of it and helped herself to stand.

As she and Lilly walked away, Tess felt the crisp fall air against her cheek. Looking up, she swore the clouds above were making the shape of a smiley face and pointed it out to her sister. "Look, it's a smile."

Snorting, Lilly swung an arm around her sister's shoulders and grinned. "Yep. It wouldn't surprise me a bit if the angels put that in the clouds just for you."

They made their way back through the rows of gravestones to the paved road where Hudson and Ford Marks waited for them. Together they leaned against Hudson's pickup and both offered smiles as they approached.

Still out of earshot, Tess snickered. "Who'd have thought two sisters would end up with two brothers?"

"Sure as hell not me," Lilly mumbled. "I still think I got the hotter one, though."

Tess laughed and nudged her sister. "Keep tellin' yourself that, sis."

THE END

About the Author

J. Thomas-Like is a writer born and raised in Michigan. She lives with her doting husband, brilliant son, a passel of cats, and a dog. This is her second novel. She started writing at a very young age, and is making her dreams come true, one story at a time.

Note from the Author

I hope you enjoyed this story!

Please take a few minutes to leave an honest, constructive review at Amazon or on my Facebook page. Reviews are just tips for writers, like a gratuity for the waitperson who brought your meal the last time you dined out. It gives us encouragement for bad days when we think we'd be better off taking up poking badgers with spoons for a living.

Connect with me at
www.jthomaslike.com
www.facebook.com/jthomaslike
http://twitter.com/jthomaslike

Cover art by James, GoOnWrite.com

Author Photo by Chasing Light Photography

Made in the USA
Charleston, SC
06 April 2016